'One hardly knows where to start in describing this idio-syncratic and very funny novel. For one thing, wacky things happen to the characters... for another, *they* are wacky. Such connections as they make with each other are fortuitous – often disastrously so... By themselves, these events may sound too exaggerated and grotesque to be funny, but the thoughts in the characters' heads render it all high comedy... the disasters accumulate with manic energy' – *The New Yorker*

'Wildly amusing... eccentric characters are drawn into and out of each other's orbits in the course of *The Planets*. Boylan directs their zany progress with a conjurer's manic zest, effectively combining hilarious absurdity with moments of unexpected poignancy' – *Los Angeles Times*

'A real flair for comic detail and contemporary absurdity' – *Washington Post Book World*

D0774046

THE PLANETS

THE PLANETS

James Finney Boylan

BLOOMSBURY

First published in Great Britain 1991

Copyright © 1991 by James Finney Boylan

This paperback edition published 1995

The moral right of the author has been asserted

Bloomsbury Publishing plc, 2 Soho Square, London W1V 6HB

A CIP catalogue record for this book
is available from the British Library

ISBN 0 7475 2118 2

10 9 8 7 6 5 4 3 2 1

Print in Great Britaiin by Cox and Wyman Ltd,
Reading

FOR DEIRDRE
BRIGHT STAR

THE PLANETS

THE PLANETS

MERCURY

◗

The Winged Messenger

*The planet is believed to have no atmosphere. Its
surface has been described as rough and
mountainous.*

Early Easter Sunday, Edith Schmertz set the clocks in her
house back two hours and went outside, carrying a small
parachute she'd stolen from her wicked sister-in-law. Smoke
from the mine fire hung in the air. It had been burning now for
twenty-two years, almost as long as Edith herself, except that no
one wanted to put her out, besides maybe her ex-boyfriend
Dwayne. She was going to have to walk right by his house on
her way to the airfield, which would be the worst part of the
ordeal. Dwayne might open a window and yell something at her,
the kind of comment that would remind her that most things
were impossible. Just when you thought you had a chance, the
Dwaynes of the world opened up their mouths and made your
balloons explode. It was no sense in trying to be in love, Edith
thought.

She put down the parachute and paused to catch her breath.
It weighed more than she'd expected. Up ahead was the hollow
tree. When she was a child, her father used to put her on his
shoulders and let her stare down into the trunk. You could look
through a big hole where a branch had been. Her father had said
that elves lived in there. They fix your shoes.

It was a bright, warm day in Centralia, Pennsylvania. There
wasn't much left of the old place now. Since the mine fire, it had
become a ghost town, with the elementary school torn down, the

stores and homes boarded up and abandoned. Columns of smoke and carbon monoxide rose from the ground, erupting from cornfields, pouring from boreholes.

Behind the hollow tree was a patch of earth where the Snelsons used to live. There was something about the Snelsons that hadn't been quite right. Somehow they'd wound up with more pets than they could handle. They had chickens and snakes and a miniature gorilla that could sing. The children had a funny smell, like peanut butter. Grass was beginning to grow over the brown patch where the house once stood. A seatless swing set stood in the backyard, the rusted chains blowing back and forth in the wind.

Up ahead was Dwayne's house. Smoke was coming out of the chimney. Looking at all that smoke dissipating in the air, Edith felt a deep remorse, as if she had been erased. After all, as recently as Christmas, she had heaped wood on that fire herself, had helped collect the kindling and stack the logs in neat piles near the henhouse. She had looked out the bedroom window, watching the patterns formed in the snow by the warmth of the mine fire below ground. The snow melted where the fire was hottest.

For two years this had been her home. Now, though, she was a stranger, locked out. That front door, with the knocker shaped like the head of a gargoyle, was shut tight. And Dwayne was shut up behind it. Once she had lain in the waterbed, tracing the shapes of the moles on Dwayne's shoulder blades. They looked like groups of constellations. Near his neck was Orion, with his shining belt. Betelgeuse was a mole near his backbone. And the Twins below the skull. Dwayne had a great smell—sort of like Bosco chocolate syrup. He used to call her his "little Coconut." Sometimes she would call him "Marbles," which was the name the Snelsons had given that singing gorilla, at least until the night it suffocated in its pajamas.

She put on the parachute and continued towards the airfield. Up ahead was Whispering Winds Kennels, where a man named Meyers bred Dalmatians. The Harrisons, Dwayne's next-door neighbors, had one of those dogs. Something was wrong with it, though. The dog was listless, uninterested in the world. An unpleasant juice oozed out of its eyes and gathered on its spotted muzzle. It looked like it was crying out its own brains.

Edith stopped in her tracks again, and looked back at Dwayne's house. Did he think about her, ever? Did he remember the way she had connected the constellations with her fingertips, the feeling of her cheek against his chest? What was he doing at this moment? Sitting in front of the fireplace, holding a picture of Edith in his hands, sniffing back the tears? It wasn't out of the question. He was probably cursing himself for his own insensitivity. What if she were to burst through the door at that moment, ready to forgive him? She could be bringing him a rare gift of understanding and mercy, instead of trudging by, racing towards an airplane. She wondered if she were being selfish.

The ironic thing was that Edith had had a crush on Dwayne for years before she had become his lover, back when they both attended Buchanan High School. He wasn't interested in Edith then; he had gone out with Edith's friend Vicki instead, which was typical. Vicki had these great breasts and was over six feet tall and got to represent Sweden at the Miniature United Nations. Edith had had to listen to Vicki talk to her, staying over nights, wondering in the dark. She'd ask Edith about Dwayne, *do you think Dwayne likes me, why do you think Dwayne doesn't like me, is there any way you can think of to get Dwayne to like me,* on and on until Vicki would fall asleep in the midst of saying his name, "Dwuuuhhhh—" and would lie there with her mouth open for eight hours. Sometimes in the morning Vicki would open her eyes and finish it, right where she left off: "—wuhhayne."

Vicki finally did go out with Dwayne in eleventh grade. That had been in 1976, eight years ago. It hadn't been as humiliating for Edith as she'd feared. It was kind of like going out with him by proxy. Those late-night talks, although more infrequent now, were reversed. Now Edith asked the questions. What did they do on dates? What did they talk about? Vicki told all. Some of it was disgusting. The night of the senior prom Dwayne tried to have his way with her. In an old refrigerator. They were at some trash dump. He thought it would be fun. Maybe get some pillows out of the car. Vicki said that a) she was saving herself for marriage, so forget it, but more importantly, b) it was dangerous to play in old refrigerators, kids had been known to suffocate and die in them, so even if she wasn't saving herself for marriage (a), she'd still think he was out of his goddamned mind. Dwayne got all sore and drove off. He did come back for her later, but he just dropped her off at home and that was pretty much where things had ended.

Edith had listened to all this with horror and wonder. She had been taken to the prom by Scott Eunichtz (called "The Snail" by the girls at Buchanan), who had tried to make her laugh by forcing her to wear his inch-thick glasses. She didn't laugh. She told him to quit it and gave him his glasses back. Scott didn't take her to any trash dump after the prom, that was for sure.

Later, Edith was furious with Vicki for resisting Dwayne's advances. Okay, maybe the refrigerator was a bad idea, but after all, they'd been going out for a while, and it was time. Edith felt Vicki owed it to her to sleep with Dwayne. One of them ought to find out what sex was like, and it wasn't going to be Edith. This had been Edith's big chance to sleep with someone, sort of by the transitive property. And Vicki had screwed it up. Saving herself for marriage? What was the point of saving yourself if by the time you finally got around to it your kids were old before they were even born?

It was sad: People's personalities were pretty much finished developing by the time they were thirteen years old. Then you spent the next eighty years trying to cover it up. You learned all these methods of making people concentrate not on the fact that you were fat but on the fact that you had a great sense of humor, for instance, or that you had all sorts of unusual talents that they hadn't even heard of, like maybe you played the accordion or had a collection of paste or something, *anything,* to keep a stranger's attention on the fact that you were underneath it all pretty interesting, and not what you appeared to be on the surface, which was a complete and total *dork.*

Without thinking, she took a step towards the house, then

stopped again. Down Almond Street she could see the eye of the hollow tree. Smoke puffed out of a borehole. Boreholes were vents the government had dug from the surface down to the coal seam. The boreholes helped them follow the progress of the fire. Edith squinted, as if she saw something. She raised her fingertips to her forehead. As if she'd remembered something she had to go back for. That was it. She'd just go back and cross in front of the house again. Maybe she could call from Dwayne's house. Just ask if she could use the phone. He couldn't deny her that. Maybe he'd still be holding her portrait in one hand. They could have a conversation.

So she went back, looking dead ahead, towards the tree where there were no elves, down into the distance in the direction of her small home and in it her brother and his stupid wife Brenda. The golden girl. Everyone had practically fallen over themselves falling in love with Brenda. With any luck, she was still asleep. They were both in bed now, at least Edith hoped so. If not, she would be in trouble, and soon. The wife would come looking for her, trying to get her parachute back. Jesus, what then? Well, that didn't matter. Since she'd set all the clocks back. Brenda and Simon would think it was still early; they wouldn't dream of getting up at 7:00 A.M. Easter Sunday. They weren't children. If all went well she'd rendezvous there by nine-thirty or ten and they'd get the shock of their lives. It would serve them right. It was time for people to stop assuming that Edith was incapable of the unexpected.

She walked up to the front door, and touched the brass knocker with her fingers. It was cold. Last Easter she and Dwayne had run around in the front yard having egg races. This involved pushing raw eggs from one spot to another with the bridge of one's nose. It hadn't been as much fun as it was supposed to be. Edith's egg broke and her nostrils got all yolky. Dwayne went inside and got her a towel.

With a sudden fury Edith realized that she had no intention of knocking. She'd just lean her head in and say yoo-hoo. That would get him. Hello, here I am. Liberace back from the dead, or whatever his name was. The one who got his brain served on a platter. When she was little her mother used to roll up slices of baloney for dinner. Olive loaf.

She swung open the door. "Yoo-hoo," she said. She peeked into the house. It smelled exactly the same—the familiar, gentle stink of the place reminded her of days and afternoons spent here, lying around on the couch, watching "One Life" on television.

"Hello?" She closed the door behind her. "Dwayne? Anybody home?"

The house rang with an eerie silence. There was a fire roaring in the fireplace, but the living room was empty. There was a mounted moosehead above the mantelpiece which she couldn't remember seeing before. She walked into the kitchen. God, the smell of the house was unbelievable. She had completely forgotten the—what would you call it—the *essence* of the place. Written it out of her mind. And now, that gentle smell of Dwayne, that musky chocolate milkfulness, filling her senses. The minutiae of remembrance surrounded her. She had already forgotten the refrigerator magnets and the paint can with the wooden spoons in it. The sound the gears in the clock on the stove made. The fruit salad wallpaper.

He had moved the appliances, though. That was clear. They were nowhere in sight. Maybe Dwayne ate out now. He surely wasn't getting the kinds of meals he used to—Edith's special Noodles Romanov and Bang Pow Chicken. In the next room, something croaked. Like a frog in a gray pool of dead water. I'd better vamoose, Edith thought. It was too depressing. But first, what. Leave him a note. Write a note saying *Stopped by to Say Hello. Wishing you the best, Edith.* No, wishing you—the *special* best. She opened the drawer to find a pencil, and stared into Dwayne's junk. Pieces of string. Place mats. Garlic press. Raffle tickets from last year. Turkey baster. Paper crown from Burger King. Yo-yo.

She rummaged around the junk, trying not to think about the hour-and-a-half-long story that accompanied each object. She found the shaft of the malfunctioning automatic pencil with *Greetings from Miami* stenciled on the side. There was a chamber filled with water and a woman seemingly in waves and a shark that would move towards her if you turned the pencil on its side. Edith and Dwayne had gotten it during the trip to Disney World. She remembered the way Dwayne screamed in Space Mountain, and at the Lincoln Robot, and in Mr. Toad's Wild Ride. The pencil didn't work. Closing the drawer with exasperation, Edith went upstairs. Unless things had changed radically, Dwayne kept a hoard of felt-tip pens in the bureau near the waterbed.

She huffed and puffed up the stairs, still wearing her parachute, checking the time on her wristwatch. The jump was in a half hour. She was going to have to lie to the pilot and to the other sky divers, and that might take some talking. Convince them that she was her own sister-in-law. It was surely getting to be time to get out of Dwayne's house and back outside. It was creepy being in here. She knocked on the bedroom door. There was no sound from the other side.

She stood there for a moment, however, afraid to proceed. What if she walked in and he were in the midst of some tryst? Maybe that was why they hadn't answered. In the heat of the moment you lose your sense of hearing. Were they over there, listening to her listen, lying there in conjugal union, motionless, looking down towards the door? Waiting for her to leave. They might even be dead. She'd enter the room to find the two corpses, their bodies stiff, the lips light blue.

"Hello?" she whispered. "Dwayne? Are you there, honey?"

She pushed the door open quietly, hoping he would not be dead. Swinging from an extension cord, holding a note that said *I'm sorry I'm such a jerk.*

The room looked sort of like someone had pushed all of Dwayne's clothes into one of those baseball-pitching machines and left it on for an hour and a half, just letting the device strew pants and shirts and socks and shoes and scarves in every direction. It was amazing. Edith had a feeling of strangulation. She wished that there was someone around who could give her the Heimlich maneuver, or tell her a story.

On top of a small stand in one corner was a strange little cage.

A hutch, to be honest about it, for in the midst of this metallic superstructure was a white Angora rabbit. It had enormous whiskers radiating from either side of its disgusting rabbit maw, like the antennae of a lobster. And its little nose. Vibrating at several hundred spasms a minute.

She swallowed. What could possibly be going on here? She took a step forward towards the desk. Something pink wrapped around her shoe.

Edith bent over to disengage the whatever it was. What it was was a pair of pink panties with black fringe along the waist and around the leg holes. On the front was printed RED DOG SALOON. On the back it said JUNEAU, ALASKA.

Well, Edith thought. There it is. She dropped the panties as if she had touched a leprous growth on a brain-dead animal. The reason Dwayne's not home is because he's off with some Alaskan mopsy-top. Typical. But no, if this were true, then who had lit the fire downstairs? At the very least the rabbit wasn't Dwayne's. It was obvious: Dwayne was not only going out with someone else now, but had reached the stage of the relationship where the woman had decided to move her pets in.

Edith walked towards the desk to get a pen, so she could write some kind of note along the lines of *DROP DEAD*. But even as she picked up the felt-tip, she realized that there was something wrong with Dwayne's bedroom, something even worse than the fact that it had a rabbit in it. The television was gone. So were the stereo and the tape deck. Even his clock radio had vanished. Realizing what had happened even before she turned, she looked at the bureau drawer where Dwayne hid his mother's silver. The box was on the floor, empty.

Dwayne's house had been robbed.

She stood there, looking at all the shoes and underwear, holding her felt-tip pen. Her first reaction: Fine. Serves him right. Her second reaction: Maybe the Alaskan bimbo had made off with all the stuff. That's where Dwayne was now. Off chasing her. Trying to get his stuff back. Third reaction: They had gone to the police. To report it. But none of these reactions really made sense. His car was still out front. Where could they have gone? Had they stolen their own things? Can you do that?

But even as Edith stood there in wonder, the front door opened and closed downstairs and the house filled with the sounds of Dwayne and his new girlfriend returning. They were laughing and choking, stunned by the extremity of their own merriment.

"Honestly, Dwayne," the woman said. "You have got to be kidding."

"Naw," Dwayne said. "That's the way it was."

"But what a dope," the woman continued. "She musta been a imbecile or somethin. A screw loose."

"She was just like . . ."

"What? Go on. She was just like what?"

"Was, uh . . ."

There was a momentary silence downstairs while Dwayne thought. Edith knew what this was like. It was agonizing to wait for him. You could almost hear the rusted gears and springs desperately trying to revolve within the depths of Dwayne's brain.

"Was what, Dwayne?"

"Huh?"

"You were going to say something. You said, 'She was just like . . . ,' and then you trailed off. What was she like?"

"Aw, I don't know," Dwayne said. "She was just unlucky, I guess is what it was."

"Unlucky? There's more to it than that. Honestly. Eggshells in her nose?"

"Yeah. She sure got, uh . . ." He trailed off again.

"Dwayne?"

"What?"

"You were saying something. You said, 'She sure got' something."

"Uh. Yolky."

"Yolky?"

There was another agonizing silence.

"Yeah," Dwayne said at last, softly. "She got yolky."

They started laughing again. It was as if they had never heard anything funnier in their lives. They were pounding on the floor like referees at a wrestling match.

"Listen," the woman said. "Dwayne. Wait right here. I got something for you."

"I'll wait right here," Dwayne said. Suddenly he sounded depressed. "No place for me to go."

Edith heard them lumbering into the living room. That bought her a little time. The second they go into the kitchen, they're going to find all the appliances missing. And call the cops. On the phone upstairs. *And find Edith.* They'd think Edith had robbed them! They'd call the cops and throw her in jail and Edith would spend Easter Sunday in a cell with the Outcast, the guy they kept mentioning on the radio who rode around on a donkey holding up hardware stores.

"Oh, baby," Dwayne was saying. "You shouldna. You really shouldna given me this."

"I wanted you to have it," the woman said. "It was my daddy's. My daddy woulda wanted yuz ta have his."

"Aw," Dwayne said. "I miss my daddy." He sniffed.

"I miss my daddy too!" the woman said.

"We both miss our daddies!" Dwayne said.

"Oh, Dwayne!" she said. It sounded like they were both sobbing now. "Oh, my little Dwayne!"

"Buh, buh, buh," Dwayne said, crying. "Buh."

Edith listened to this scene in horror and wonder. She recognized that sound. It meant that something deep inside of Dwayne had been touched, maybe a part you'd better leave alone because Dwayne isn't really all there, and the part you've touched is the part that was never there in the first place.

Edith considered her escape routes. The most obvious one, of course, was to use the parachute. But there wasn't really enough wind to make a jump from a second-story window. The chute wouldn't even open by the time she smacked into the backyard. This was all Edith's guess. She had never gone skydiving before, simply assumed that at some point you yelled *Geronimo.* But that was from an airplane. This was from a back window. She needed something quieter.

The only other option would be to run down the front stairs while Dwayne and whoever she was looked the other direction. But there was no other direction. There were only two rooms on the first floor, the kitchen and the living room, and you could see the stairs from both of them.

Maybe she could make some noise upstairs, and when the two of them came up to investigate, she could hit them on the back of the head with a frying pan. Conk them out. Except that the frying pans were in the kitchen. Something else heavy, then. What was there heavy enough in the bedroom? A book by Danielle Steel? No, only three hundred pages. Why couldn't Steel have written a little bit longer? Put in some subplot about guys trying to blow up the KGB in a submarine with naked women, or something. Or had the heroine have a second affair with the handsome and mysterious man's twin. The problem with most literature nowadays was that there wasn't enough heft to it to really conk someone out with. Your best bet was still the encyclopedia.

"I have something for you, too," Dwayne said. "A gift."

"What? What is it?"

Dwayne didn't answer. They were probably making out now, right there in front of the fireplace. Edith wanted to throw up. If she got out of here alive, she would throw up, retroactively. She looked out the window. The Harrisons' house was about thirty feet away. Maybe she could get their attention. She opened the window. The cool air from outside blew in, rustling the bag of McDonald's french fries and take-out portions of Chinese food on the floor. Maybe she could throw something. She picked up a black high-heeled shoe and tossed it towards the Harrisons' house. It twisted through the air, rotating like some sort of South American weapon, bounced off the side of the Harrisons' house, and landed in the rhododendrons.

A dog barked. Buddy, the Harrisons' foul and overweight Dalmatian, walked towards the shoe. Buddy was the runt of one of the litters from Whispering Winds. The Harrisons had gotten him out of pity. The dog was more liquid than solid. It had streaks of brown goo on its muzzle that were the results of the curious jam that oozed from Buddy's eyes. Sometimes this same substance came out of the dog's ears, particularly when the dog was near electrical equipment. The dog's presence, for some reason, interfered with the reception on the Harrisons' televisions and radios, which was why they kept it outside. It was about a hundred pounds and had no hair on its tail.

Buddy sniffed the shoe and growled. That's good. Bark a little, get Dwayne and his friend to go outside. What seems to be the problem, Buddy? Then while they were trying to figure it out, Edith could run downstairs and be on her way.

Buddy looked up at Edith. He was confused. The smell of the shoe belonged to the foot of the woman from next door. But there was also the smell of Edith on the shoe. Because she had thrown it. Yet Edith, up until a few months ago, used to *be* the woman from next door. Now Edith was waving at Buddy from a second-story window. He got a lost look on his face. Thinking his special dog thoughts.

Edith threw another shoe. The spike on the high heel rotated round and round as the pump whisked through space. It really did look like some kind of weapon. Edith wouldn't have wanted to have gotten hit by it.

Unfortunately, Buddy did get hit by it. The heel struck him just behind the head. He fell over. *Oh Jesus,* Edith thought. *I've killed Buddy.* Dwayne is going to find me up here, will strangle me to death, then after I'm dead they'll blame me for the robbery. All of which wouldn't really be so bad if you compare it to some other things, but now, on top of it all, she will have to go to hell with the murder of Buddy on her hands. Buddy will be up there in heaven, licking hot dogs off of a rotisserie, while Edith, whose goal in life was just to remain out of people's way, will spend eternity in Hell for Buddy's cold-blooded execution.

No, wait. He's up again. Buddy was only knocked out for a second. He's looking up at Edith in wonder. Maybe he died for a second, like one of those experiences you read about in the

National Enquirer, and Buddy went for a few precious seconds into hot dog heaven and saw the snout of the Dalmatian god, who extended his paw and said: NO, BUDDY. NOT YET. BUDDY, GO BACK.

Buddy leaned over and licked the second shoe.

From downstairs came a low moan. Edith recognized that moan. Dwayne.

Was there no way to get him to bark? The problem was that Buddy recognized Edith. She used to live here, after all. Why shouldn't she be throwing shoes out the window? They had less right to be here than she did. They were alien shoes. Not native to this area. Poison shoes.

This was when Edith looked at the rabbit again. The rabbit. Sure. She could show him the rabbit. That would do it. She moved towards the hutch, opened the little gate. The rabbit looked at her, vibrating its disgusting little nose. Its whisker-antennae pricked up, as if the creature were puckering its snout. With a mixture of courage and revulsion, she picked up the rabbit and looked it straight in the eyes. The rabbit looked back.

She went back to the window. Buddy was still standing there. She waved Bunny back and forth. "Come on, Buddy," she said. "Ruff, ruff ruff." She held the rabbit out towards him, beckoning to him with it. "Ruff ruff ruff," she said, quietly. There was a clear urgency, yet a trace of sadness in her voice as well. "Ruff. Ruff ruff."

Buddy cocked his head to one side and raised his ears.

He's probably still stunned from being hit with the shoe. But he knows this is a rabbit here. It's evident something inside, some dog hormone, is being affected. But Fluffy's still too far away. We need to get it closer. Right under his little dog nose. That should do it. Then he'll bark and Dwayne and the Bimbo will go outside and Edith can get back on the road towards the airfield and make the jump and be back at her own house before everybody wakes up and realizes she's changed all the clocks in the house.

Okay, okay, so now we've got to get the rabbit closer to Buddy. Edith looked around. Maybe she could lower it on some string. But no, there's a fence dividing the properties; she'll have to get it over the fence. Right.

So she could throw it. But Jesus Christ, then Fluffy might die even before he got to Buddy. Do dogs bark at dead animals? Usually not, but you couldn't tell with Buddy. He was the kind. But if not, then that would be it. She wouldn't get a second chance. And Edith had pretty much put all her resources into this rabbit concept anyway. There's not much time left. All was quiet downstairs—were they calling the cops already? It was time for something to happen!

So: what she needed now was something soft, something to wrap the rabbit in. That way it wouldn't die on impact. She put the rabbit down for a second, went over to the dresser, looked through one of the open drawers. There was a sweater. A sweater with a zipper. Jesus Christ. Obviously property of the Moron downstairs. Wrap up Fluffy with it. It was nice and soft and— hey, it's angora! Now what? Would that make the rabbit sad, being wrapped up in angora fur? Probably not as sad as being thrown out the window for Buddy to sniff. Now where was that rabbit, anyway?

Bunny was not to be found in the room. He had not hopped back into his cage, nor had he gotten lost under the bed, nor had he merged into one of the soft fluffy piles under the bed. Bunny was on the lam. Bunny had flown the caboose.

But wait—there at the top of the stairs, looking down on all creation, his antennae twitching, his ears flopped down on either side of his head. Edith moved slowly towards him, trying to have as much grace in motion as one can have while still wearing the goddamn parachute on one's back. One false move and Bunny would hop downstairs, and Dwayne and the Bimbo would look up. *Hey. Rabbit's out.*

"C'mere," she whispered. "C'mere." She held out the angora sweater, tried to make it look like another friendly bunny. "Hullo," she made the sweater say. "Let's talk about carrots."

From downstairs, the woman said: "Dwayne, you are an absolute doll. Thank you. This is a very precious gift. Now how about a drink? You want a Bloody Mary or something?"

Edith pounced. Got him. She grabbed him by the ears and wrapped him up in the sweater and moved back into the bedroom and over to the open window.

"Okay, Coconut," Dwayne said. "Anything for you."

Coconut! Jesus! That was what he had called Edith! The pendant that she still had at home said I LOVE YOU COCONUT on it. He had given Edith's nickname to this moron with the Juneau Alaska underwear! Coconut! What a complete and utter sleazeball!

Edith flung the rabbit out of the window with all her might. Son of a *bitch*!

Thinking about it later Edith figured there must have been buttons on the sweater. In addition to the zipper. For ornaments. Or something hard. Either that or the window which Fluffy hit had already been broken, or had a hairline crack in it, like you see in glasses sometimes. Anyway there must have been something, because the window shouldn't have broken. Maybe the rabbit weighed a whole lot more than anybody thought. That was possible. It was big.

There were a few moments of silence, a few precious seconds while everyone reacted. Edith stood in Dwayne's bedroom, looking at the hole in the neighbor's windowpane the bunny had made. Dwayne and his girlfriend downstairs stopped kissing and looked up, hearing the sound of tinkling glass. Buddy stood on the ground, looking up at the place overhead where a moment ago something had streaked across the sky. In the Harrisons' house, little Phoebe Harrison opened her eyes, and for a moment thought that perhaps her Easter wish had come true. Of course she had wished for a pony, and this was more the size of a rabbit, but who knows, maybe it really was a pony, a very small one, she'd have to take care of. She sat up in bed and turned the fluffy animal over, trying to figure out where the mane and hooves were and then she saw the blood and this was the moment she began to scream.

As Phoebe screamed, Buddy cocked his head again. His tail grew stiff. He threw his head back and began to howl.

"What's that?" Dwayne said.

"It's okay," the woman said. "It's just that dog again."

"What's wrong?" Dwayne said. "Something's wrong."

"Nothing's wrong, sweetheart. That dog's just barking again. You know how it is. That dog's not right in the head."

"He's upset about something," Dwayne said. "I can tell he's upset about something."

"You certainly seem to understand that dog well," the woman said, her voice suddenly icy.

"We've got to find out what's happening. Something's happening. It is. Something's, uh, going on!"

There was the sound of people moving downstairs, and the shush of wind as the front door opened. Edith knew that this was the moment. She should move. But this was not what she had wanted to have happen. Someone, probably a little girl, judging from the scream, was very unhappy next door. And it was her fault. Edith's. She was the one who had thrown the rabbit through space.

These were the kinds of things that happened. There was never any time to stop and explain how things came to be. She had only wanted to be left alone, had only wanted to give Dwayne her best wishes on the occasion of this lovely morning. And now she had thrown a rabbit through a window. A rabbit that belonged to someone she didn't even know. And a small child was having the kind of psychological trauma that would doubtlessly scar her for life and not only that but in a moment the police were going to come over and arrest her for something she didn't even do.

In a perfect world Wedley Harrison from next door would have come out of his house at that moment and rescued her. It was Wedley she had turned to, the night she realized Dwayne was cheating on her. She'd run into his house and collapsed in his arms, begging for him to rescue her, as Wedley's two daughters looked on in horror. But Wedley hadn't saved her then, and he didn't save her now. He remained in the house with the broken window, while his daughter cried in her room.

Edith made sure the parachute was tight on her back and ran down the stairs. Dwayne knocked on the front door of the

Harrisons' house. Buddy was barking. Phoebe was still screaming.

Edith moved down the stairs like a boulder rolling off a cliff. She would have careened straight through the open door, out across the yard and back into the street, had she not looked over at the fireplace. She wanted to get a last look at that moosehead. But instead of a moose she met the eyes of Dwayne's girlfriend. She had a strange expression, as if she had been expecting Edith all along. It was an expression Edith knew well, one she had seen before on Vicki's face. It was the face Vicki used when she'd told Edith something secret, that said she had shared something that had rested deep within her heart.

Vicki looked a lot older than she used to. The last time Edith had seen her was at graduation. Now she looked like a woman, a grown-up. In the seven years since high school, Vicki had become devastatingly and disgustingly beautiful. Just being in the same room with her made Edith feel that she had stepped out of the world and into a magazine from Florida.

"Edith," Vicki said. "Is that you, honey?"

"No," Edith said. "I'm not who you think I am."

"It is you," Vicki said. "Edith. What are you doing?"

"You've got it all wrong," Edith said. "I'm somebody else entirely. I'm someone you've never met."

And having said this much, Edith ran out the door. She hoped that Vicki would take her at her word. She probably wouldn't though. Vicki had always been the suspicious type. Was she still distrustful, now that she was gorgeous?

She looked back at the house from Almond Street. The Harrisons' front door was open. Inside people were yelling and screaming. There was the sound of things smashing. Buddy was still howling in the side yard. One of the shoes Edith had thrown was hanging off of a rhododendron bush, swinging slightly by its heel in the Easter morning wind.

She ran until she got to Whispering Winds Kennels, the parachute pack bouncing up and down between her shoulder blades. All the Dalmatians were pacing back and forth in their kennels, looking at her angrily and showing their teeth. Edith, out of breath and slightly frightened, paused in front of the kennels, and tried to assume a look of complete ignorance and composure. If she showed up at the airfield distraught and confused, she was certain to give herself away.

It was a good thing she had decided not to use the chute to get out of the second-story window. She would never have had time to repack it on the ground. Anyway, she didn't know anything about packing chutes. The only reason she could do the jump at all was because Brenda had packed it up last night before going to sleep.

The members of the Centralia Aerharts—the all-women's skydiving club—were walking towards the plane when Edith arrived at Centralia Airfield. The pilot looked over at her and said, "You must be Brenda."

Edith said that she was.

"We almost left without you," he said. "You're late."

"I know," she said. "I got tied up."

"I've heard so much about you," said a horsey-looking woman wearing a blue jumpsuit. "Your friend Chip knows my boyfriend Huff."

"Oh yeah," Edith said. "Huff. I've heard of him."

"My name's Jenny," she said. She pointed towards a thin woman in front of her. "That's my sister Jody. Up there is Jane Peabody and Rosalee." Jenny looked at Edith's clothes. "You're going to jump in that?" she said.

"Sure," Edith said. She realized at this moment that she was just wearing blue jeans, her coat, and a pair of gloves. Everyone else was wearing special goggles and jumpsuits. All very official. "This is what I always wear," Edith said. "Keeps it simple." Jenny nodded.

"Whatever," Jenny said. "I suppose they do things their own way in Philadelphia." Edith shook her head yes. The five women and the pilot walked towards the plane. It was quiet there, except for the distant barking of the dogs at the kennels. A wind sock lay gustless upon a pole.

The plane had no seats in it, just two long benches on either side. Everybody leaned forward because it was impossible to lean back with the parachutes on. The pilot muttered some numbers into a radio, then looked over his shoulder at the women. He pressed some buttons and the propeller in front began to spin. The tiny plane sounded like a lawn mower.

Edith was seated on the bench behind the pilot's left side. She watched the blades of the propeller spinning, gaining speed until they seemed to become invisible. You could look through the space where the propeller was and hardly know it was there, except that colors seemed more monochromatic, as if the blades were spinning the reds and blues out of the world.

I hope that thing is connected to the front, Edith thought. Probably just hanging on there by a single nut. What if the propeller gets loose? It would probably keep spinning, soar below them. But maybe it would slash right through the plane, cut them all up into little pieces. Probably be fast. You'd never know it. Not the worst way to go. Not unless it got the pilot and everybody else but not you. Then you'd have to sit in the fuselage, waiting for impact. You wouldn't mind the crash, but you'd have to wait for it for so long.

Brenda said it was easy. That you just stepped out of the doorway into oblivion and fell through the sky (this was where Brenda had started waving her arms around) and reached a kind of special quiet place deep within your hurtling, velocity-gaining being. The still point of the turning world. The wind rushed through your ears as the horizon tilted upside down and you could open up your hands so they looked like starfish and stretch for miles and miles and never touch the earth. It was a kind of freedom, Brenda said. Maybe the last place on earth you could find that kind of freedom, maybe because you weren't on earth. For a moment you were cut off from the agony of it all, separate from the teeming sadness down on the planet. Cut away from crying children and singing gorillas and suspicions of burglary and inarticulate men incapable of love. She said it made her more alive, that after each jump she felt like she had stuck her tongue into an electric socket connected to the omnipotent dynamos of the planets.

The plane twisted around to the left and bumped towards the runway. Everybody else was talking and laughing. Rosalee had some sort of liquid in a thermos she was handing around. Her friend, the short one, handed Edith a Styrofoam cup. Edith sipped. The plane bounced once on the runway and was airborne. Irish coffee.

"Wait a minute, lemme give you some nutmeg," Jane Peabody said. She had an interesting face—tired and lined, her cheeks red and rosy.

"I'm okay," Edith said, holding the cup in her hand.

"Ah, gowan. Hold it here." Edith did. "There ya go. Happy Easter to ya." Jane toasted Edith. Below them, the rooftops of Centralia grew small. Squares of yards and barns and fields moved slowly beneath the plane.

"Hey, honey," Jane Peabody said. "Looka here." Their eyes met. "You okay? You aren't getting the jitters, are ya?"

"Nah," Edith said. "I'm okay. I was just thinking, that's all."

Jane Peabody looked towards her, waiting for Edith to say more. Somebody wanted the nutmeg. Jane handed it to Jody across the aisle. Jody and Rosalee were laughing it up. Jane reached over and rubbed Edith on the back. "You sure you're all right?"

"I'm fine," Edith said. "It's just me and my husband had a fight."

"Gee, I'm sorry, Brenda," Jane Peabody said. "Isn't that always the way? Well, don't you worry. Soon you'll be floating and he can go fuck himself." She smiled self-consciously, as if to let Edith know she was not by nature a profane woman. The Irish coffee felt good inside. It tasted like it was spiked with lighter fluid.

"I always forget about everything when I'm jumping," Jane Peabody said.

"It would be nice if you could just keep falling forever once," Edith said.

"Wouldn't that be the best?" Jane Peabody said. "But there's no sense in thinking that way. You do and it's bam, *sayonara.*"

The thermos went around again and everybody took a little more. Jenny and Jody were hysterical about something, some story about a woman getting a tattoo of a skunk. Edith didn't really follow. She looked out at the sky through the invisible propeller. The blades turned the horizon gray.

Edith was not particularly nervous about the jump. She had heard Brenda talk about how easy it was so many goddamn times it was like she had the whole process memorized. There was a metallic taste in her mouth, as if her teeth had turned to aluminum foil. The parachute was supposed to be specially designed. So you could steer it. It was a whole new age. Edith figured with a little practice she could land straight in her backyard. Shock the hell out of them. Then they'd shut up. Brenda might be a little annoyed, but that was part of the plan too. We might finally stop hearing about how wonderful she was and get a little peace and quiet.

Everyone assumed that Edith was incapable of anything. It was just taken for granted. Edith had a rule: treat someone like an idiot long enough, and that person will start to act like an idiot. This had been going on since high school. Vicki going out with Dwayne and leaving Edith on her own. Everybody going off to college, leaving Centralia, selling their houses to the Department of the Interior, having them torn down. Well, let them leave. If that's their attitude. The town would be fine once they tore down the abandoned houses. It would look almost like it used to.

That was really something, though, running into Vicki at Dwayne's. The nerve of the woman. Vicki had moved away in 1978. As soon as Vicki got out of high school her family decided to give up. She and Vicki had run into each other in the Bob-In in Mount Carmel the week after graduation. They drank Tequila Sunrises, just like in tenth grade, talked about the people they knew. When they finally got around to Dwayne, Vicki just said, "He likes you. I know." The next week, she and her mother had moved to Reading. Last thing Edith had heard Vicki was working in a piano showroom.

She called him four years later, the day after Hurricane Hildegarde. Right out of the blue. There was this big tree down across her driveway, and he had a chain saw and his pickup, so why didn't he come over and help her out. She wasn't nervous. It was completely natural. He stood out there sawing the tree in half while Edith watched him from the kitchen window, drinking V-8 juice. Afterwards he cut it all up into firewood and stacked it on the porch and came inside and had a beer and it was just as natural as could be. He talked a little about Vicki, how he missed her a bit, but he remembered the good reasons they broke up and didn't want to "see that movie again," as he put it. "She wasn't who I thought she was," he added, and talked about everything he had done with Vicki in high school, as if they had spent all that time together in order to prove who they were, and Vicki had gone back on the promise. "Maybe it wasn't Vicki you were looking for then," Edith said.

It was brilliant. Vicki had spent all that time going out with Dwayne, then talking about the relationship so that Edith could secretly go out with him too. And in the end Dwayne felt that Vicki wasn't who he thought she was. Maybe who he thought she was, was Edith. So that whole time it was as if Dwayne was going out with Vicki *because* she told Edith everything. Vicki had only been the stand-in. The prelude.

Jody crawled down the center aisle, held on to an iron rung near the door, and told everyone to "hold on to their hats." She opened the door and a mad rush of air filled the fuselage. Jody's empty Styrofoam cup blew over and rolled towards the back of the plane.

She let go of a small red streamer. Everybody looked out the windows and watched it drift. The streamer blew down towards the town, falling swiftly into the midst of a field. A steaming borehole at one end betrayed the presence of the mine fire. Even from this altitude, smoke from the fire was still visible, drifting over the hills and fields.

Edith looked out on her hometown. So little of it was left now. In another twenty years, would it still be on the map? Already they were taking the names off the signposts. There was no town there to direct people to. The only major structure remaining was the Orthodox church up on the hill. And the Odd Fellows' graveyard. It was in a junkyard beyond the cemetery that the fire first started. Twenty-two years ago now. Some kids playing with matches. The dump fire caught on to a coal vein near the surface, and that was it. Twenty-two years later, the fire had spread through the mountains, under the streets and homes. You couldn't stop it.

For a while there, it was as if Edith were living in her own most desperate and wonderful dream. She would wake up in the morning next to him, his arm around her even as he slept, emitting his lovely chocolate smell. She would kiss him awake, and they would begin to make love. Later she'd go downstairs and make him scrambled eggs and toast and bring them to him, and then go outside and get the paper and they'd sit there in bed reading and drinking coffee in the warm aftermath of their passion.

They had been living together for almost a year when Dwayne seemed to change. When she'd kiss him awake in the morning, he'd get up and immediately get in the shower. She'd make him oatmeal and he'd come downstairs for it. They'd read the paper, sitting in separate chairs, and then he'd give her a quick peck and drive off to work.

And that was all right for a time. Even true love needs a rest. But he'd come home late, or he'd call her and tell her to meet him at the Bob-In, and when she got there, there he'd be with all the guys from work and their wives, many of them from the same high school crowd that had included Dwayne and Vicki and had excluded Edith. And again she came up against this problem of everyone being the same person they were in ninth grade except that now instead of complaining about their parents they complained about their children. Something about that circle remained tight and rigid, and Edith, even though she was Dwayne's lover now, was still not included. One day she had found someone else's panties under their bed. That was how it had ended, but the end had started before that.

The only person who had ever acted like she was a real human being had been that Wedley from next door. Once when Dwayne refused to let her come to the Bob-In with him she went next door and drank lemonade with Wedley. He was a sad man—you could tell just by looking at him that his wife had left him—but there was something sweet about him too. He listened to her problems and he didn't tell her she was weird. He just said something like everyone has to find their own answers, just like that. Then he kissed her ear and led her back to the house. It was a shame that Wedley was so much older than she was. He was almost twelve years her senior. If he'd been younger, then maybe something could have happened. But he was beyond Edith's grasp, like everything else worth having.

There was this one time Edith and Dwayne had been walking out near the farm where Dr. Meyers had had his veterinary practice in the sixties. The farm had gone to pot and the farmhouse was practically caved in now, and the lone windmill stood at the edge of an old sulky track, spinning in the wind. They were burying Dwayne's cat. He said there were a lot of animals buried out there, that it was the logical place to inter Sneakers. The field was pretty close to the fire zone, and there was a borehole out in the middle of the field with a lot of smoke coming out of it. Dwayne's shovel had come into contact with bones almost as soon as he started digging, and all kinds of tiny skulls and little thighbones and vertebrae from pets long gone started coming up with the dirt. Dwayne said not to cry, but he kept digging, and the pile of bones kept getting larger and larger and Edith asked him couldn't he just put Sneakers in there now but Dwayne insisted on burying her three feet down. So he kept digging and the bones and skulls kept coming up with the dirt and soon Edith was crying. She wasn't even quite sure why, but she knew what she wanted more than anything else in the world was for Dwayne to stop what he was doing and hold her. To tell her that she was more important than some dead cat. Dwayne just looked up at her and said, "Squeamish, huh?"

And soon she was crying so badly that she was shaking, and each new sob seemed to thrust three more out of the cavern from which they were leaking. Finally Dwayne came over and gave her something. It was a little tag, covered with dirt. It said: JOCKO. He wanted her to have it.

Edith started crying harder and harder. And Dwayne just shook his head and went back to burying Sneakers. She needed him to comfort her and all he did was give her a dog tag from somebody's JOCKO that had been dead god only knows how many years. Edith got up and turned and started walking across the field, towards the borehole where the smoke was coming out. The air smelled like sulfur and ozone and snow, and there were tears on her cheeks, and behind her she could still hear the sound of Dwayne's shovel digging in the field. A plane went by overhead.

"Edith?" Dwayne said, from a distance, and soon he was running after her, and she was running away from him, and when he finally caught her he still had the shovel and she somehow managed to move his arm too hard when she spun around and the flat side of the shovel conked him on the forehead. His face went blank for a minute, as if his skull was a bell that had just been rung. Then he raised the shovel over one shoulder as if he was going to strike her, and the two of them were just looking each other in the eyes when he dropped it and held her tight. Edith was still crying. Dwayne didn't say anything, but he could see the smoke coming out of that borehole over her shoulder and he watched the smoke move through the air as he held his sobbing lover in his arms.

Edith looked over at Jane Peabody. "Can I borrow a pen?" she said.

"A pen?"

"Yeah. A pen. I gotta write something down so I don't forget."

Jane Peabody handed Edith a pen, and Edith hunted around in her pockets for something to write on. There was a laundry ticket from last month she thought she had lost, and she jotted a quick note for them to read. A message. She handed Jane Peabody the pen, put the laundry ticket in her pocket. That field, with all the little bones and skulls in it. Somebody's JOCKO.

They never talked about that scene, the way they never talked about most things, but what was clear to Edith was that after all these years, he wasn't who she thought he was either. For a while she thought that meant there was some other phantom Dwayne, the true Dwayne, waiting for her out there, just as there had been a true Edith for him, waiting beyond the phantom Edith which had in reality been Edith's friend Vicki. She wondered about this other person, this True Dwayne, wondered if he knew there was a phantom Dwayne taking up space with Edith at that time, wondered if he was ever thinking about her. Maybe the two of them were both thinking about each other at the same time, looking out into the night. Perhaps it was that Wedley Harrison from next door. How strange it would have been if Wedley turned out to have been Dwayne all along.

Jody gazed through the open door, down at the fields below. In the back the other girls were still laughing about something and the Styrofoam cups were all rolling on the floor. The Aerharts were smashed. They were poking each other in the stomach and laughing and poking each other in the ribs and laughing and poking each other in the stomach again. And laughing.

You'd at least think they'd let me in on the joke, Edith thought.

Jody jumped out of the plane. Jenny and Rosalee stood by the door, checking their gloves. Edith stood up.

The sound of the air rushing by was amazing. She looked out over Centralia. Yes, there was her hometown. You could see almost every place Edith had been in her entire life from here. There was where the elementary school had been, and beyond it the gentle mountains where her grandfather and father had worked in the coal mines. There was the road that led up to what had once been her parents' house, not so far away. It would be easy to negotiate.

Jenny jumped out of the plane. Rosalee jumped out of the plane. It was quiet now. All that laughing and poking and smirking had gone overboard. It was just Jane Peabody and Edith now. They stood by the door. It didn't seem hard to do. Edith had wondered if she was going to have a final attack of nerves at this point, but it was completely simple. Three open parachutes drifted below them. The air was clean and crisp. For once, Edith thought, I'm out of the drift of smoke.

Jane Peabody turned to Edith and rubbed her shoulder. "Feeling better?" she said. Edith nodded. "You gotta look on the

bright side," she said. "If ya don't, ya make yourself a nutcake."
She smiled, waved once, and jumped.

Down on the ground a police car moved down a country road,
its beacons strobing blue against the green grass. The wind blew
in Edith's face. For a moment she thought about Scott Eunichtz,
putting his glasses on her face. That underwear from Juneau. That
refrigerator in the dump.

Edith Schmertz stood alone by the door. Below her Jane
twisted around and around, sometimes drifting on her back,
sometimes rolling on her side, like a body in water. Edith placed
one hand on her neck, feeling the hollow at the bottom of her
throat. For an instant her fingers looked for something. The
necklace, the one that said I LOVE YOU COCONUT. But that was
back at home, and she was not likely to see it again. She shook
her head and sighed, took a deep breath, and stepped forward.
The sound of the airplane immediately grew louder, sounding
like cannonfire, then softly faded, until at last it vanished into the
gentle blue rush of air and earth and sky.

V E N U S

◑

The Bringer of Love

*Little can be learned of the true surface of the
planet, as observers cannot penetrate beyond the
enveloping layers of clouds or vapor.*

Meanwhile, a few miles away, Dent Wilkins was regretting
his halfhearted tryst with Judith Lenahan, who, as it turned
out, was a mime, an orphan, and a nudist. To his aggravation,
the morning after they had slept together she had tried to coerce
Wilkins into her depraved lifestyle. Judith, for her part, didn't
understand how a sane human being could sanction clothes. There
was something about the state of being dressed that filled Judith
Lenahan with a vast sense of aggravation and loathing, a sarcastic
mumpishness that only nakedness could allay.

Judith Lenahan lived in Bryn Mawr, which, she now realized,
was a much better place for nudity than Columbia County. She
lived in a small apartment building near the firehouse on Lancaster Pike called The Blackthorn. There was a cast-iron coat of arms
over the door that featured a woman on horseback encircled by
the blooms and briars of a black rosebush. On a typical day Judith
passed beneath this heraldic shield at six, and was naked by
six-fifteen. She liked to peel her hated work clothes off in the
kitchen, put some loud music on the stereo, then get a sixteen-
ounce can of Pabst Blue Ribbon from the refrigerator. In the
summer she liked to consume it standing right there in front of
the refrigerator with the door open. It was good to feel all that
cool air on her body, and to listen to music as loud as it could
possibly be. The beer, and the music, and all that refrigeration,

were an antidote to a poison that Judith Lenahan had spent the
working day reluctantly ingesting. The Blackthorn Cure, Judith
called it, as if that woman on horseback could help her to ride
away from the world, leaving its obnoxious non-naked putrescence stranded behind her, tangled amid those strange black roses
and brambles.

The possible volumes of her stereo were precisely determined.
The people next door were Quakers, the people on the other side
were students at Haverford College, the guy across the hall
collected worms or something, the woman upstairs was a certified
public accountant, the couple downstairs were park rangers at
Valley Forge National Historic Park. Judith knew exactly what
volume got each of them out of bed, and at what time. The main
problem was the worm guy from across the hall, in whose
apartment her music was probably the softest, but he was the kind
of person who always had to have his finger in your face or he
wasn't happy. So Judith sat there after work in her chair buck
naked, drinking her second beer and listening to her music as loud
as she could get it, which on account of the worm wasn't very.

Judith didn't think there was anything particularly interesting
about the fact that she spent most of her time naked. It was
boring, something she had accepted as part of herself for years.
Clothes were stupid. All you really needed was to be warm. The
rest was all fashion, and fashion was idiotic. You ended up
making some sort of statement, no matter what you did. There
was this whole secret code, especially for women, about who you
were and what you were saying about yourself when you dressed
a certain way and she didn't want to know about it. It was the
same experience she had had when she found out she needed
glasses. All you wanted to do was see. But oh no, they wouldn't
just give you a pair of glasses. You had to pick out the goddamn
frames. And there were tortoiseshell frames for preppies and John
Lennon glasses for hippies and Benjamin Franklin glasses for
librarians, and she was supposed to use the fact that she was
practically blind as some sort of opportunity for making a complex statement about herself. The fact of the matter was that it
was nobody's damn business who she was. If people wanted to

know who she was, they could ask her a question. Talk to her. Rather than making some sweeping and condescending snap judgment based on her glasses. She got contact lenses in the end, which she also hated because contact lenses were another form of statement, but what could one do? Contacts were less of a statement than anything else, and a lack of statement is what Judith was aiming for. The hell with it, Judith thought. She wasn't going to spend her life providing secret signals for strangers to misconstrue.

It was this kind of thinking, of course, that had led to the decision to shave her head. Judith had long reddish-brown hair that fell below her waist; she figured that just letting the damn stuff grow was the closest thing to making no Hair Statement whatsoever. It never got much longer than that; by the time her hair got to her waist it tended just to fall out. So that was great: she didn't ever have to set foot in a hair salon where some ditzy woman came up to you and asked you what "you'd like." Hair was worse than clothes, in a way, because you had so many options, none of which were practical. If you got a perm you were presumed to be stupid and if you got it dyed you were presumed to be superficial and if you just had it trimmed you were assumed to be a coward. Judith's answer was just to let it grow, and tie it back and out of the way. When she wore a coat, she'd keep her hair under the collar in the back so people wouldn't look. This seemed like the perfect solution for a while, but then at this temp job she had for the month of April, one of the other secretaries said she "looked like a gypsy." It was the worst. What the hell business was it of some stranger who she was? So: off it would go, right down to the roots.

It was the perfect solution. She figured she would buy some wigs for those occasions that she needed to look normal, like in the office. When she got home she could take her hair off, just like everything else. And it would come in handy for her mime work. Judith only worked as an office temp when the mime business was slow; unfortunately, this was turning out to be most of the time. But with a shaved head all kinds of things might become possible.

On the day after Palm Sunday, Judith had risen and donned her dress-for-success things and taken the train downtown to Market East. She was temping at a bank on Chestnut Street. Temping was the perfect job for Judith because everyone pretended she did not exist; it was a job you could step out of at the end of the day. Judith was temping at a bank she thought was called Melon. All she knew about Melon was that it used to be Girard Bank and some clowns from Pittsburgh had bought them out. So suddenly everybody that had a Girard account got a letter saying that now all their money was in the hands of something called Melon, and weren't the customers just wild about that? Companies did these kinds of things. When Judith was a kid there used to be Esso stations, with signs over the garages announcing HUMBLE OIL, or HAPPY MOTORING. Now Esso was called Exxon, and nobody said anything about Happy Motoring, let alone being humble. They were too busy spewing gallons of Vitalis into the ocean to worry about being humble.

She was working a telex machine for this guy Wilkins in the Trust Department. She didn't quite know why they called it Trust. It seemed like Trust was the last thing you'd have in a bank. Everybody knew that only insane people liked going to the bank. Most people would rather get German measles than have to go to the bank and stand in line. A line that, more often than not, led to a teller who would explain that the thing that you're trying to do is impossible and you'll have to get special permission from some goon behind a desk who won't be free for another hour because he's busy with some deranged person. Or else you'd get stuck behind a guy who wants his paycheck in two–dollar bills, silver dollars, and dimes. There ought to be two lines in banks, Judith thought, one line for the insane people, and one for everybody else.

Anyway, at twelve-thirty, Judith got up from the telex machine and took the elevator down to the street to get her head shaved. She felt a grin deep within her body at the brilliant simplicity of what she was about to do. Judith walked out on the spring scene—on Chestnut Street people were wearing light-colored clothes and going without their jackets. There was a woman selling flowers on the corner of Chestnut and Tenth. Tourists down the block were gathering in front of Independence Hall and taking pictures. She remembered going there with her father years ago. That was the last memory she had of him: her tiny hands feeling the cold iron of the Liberty Bell's clapper, and trying to read the writing around the bell's shoulder: *Proclaim liberty throughout the land*.

Judith stepped westward into the stream of people on Chestnut, walked down towards Broad Street. She had seen this salon called Hair Today Gone Tomorrow, figured it was as good a place as any. When you got your head shaved, would it matter who did it? Would different places do it differently?

She walked into the salon, which was almost deserted. One woman sat underneath a hair dryer in the back. The place was not doing well. A girl with hair like a pineapple approached and asked what she'd like. She was wearing a name tag that said SHIRLEY.

Judith froze. She was, without warning, completely unnerved. Shirley just stood there staring. In the distance the woman under the dryer looked like she was having a brain transplant. Rows and rows of hair spray and shampoos glistened from a shelf.

"Head shaved," Judith said.

"Shaved?" Shirley said.

"Shaved," Judith said. "Head. Mine. I want mine. My head shaved. I want you to shave my head."

"Now?" Shirley said.

"Yes," Judith said. "I would like for you to shave my head now. You do do that kind of thing, don't you?"

Shirley looked surprised. Insulted. "Sure," she snorted. "Naturally."

She seated Judith in a chair in front of a window. She tied a cloth around her.

"Didja wash yer hair this morning?" said Shirley. She had an incredibly high voice, as if her parents were elves.

"No," Judith said.

"Lean *be-*yack," said Shirley. Judith found herself being eased backwards; the back of her chair reclined so that Judith's head could be lowered onto the edge of a sink with a neck-shaped cut built into it, kind of like a guillotine sink. Shirley began to moisten Judith's hair, and she felt the warm water seeping into her scalp. It felt good. She closed her eyes and relaxed, feeling her hair being washed. She thought about her baby days again. Once her Grandma Watson, who was not related to her family at all, had made her a batch of Marshmallow Octagons. This must have been right after they got the news about her father. Grandma Watson was a friend of her father's who came to stay with them for a while. Judith remembered looking up in the sky at an airplane and waving.

"Up," said the hairdresser.

Judith felt herself rising, almost as if she were filled with helium. Her hair was wrapped up in a towel. The chair rose up and the back made a clicking noise. The hairdresser looked her in the eye.

"Shaved?" she said.

"Uh-huh," Judith said.

Shirley took an enormous pair of shears and cut off a huge chunk of her hair on the left-hand side. Several feet of hair fell to the floor.

"Can I have it back later?" Judith said.

"Hah? Back?"

"My hair. I want to keep it after."

"Ya want it I'll give it to yuz."

"Thank you."

The hairdresser clipped another huge chunk off of the other side. In ten or eleven snips, all the long tresses were gone. The hairdresser changed scissors and started clipping the nubs close to her scalp.

Judith looked up, towards the window that looked out on Chestnut Street. Three or four women had stopped to look in the window of Hair Today Gone Tomorrow to watch what was going on. Their eyes were frozen wide open in horror.

"Aw, doan chew mind 'em," the hairdresser said. "Buncha *am*-bulance chasers."

Shirley popped some gum in her mouth. "Ya gonna look *fab*-u-lous," she said.

The crowd at the window was slowly growing larger. It was beginning to feed on itself, drawing in people who wanted to know what was going on.

The hairdresser put her shears down and flipped on an electric razor. "Yuh ready?" she said.

Judith wasn't really ready. Suddenly she felt unsure, regretful. But before Judith could say a word, Shirley moved the electric razor down the middle of her head. Something in Judith's throat tightened, as if she had swallowed a potato. At the window, a woman with a shaved head walked by. She looked in, smiled, and walked on. The crowd outside looked at the other woman, then looked back in.

Shirley shaved the sides. It was getting very, very smooth up there.

All at once something burst within her. Judith gasped for air. It took her a moment to figure out what was going on. Tears were rolling down her cheeks.

Dammit, Judith thought. Where is this coming from? But even as she wondered at herself, she began to sob even harder. She looked at her hair on the floor, then up at the crowd of people, and hated herself. She was being victimized by some suppressed emotion, and yet the more she tried to suppress it, the more her tears came. She clenched her teeth and tried to concentrate on the fierce independence of her life. The hairdresser was finishing up now. Her long auburn hair lay on the floor.

It was those Marshmallow Octagons that had gotten her started. Damn those marshmallows, god *damn* them to hell! When she was a child, her mother used to brush her hair, setting it in braids. She called Judith "Bunny Rabbit." Judith sobbed again. She was glad the crowd outside was thinning. She was completely bald now. She could feel it. Just before the crowd outside cleared altogether, she made eye contact with a man who had been standing there, watching her, and it almost looked as if he were going to cry too.

Dent Wilkins, standing in the window, nodded to her, as if sending a secret message across a crowded room.

Then, embarrassed, he moved on.

"All done," Shirley said, and held up a mirror. Her voice was higher than a piccolo. "Ya like it? Whaddya think?"

Judith looked into the mirror. The first thing she thought was: *I look like an alien from outer space.* She did not recognize the person in the reflection as herself. And the second thing she thought was: *It really isn't all that bad.* In fact: *I kind of like looking like an alien from outer space.* She'd have to think it over. She smiled, reached up with her hands, holding a corner of the sheet, and dabbed at her eyes.

"It's perfect," she said.

"It's thirdy bucks," the hairdresser said. "Ten for the shampoo, twenny faw the shave."

Judith was still a bit shaken. Later, she didn't really remember leaving the salon, although she'd ended up buying a wig there before finally paying up. She bought some hair that made her look like a housewife from the nineteen-fifties. To wear in the office. And to keep warm. The world had suddenly become much cooler.

Soon she was walking back down Chestnut Street through the crowds. In her handbag was a plastic bag with her old hair in it. It was good to know it was down there. Made her feel more assured. On the street, jazz xylophonists were performing in front of Wanamaker's. Hot-pretzel vendors cried on the corners. She did not look in windows to observe her reflection. It was enough to know she had gotten through the ordeal, and she was pleased. In a week or two, she would arrange to have a wig made out of her old hair, and the plan would be complete. Get a wig made out of the hair she'd just had shaved off, so she could look like herself without having to make a statement about it. Until then, she would masquerade like this, let people think what they thought.

When she got back to the telex machine, it was remarkable how few people seemed to notice any change. That was the thing about being a temp. No one had noticed that she existed in the first place, so no one observed any alteration. She sat at the telex desk, sending out messages, listening to WMMR on her Walkman. No one said anything. She was so pleased with herself that she got up at a little past four to go into the women's room and look at herself. The place was deserted. She took off the wig. I'm really, *really* bald, she thought. You couldn't even see the little stumps of her hair. Her head was as smooth and round as the egg of some prehistoric bird. In a single morning she had become a rare and exotic creature.

Amazed and transfixed, she walked back out to the hall, turned left, and immediately knocked over Wilkins. He had been coming around the corner and the two of them collided and fell onto the floor. Her wig came off. For a moment they sat there, looking at each other, horrified.

Finally Wilkins said, "Who are you?"

"Judith Lenahan," she said. "You know me."

He reached out his hand to her, to feel her head. "Do I?" he said. She felt his fingertips on her scalp. He drew back his hand as if he had received an electric shock.

She picked up her wig and put it on her head.

He looked like he was going to have a heart attack. He tried to say something. "That's wrong," he said finally. They stared at each other. What he meant was that she had the wig on sideways. He reached out again and turned it on her head. "There," he said.

Judith Lenahan and Dent Wilkins stood up.

"Are you okay?" he said.

"Yeah. I'm fine. You're okay too, right?"

"I'm all right," he said. "I'm all right. Well. Anyway." He turned on his heel and ran down the corridor, scurried into his office, and slammed the door. Judith stood there looking after him, feeling a strange new sensation. All she had to do was look at him, and Mr. Denton Wilkins, vice president in charge of Special Trust Projects, had had to run away from her.

For the first time in her life, Judith Lenahan felt in firm possession of a new and alien emotion. It was as if she were floating outside this world, looking down on things from a vast and majestic distance.

She rode the Paoli Local home that evening, and, as always, got off at Bryn Mawr. She walked underneath the railroad bridge that had LIONEL painted on the side, then up to Lancaster. Took a right on Lancaster, walked down the hill, past the firehouse to The Blackthorn. Walked up the three flights of stairs and unlocked her door. Yanked off the dress-for-success tie in the foyer. Undid zips and buttons and kicked her shoes into the corner. She paused to wriggle out of her hose. Halfway to the bathroom she was buck naked. In triumph, in ecstasy, in truth, she reached to her head and grabbed her hair. It fell to the floor. She stepped into the shower, turned up the water, and sang at the top of her lungs. Judith Lenahan was filled with the pounding, visceral rhythm of her own complex life.

Later she sat in her favorite chair listening to some tapes, drinking her beer. She had very few possessions, but in the middle of her living room stood a telescope on a tripod, a gift from her Uncle Flip, the man who had been thrown out of the U.S. Marine Corps Marching Band for poisoning edelweiss in Switzerland. She adored the telescope, but she had to open the curtains to use it, and Judith preferred to keep her curtains closed. So the telescope stood there, resplendent on its tripod, unused. Once she had used it to look out at Bryn Mawr. She had seen a wooden horse in front of a hardware store a mile away. She had zeroed in on the eye, and got the creeps. She was afraid it was going to blink.

Judith threw her empty beer can on the floor. Her hands traveled to her scalp and ran over its smooth, ovoid surface. There's no shortage of miracles, Judith thought. The tape she was listening to came to an end.

Standing up, she turned out all the lights in her apartment and opened the drapes. Before her, stretching westward towards the Appalachians, were the cities of the Main Line: Rosemont, Villanova, Radnor, St. Davids. She folded her arms and stood by the window for some time, watching the traffic on Lancaster. Clouds covered the stars.

When the rain began to fall, she left the window and sat down again in her black chair, the apartment still dark. Holding her knees against her chest, Judith hummed quietly, off-tune, to herself. From outside came the quiet rush of tires on the wet pavement.

I feel like a statue by Rodin, she thought. *Nude Woman Reclining*. There was a copy of Rodin's *The Kiss* in the museum on Benjamin Franklin Parkway. Once she had gazed at the statue all afternoon. There was something terrible in the all-consuming passion of those frozen lovers.

It had been three years now since she had run her life through what she called the Purifier. One day, quite suddenly, she had seen, with terrifying clarity, the magnitude of the world's falseness. And just as suddenly she had decided to detach herself from the world, and from its insipid contrivances. She quit her job as an actress; she broke up with her boyfriend Muggs (who played the ocarina); she threw out most of her records and clothes and keepsakes. When the Purifier's work was through, all that was left was mime. Its wordlessness guaranteed its honesty, and the integrity of her passion.

She went to the refrigerator and got another cold beer. She opened the top and felt a satisfying exhilaration as the compressed air escaped from the can. Leaving the refrigerator door open, Judith returned to the window and looked out upon the world. It was getting late.

She moved one arm into an arc over her head, and looked out at the Main Line with a beseeching expression. This was a movement from her repertoire called the Human Question Mark. Judith wasn't quite sure what this movement meant, but she did know that it was something that belonged to her.

Judith stood naked by the window, frozen in pantomime, watching the falling rain.

•   •   •

Judith's metamorphosis passed unnoticed by everyone at Melon—everyone, of course, except for Dent Wilkins, who had been suffering from the desire to dedicate his life to her ever since the moment when, distracted and morose, he had accidentally knocked her over in the hallway. A creature from his unconscious imagination had looked back at him. Big green eyes. Big bald head. "Who are you?" he had said, feeling himself dissolve.

"You know me," she had replied.

That was Monday. He had spent the previous weekend in a strange solitude; his wife Tawny was gone, escorting the kids out to Saginaw to spend Easter with her parents. Business the following week necessitated his remaining in Philly. It was the first time he'd been away from his wife and children in years. It had all been very cordial and diplomatic, and he had acted sad about being apart from them. Yet it was also true that immediately after his family's departure he had played his Little Richard records as loud as he could get them and danced on the dining room table. On Sunday night he had ordered pizzas for dinner and ate them in front of the television and left his dishes in the sink.

Wilkins had been thinking dark thoughts for some time. He thought sometimes about making a voodoo doll of his wife that he could stick pins in. Tawny had a particularly Philadelphian affliction called Main Line Lockjaw. Her mouth was kind of like Katharine Hepburn's, except that it looked good on Katharine Hepburn, whereas on Tawny it looked like her upper and lower teeth had somehow become welded together. When they had sex, more often than not he found himself kissing her incisors. Anyway, even if he got to kiss her teeth, which was not all that pleasant in the first place, it was in the dark and after she had forced him to watch public television.

The day his wife left he had found himself lingering in front of a store called Doc's Love Products. Inside there were men in plaid, looking at pornographic magazines. He burned with a desire to go in and look around, to join these men for a while. But it was wrong, repellent, and he knew that. If people saw him, they would talk. Still, his heart pounded in his chest, and he wished he had the courage to go in and look around. But he turned away, glad that he had obeyed his conscience, and yet still wishing he had more courage.

It had been some time since he had done anything questionable. Wilkins was forty-eight years old, and had spent the last twenty-two years in Trust. He had gotten married in 1961, had joined what was then called Girard Bank the following year, and had three good-looking children, Peter, Denton Jr., and Tiffany. He had a box at the Devon Horse Show, a pair of woolen trousers he wore to the Union League, and a squash racquet. By Main Line standards, Wilkins had hit the jackpot.

He hadn't thrown Corky Chorkles in the garbage just yet, however. Corky Chorkles still remained in a dusty case in the attic. It had been nineteen years since Wilkins had put his hand up Corky's neck. It was amateur night at the Main Point, June 1965. At Princeton, everyone had thought Wilkins' ventriloquism act was hilarious. A regular riot. He had been doing a routine with Corky Chorkles since he was thirteen. He'd bought the dummy with the money he'd made mowing lawns.

Corky had red hair and a polka-dot bow tie. He would roll his head towards Wilkins and say, "My dog has no nose."

Wilkins looked at the dummy and said, "No nose? How does he smell?"

Corky said, "Terrible!" and laughed.

No one at amateur night had laughed, though. Wilkins and Corky Chorkles had stunk up the house. When he came home, Tawny had said, "I told you so." She thought it was humiliating that her husband would be seen throwing his voice in public. So Corky went back in the box, and that was the end of Wilkins' voice-throwing days.

He hadn't taken much notice of Judith Lenahan when she first started working for him. Just her hair. She had the kind of long reddish hair he often admired on models. That swimsuit issue of *Sports Illustrated*. Va boomba boomba boomba. He had once asked his wife if she wouldn't like to grow her hair out. Tawny had just laughed and said, "What, you want me to look like Cher?" She was different, this Miss Lenahan. She seemed both vulnerable and hostile. The combination was unsettling and alluring.

He hadn't been thinking about her on Chestnut Street, though, when he noticed the crowd. It looked like something terrible was happening. He'd looked in, and it was like a horror movie. There she was, the girl from the office. He wanted to yell, the way you could sometimes yell yourself out of a dream. All that hair on the floor. His mind raced ahead. Maybe he could get that hair, and do something with it. Glue it onto Tawny's head while she was sleeping. No, impossible. She'd smell the glue and wake up, and ask him what he thought he was doing, and then he'd have to explain.

He was thinking all this, dumbstruck, when suddenly he saw tears, spilling out of her eyes and down her cheeks. The young woman was shaking, like there was some sort of inner earthquake going on. His heart broke for her. If only he could help her. Wasn't there anything he could do?

He realized she was looking right at him, and with a sudden sense of embarrassment he turned and fled. He went back to the bank and stayed in his office all afternoon. Keeping to himself. Around four he thought he'd go out for a candy bar. Maybe one of those Kit Kats. A Chunky. Suddenly, out of nowhere, they collided. Her wig came off. There she was again, her head like the full moon, looking at him, with such eyes! He found himself reaching out to her, his hands brushing against her smooth head, the tiniest friction of stubble against his fingertips.

"Who are you?"

"You know me."

The next thing he knew he was on his feet, running down the hall, bleeding, as if she had run him through with her mighty and invisible sword.

That night, on his way home, he'd finally gone into Doc's Love Products. Just took a right-hand turn, and there he was. Treading water in an ocean of low-grade smut. A weasely-looking man with a Phillies cap sat behind the cash register. Beneath the register was a glass display case full of plastic penises. Some of them were not pink.

He turned away, in panic, and saw a man he knew in the back of the store. It was Ken O'Donohugh, the junk bond man. He was reading a magazine called *Bounce,* oblivious to Wilkins' presence. Ken's mouth was open, his eyes full of longing and surprise.

Wilkins ran out of the store. People looked at him as he came back out into the street, with glances full of disgust and recrimination. They're right, too, Wilkins thought. I'm becoming evil. What can I do to remain myself?

On the train home he looked out the window at the empty freight yards of the Penn Central. Workmen were tearing up the rotted ties in front of what used to be the Food Fair building, before it closed, near what used to be the *Evening Bulletin* building, before that closed. The Schuylkill River moved, in its lovely polluted brownness, off towards the horizon. For a moment he thought he heard the voice of Corky Chorkles.

"Let me out of here," he said.

The woman across the aisle from him looked up suddenly. She didn't know where the voice was coming from. She got a hanky out of her pocketbook and mopped her temples.

"I said, let me out of here," Corky said again. *"Bastard."*

That night he opened up a bottle of Chateau Haut Brion 1970 and drank it by himself. He found himself growing drowsy, though, unable to enjoy his own intoxication, and he halfheartedly took off his shirt to get ready for bed. Wilkins sang "The Wells Fargo Wagon" drunkenly to himself.

"Oh-ho the Wells Fargo Wagon is a-comin' down the street. Oh don't let him pass my door."

He saw his wife's binoculars, sitting on the windowsill. She put out suet for grackles.

"It could be somethin' from someone who is no relation, but it could be somethin' special just for me."

He looked out on the darkened buildings of Lancaster Avenue, the closed stores and the empty houses. You'd never know, he thought, looking at the world, that this is a place where people live.

And for an instant, illuminated by faint refrigerator light, he thought he saw her, standing by a window, looking out at the Main Line, watching the rain. He put his binoculars down and turned his back. It was insane. Now he was inventing her out of silhouettes and shadow.

But again he saw the smooth head of Judith Lenahan in his

memory, looking at him. The tingle of her stubble beneath his trembling fingertips. What did she know that enabled her to reinvent herself? What kind of secret courage did she possess that continually and tragically eluded him? He had reached out to her, touched her head. "That's wrong," he'd said. She'd looked at him with those vast green eyes of hers, as if drinking him through her pupils.

He was going to have to track her down. Would she go away with him, if he asked? Surely he was not the only one feeling this wild current of electricity. They could go up to the summer house in Centralia together, where no one could find them. They could sit in that old bed looking at the roaring fire and she could tell him how she had found the courage that infused her. Surely such a conversation shouldn't be against his morals.

Dent Wilkins turned off the lights in his house and stood by his open window, holding his wife's binoculars, thinking about the future. He was stunned by the wonderful depravity of what was suddenly, finally, possible.

• • •

On Good Friday, Judith sat at her telex desk, reading the Philadelphia *Inquirer*. There was a column on page three called "The Scene" about talking cactuses and chili-eating contests. It was giving Judith a headache. Wilkins was standing in his office door, looking at her. She tried to ignore him, but he just kept staring. Finally she looked over at him.

"Mr. Wilkins?" she said.

"Yeah," Wilkins said.

"Is there anything I can do for you?"

"Well, I don't know," he said. Wilkins seemed nervous. He walked over and stood next to her. "What are you doing this weekend?"

Judith smiled. He had to be kidding.

"I mean," Wilkins continued, "are you going to be with your family for Easter?"

"Me?" she said. "No. I live by myself. Anyway, I don't do holidays, if you know what I mean."

Wilkins didn't know what she meant. She didn't do holidays? Was not celebrating holidays part of what made her different from him?

"You don't have any plans, then?" he said.

"I didn't say I didn't have any plans," Judith said. "I always have a plan."

He tried to smile naturally. "Listen," he said. "Miss Lenahan. Would you like to have dinner with me, maybe tomorrow night? I'm on my own too, right now," he said, "and I could sure use the company. Would you consider?"

Judith looked at him with a big smile.

He was standing there in his blue pin-striped suit, his perfect hair all streaked with dried Vitalis. He'd never greased it before. He looked like a high school kid on his way to the prom.

"Mister," she said, "you have got to be out of your goddamned mind."

He just stared at her. She stared back. He looked at the floor, and shrugged.

He looked around nervously to see if anyone was listening. "I'll pay you," he said.

"You'll pay me to have dinner with you?" she said.

Wilkins nodded.

"How much?" she said.

He thought. "Two hundred dollars," he said. He looked around again.

Judith looked at him. He wasn't really all that horrible. You could tell he must have been a human being at one point in his life. What had happened to Wilkins, to change him from what he might have been into this? She thought about his invitation. It was supposed to rain this weekend, so the mime industry was going to be closed.

"Two thousand," Judith said.

He shook his head. "I like you," he said. "You've got something."

He was trying to sound suave. But he was shaking all over. In a way, it was very flattering.

"I like you, too," Judith said. "It's still two thousand."

He thought some more.

"A thousand," Wilkins said. "For the whole weekend."

"The whole weekend?" Judith said. "You want to have dinner for the whole weekend?"

"More than just dinner," Wilkins whispered.

"You're insane," she said.

"Please say yes," Wilkins said softly. "I have to know about you."

"You want to know about me?" Judith said. "Why don't you just talk to me? Why do you have to give me money?"

"Would you spend the weekend with me if I didn't give you money?"

Judith thought about it. "No way," she said finally. "No way in hell. You're disgusting."

"So take the money," Wilkins said. "Please. I'll give you the whole two thousand. Make it just one night. Saturday. Please say yes."

"Aw jeez," Judith said. "You're pathetic."

She had no intention of taking his money. But it might be possible to have some fun with him. Especially if he took her someplace nice for dinner. She could let him see what it was like to live a life without pretensions. She might be able to be a good influence on him. It seemed wrong to let this adventure slip between her fingers.

"All right," she said. She hit a few keys on the telex machine to take herself off-line. "Two thousand dollars. For a weekend with you, Mr. Wilkins. I'm thrilled and honored. So where and when, then? I mean how do you want to do this?"

"Tomorrow," he said. "I'll pick you up." He walked away from her desk, swinging his arms.

"Mr. Wilkins," Judith said. He spun around suddenly, fearful. "What?" he said. "What?"

She looked insulted. For a minute Wilkins was afraid she was going to cry.

"Don't you even want to know where I live?" she said.

Twenty-four hours later they were in Wilkins' Saab, soaring

up the Pennsylvania Turnpike towards the summer home in Centralia.

•   •   •

Judith sat to his right, watching the scenery. Signs along the highway advertised Indian Echo Caverns and the Pennsylvania Dutch Anti-Gravity Park in Mount Joy. It was getting dark out now; Judith's silhouette was lit by the beams of headlights of oncoming cars. Wilkins' heart pounded in his chest, as each mile brought them closer and closer to Centralia. Wilkins was overwhelmed by the simultaneous and contradictory demands of his gathering lust and its accompanying, unbearable repercussions.

The fact that he had chosen the Centralia house for his tryst was perhaps the most unforgivable aspect of this transgression. It was the locale of the best days of his marriage, back before the trust industry went crazy, back when he lived only for the weekends. Dent and Tawny used to go up there and stare into each other's eyes all weekend, making love "haunted house style" (which was something Wilkins thought he'd invented). Later they'd collapse under the covers and lie there, talking into the night, listening to the sound of the Catawissa River rushing by, the crickets and cicadas making the night vibrate. Eventually they'd fall asleep and in the morning they'd make love again, quietly, tenderly, and then they'd put on big shirts and go into the kitchen and make pancakes and eggs. They had this thing they called Flapjacks Benedict which was three pancakes in a stack with two eggs over easy on top of that, smothered in Hollandaise sauce. They'd get back in bed and eat their Flapjacks Benedict with the morning newspaper and sit for hours afterwards reading about the world until at last they'd throw the papers on the floor and make love again.

Back then, Wilkins made love with his eyes open. Not like now. I wonder when that was, Wilkins thought. If he could find the exact day when his eyes shut. Then he could have changed things. Make things back the way they were. But on the other hand, who wanted things back the way they were? He didn't want to look at Tawny now, with those enormous teeth and that jaw sticking halfway out to Pluto. The hell with it. Now the lights were out anyway. Even if he opened his eyes, he'd still see the darkness.

Wilkins watched the hills getting higher as he followed the northeast extension of the turnpike into the mountains. Centralia was a long drive. He shook his head. Why go all the way up there? What if the place was a ruin? Why not just get a motel room somewhere and have done with it? Why not have her at his own damn house? Tawny wasn't even there. How would she know?

But of course she would know. That's how women are. They see you when you're sleeping. They know when you're awake. They know if you've been bad or good. He could see the scene now: Tawny lying there, reading some deplorable novel, silence in the room, then suddenly, the announcement: "I found something unusual today." What? What had she found? After they'd been so careful, too! What? Underwear? A toenail? Impossible! "What's that, darling?" Waiting to deliver the line that would end his life. "I'm not quite sure what it is. Maybe you can explain it to me." And then she'd hold up the single long strand of reddish hair. Raise one eyebrow. "I found it underneath the pillow. Maybe you know something about it." But you see, you think you're so smart, Tawny! It can't be Judith's. She's got a SHAVED HEAD, see? So what we've got here is a plant! A long red hair Tawny got someplace, put under the pillow, just to snare him with!

But look: If it wasn't a long red hair, it would be something else. A piece of tissue paper bearing foreign lipstick smudges, found underneath the living room couch. A strange fragrance in the bathroom. A piece of furniture rearranged. A half-consumed bottle of champagne in the refrigerator. She'd know. Even if she didn't find any evidence, she'd know.

So it had to be somewhere other than the house. Keep the house clean. Away from the radiation impact zone. He had thought about a motel, sure. Why not? People did it all the time. But not Wilkins. It seemed too tawdry. If he was going to have an affair with this Miss Lenahan, it ought to be something worth risking his marriage for. So go up to the old house. Get the old hearth warmed up again. It had worked so well at one point in his life.

And this was really the essence of it all: In a sense, going up to Centralia was a symbolic voyage for him, a trip back in time to visit the landscape of his lost passion. Back up there in the hills of Pennsylvania he would find what it was like to be alive again, find what it was like to make love with your eyes open, find that sense of fire that had once burned so maniacally within him. Get back to the haunted house position, and Flapjacks Benedict.

It was funny, when you thought about it. That the Wilkinses hadn't sold the old house altogether. There was no chance of being able to live there again. What with the smoke and the fire. But it was sentimental. It had been Tawny's parents' summer house when she was growing up. They used to go up there in the summers, fish in the Catawissa River. There were heads of deer mounted on the wall, plaques with widemouth bass. There was a porch that looked out over the river. You could hear the water moving when you went to sleep.

They hadn't known it would be the last time, that last time. It was 1977. They had put sheets over the furniture and cleaned out the refrigerator and unplugged the appliances and that was that. They drove back to Philly and never came back. A few years later, the Department of the Interior was buying people's houses for ten thousand dollars a lot and demolishing them. Tawny said she'd go to hell before she'd sell the old Newton family lodge for ten thousand dollars. She said they'd just be patient until the fire was extinguished. Until then, the place would wait. They had a caretaker, a young man named Billings who came by once a month or so to make sure the place hadn't been vandalized. The Wilkinses and their children spent the summers in Cape May now. No hunting, of course, but no mine fire either.

Judith settled uncomfortably in her seat. It was up to him to get the ball rolling, Wilkins guessed. After all, this was his idea, and it had been his money he'd forked over to her. He'd given her the check before she even got in the car. She seemed kind of reluctant to take the money, but he made her. Of course, at the time, he figured this meant that she'd take care of the rest. But this Judith Lenahan didn't know what the rules were. Which was why she was sitting all the way over there, and he was sitting all the way over here. He hadn't gotten so much as a peck on the cheek for his investment.

As he followed the highway north, he felt his blood raging within him. He kept stealing glances at her. She didn't seem to notice. You'd never know she was wearing a wig. Amazing the things they can do with technology. Was it human hair? This bothered him. Or synthetic? Which was to say, had the stuff on her head been spewed out of some machine somewhere, a Hair Producing Plant? For a moment he imagined hair coming out of thousands of machines, being hacked back by enormous industrial-strength threshers, rolling down lines, around pulleys and gears, into a Curling Device. He could see it: The smokestacks belching black smoke into the sky; the Delaware River filling with the foul residue of Synthetic Hair by-products. People going swimming in the river, guys who fell out of their University of Pennsylvania rowing shells, who swam ashore only to find themselves covered from head to foot with a rank vomit-colored synthetic hair *growing from their own bodies?* Okay, fine, that was one image, the one of the hair-producing plant, and on the other hand was the idea that the hair had been previously grown, by some previous scalp atop some previous human. Was it a job you could get? Hair grower? Every six months or so you lopped it all off? Who would you sell it to? A Hair Broker? What was she like, this other woman? Why had she had to sell her own hair? Did she live in poverty, or did she just like selling her hair, like some kind of low-key hobby. Not one that would take up a lot of your time. He found himself wondering about her. What did she do? Did she know that her hair would be placed atop Judith Lenahan and driven up to the country house in Centralia? Did she ever have some sort of deep feeling that a man would be looking at her hair with desire after it was no longer on her head? Was she thinking of him, even now, on this spring evening?

They drove in silence as far as Allentown. Then, suddenly,

when Wilkins looked over at her, he found that she was staring at him. There was an odd expression on her face.

"What?" he said. "What is it?"

She shook her head.

"You don't look the same outside of the office," she said.

"Is that bad?" he said.

"No," she said. "Just the opposite." She shifted in her seat. "You look like someone I used to know, to tell you the truth. It's weird. One minute you were a banker, the next I felt like you were almost human."

"I am almost human," Wilkins said. "Who was it you thought I looked like?"

"Some guy," Judith said. "Someone I used to know."

"Someone . . . you went out with?"

"Yeah," Judith said. "My ex-boyfriend Muggs. You have his lips."

"Muggs?" Wilkins said.

"Muggs," Judith repeated.

"And what did he do for a living?" Wilkins asked.

"Animal husbandry," Judith said sadly, looking out the window.

There was a silence.

"Animal husbandry?" Wilkins said. "I . . . , uh, I'm not sure I know what that is."

"You know," she said. "He got horses pregnant." She sighed. "At least he was supposed to."

They did not speak for another half hour.

Then, as they entered Frackville, Wilkins looked over. She was staring at him again. "What? What is it?" Wilkins said.

"You still look like him," Judith said regretfully.

"Well, I'm sorry," Wilkins said.

"Don't be," she said. "Why don't you tell me a story? As long as we're stuck here together. Tell me how you became whoever it is you are. I mean, was it on purpose, or what?"

Wilkins told her his story. Judith listened. She made him tell her all about Tawny and her teeth. She made him tell her about Flapjacks Benedict. She made him tell her about Corky Chorkles.

This last seemed especially important to Judith Lenahan. She asked a lot of odd questions, like what kind of wood was he made out of, and what color were Corky's eyes, and did he have an Adam's apple in his neck.

"My friend Muggs had a ventriloquist's dummy," she said at one point.

"Did he?"

"But it got Dutch Elm disease and died."

She shook her head.

"I'm sorry," Wilkins said.

"Don't be," said Judith Lenahan.

At ten-thirty they arrived in Centralia.

He would not have recognized this place if he had not prepared himself for the change. So much was gone now, torn down and demolished. The houses of their friends, gone; the stores downtown, gone. As they came through the center of town, they passed the Odd Fellows' cemetery on the left. Behind the cemetery was the dump where the fire had started, twenty-five years ago. There was a sign someone had put up: CENTRALIA: MINE FIRE IS OUR FUTURE.

Judith watched the town of Centralia surround her. The houses were all boarded up; smoke and steam rose in columns from fissures in the earth. Wilkins drove through the smoke, climbing the long hill of Locust Avenue, then turned right onto Almond. A short time after, he turned left into the woods where once there must have been a driveway. The car rocked from side to side.

Wilkins turned off the motor in front of a small dilapidated cottage. There was moss all over the roof. It wasn't as bad, actually, as Wilkins had feared. The place looked worn, but it was not a ruin. One window was boarded up. Judith Lenahan stood by the car, holding her black bag, looking at the old place.

"Is it haunted?" she said.

"Naw," Wilkins said. His heart went out to her. She seemed frightened. He went over to Judith and put his arm around her. "Not yet," he said.

She raised one hand to his cheek and kissed him back. For a

moment they stood in front of the old house, intertwining. Then Judith drew back from him. She looked confused.

She sniffed the air. "What's that smell?"

He picked up his own bag and walked towards the house. "The fire," he said.

He unlocked the door, using a key he had not used for seven years. The old door swung open, and they walked inside. He banged around in the dark, looking for a light. There used to be a lamp right near the door, but it was gone now, and he had to feel around, looking for the wall switch near the closet. Something crashed to the floor.

"Are you all right?" she said. "What was that?"

"I'm fine," he said. "I don't know."

He hit the wall switch, and the room was bathed in dusty light from an overhead chandelier. The living room looked much as he remembered it. The deer and fish trophies were still hanging on the wall, along with the old lithographs of hunting scenes. The dining room table lay before the picture window.

"Look at everything!" he shouted. He flicked a wall switch that turned on some spotlights outside. "Just look!" He pointed out the window. "You see, there's the river. It's running high."

"Doesn't look like much of a river," she said.

"It's really just a creek," he said. "But everyone calls it a river."

"It's pretty," Judith said. She was walking around, looking up at the old rafters, gazing at the faces of deer.

He looked at her, his heart beating wildly.

"Aren't you cold?" she said.

"A little."

"Maybe I'll make a fire in here," she said.

He took his next big risk. "Maybe we should make one in here," he said, and escorted her into the master bedroom. The queen size, four-poster bed had a big quilt on it. A huge Victorian wardrobe stood against one wall. There was a small fireplace at the foot of the bed.

"Okay," she said, and walked back to the living room to gather firewood.

"Oh, good," Wilkins said. He, of course, had meant "making a fire" metaphorically. Let's get this show on the road, he thought. Let's do the hokey-pokey and turn ourselves around! Judith was bent over a pile of kindling which had probably been piled there by Billings. They had never had wood in the house in the summer. Tawny said it brought in termites.

"You want a drink?" Wilkins asked. Judith was laying a fire. "Sure," she called. "I'll have a beer if you got any."

He walked into the old kitchen, turned on the lights. The kitchen looked much more abandoned than the living room. There was no sign of life there, no fruit in the fruit bowls, no flowers in the flowerpots. A cereal bowl lay in the sink, and he vaguely remembered leaving it there seven years ago. He opened the refrigerator, and found, to his surprise, a case of Beck's beer. Wilkins smiled. Billings again.

He brought two beers back to the bedroom. All the lights were out. The crackling fire threw a beautiful orange light onto the room. Judith was lying in bed, wearing a lacy black nightgown. The outline of her lovely, full breasts could be seen through the lace. She was still wearing the wig. The orange firelight, softly flitting against the coverlet, bathed her with sweet, haunting shadows.

"I'm back," he said.

"Oh, boy," she said. "Beer."

Wilkins walked towards the bed, handed her one of the beers. "If you want a glass . . . ," he said.

"No, that's all right," she said.

He put his beer down on the night table and turned his back to her. He took off his shoes and his pants and his shirt, everything except his white undershirt, and sat down. Wilkins lifted himself slightly, in order to pull the coverlet down, then pulled the covers up and over his body as he leaned back onto the pillow.

He picked up his beer. "Cheers," he said. They clinked bottles. She had almost finished hers. Their bodies were touching.

He put his arm around her. "Do you like this nightie?" she said.

"It's very beautiful," he said. "As are you."

"Ah, go on," she said. "My old boyfriend gave it to me. I never wore it before. I don't usually wear stuff like this."

"What are you wearing it for?" he said.

"I don't know. I thought you'd like it. It's lace and stuff."

"It's beautiful," he said again.

The two of them sat back against their pillows, staring at the fire. He had never been in this room before when a fire was going. It had always been a summer place. How strange it was to be in that room, to be lying in the bed in which he and his bride had made love hour after hour. He recognized every detail—the crack on the ceiling just above the doorway, the old painting of hounds at the hunt that hung above the fireplace, the scratches on the old wardrobe. It was wonderful to be back at his starting point, the point from which his life had begun. And the woman sitting next to him, with that wig that made her look like a 1950s housewife, it was almost as if he had traveled back in time and was about to make love with Tawny again, the way she used to be. How he had loved her then, when they were both starting out! The things he used to do for her—buying her chocolates at the Reading Terminal Market, buying her flowers from the guy in the central courtyard of City Hall. Suddenly he felt a tremendous pang of guilt for what he was about to do. This was sacred ground. He was about to—no, he already had—defiled it. Here he was, on the bed of his most sacred lust, coddling a twenty-six-year-old temporary lunatic with a shaved head! What could have gotten into him? He took a long swig of his beer, and turned to Judith, turned to her for reassurance, as if she could remind him how this had all come about.

But Judith was sitting motionless, looking at the fire, as tears poured out of her eyes and dripped onto the quilt. It was astounding, a terrible and affecting sight: the young woman didn't appear to be moving—her lips remained steady, even though they were slightly parted; her hands remained clasped over her stomach, above the coverlet, and her eyes did not blink. But water was flowing from her eyes in a quiet stream. Wilkins was suddenly, genuinely frightened.

"Hey," he said, and put his arm around her. "Are you okay?"

She sighed a loud sigh. "No," she said. "I'm not. I don't know what's wrong. I can't figure it out."

"Do you think this is a mistake?" he said, gently.

"I'm not sure." She reached over and touched the side of his arm. "Yes," she said. "I think I do. I'm sorry. I don't know how we got here."

"Just relax," he said. "It'll be okay. Really."

"I don't feel like myself," Judith said.

"I know exactly what you mean," he said. "Me neither." He took a sip of his beer. "Did you ever hear that joke about the guy, somebody comes up to him and says, 'I think we've met before, have you ever been to Pittsburgh?' and the other guy says, 'No, I've never been to Pittsburgh,' and the first guy says, 'Me neither. It must have been two other people.' "

Judith smiled wanly. "No," she said. "I don't know what you're talking about."

"I mean that's kind of what I feel like now. As if it's two other people who got us here."

"I'm sorry," Judith said. "I know I took your money and everything. I just feel a little, I don't know . . . shy."

"Shy?"

"Uh-huh."

The fire crackled and heaved on the far wall. The wood settled into the coals.

"Is there anything we can do that would make you feel less shy?"

"Yeah, maybe," Judith said. "But will you promise not to touch me if I do? Feel less shy, I mean?"

"You don't want me to touch you?" Wilkins said. "But I'm touching you now. Right now I'm touching you."

"I know, but I mean more than that. You know." She sighed. "I mean fucking. I don't think I can fuck you tonight. I'm kind of sad. Somehow I got all sentimental. You mentioned my old boyfriend, I got to thinking about him."

"You were the one who mentioned him."

"Whatever. I don't know. Maybe I was a creep to him. Sometimes I don't understand why I do half the things I do. I just want to live for real, not to live some bullshit half-life."

She wiped the tears from her face with the back of her hand.

"It's all right," said Wilkins. "Let's just relax. Why don't we? Would you like another beer? There's a case in the refrigerator."

"No, I don't want anything else right now. I just want—well, like I said, you have to promise nothing will happen."

Wilkins didn't know what to say.

"I mean, I'll even give you your check back. Or maybe, I don't know. Tomorrow. We can fuck tomorrow, okay Mr. Wilkins? I just want to get back to planet earth for tonight. I'm kind of screwed up."

"Okay," Wilkins said. "Don't worry. We can figure all this out tomorrow."

"Great," Judith said. "Fantastic." And she reached up and pulled the wig off of her head and put it on the bedside table. Then she bent forward a little bit and pulled the nightgown off over her head and threw it on the floor. "Whew," Judith said. "That thing was driving me nuts."

"The wig?"

"No, the nightie. Man. I don't know who designs those things but it feels like wearing a ball of string. I'm gonna put more wood on the fire."

Judith got up out of bed and went into the living room. She came back, carrying a good-sized log, and threw it into the fireplace. She wiped her hands, and walked towards the bed.

The sight of Judith, standing by the foot of the bed, her beautiful, full breasts now visible in all their glory, the soft, reddish delta of her pubic hair, and of course, most of all, the glistening, smooth dome of her shaved head, sent Wilkins, finally, into a complete swoon. His nervousness and awkwardness disappeared. The shy, sympathetic Wilkins vanished, and in his place appeared horny, sleazy, curious Wilkins, the Wilkins who had gotten them up here in the first place, the Wilkins whose idea all this was. Judith lay in bed next to him, and rubbed his chin playfully, almost gratefully. It was as if she were thanking him for allowing her to be herself.

He felt himself rising under the covers. This was going to be unpleasant. What was the deal he had made with her? No sex, I think that was the general gist of it. The fresh log burst into flames. The room filled with an orange light. Wilkins reached for her ass.

"Aw jeez," she said. "It's gonna be like that, then, huh?"

Wilkins did not move. He just lay there, burning for her.

"I thought we had a deal," she said.

He didn't say anything. He was hoping she would be pulled in by the force of his gravitational mass.

"Didn't we?" she said.

"We did," he whispered.

"Well?"

"But it's different now," he whispered.

"Different?"

"Yeah. Different. That was before."

"Please," Judith said. "Don't do this to me. Can't you see? I'm afraid."

"There's nothing to be afraid of," Wilkins said.

"Of course there is."

"What are you afraid of," Wilkins grunted. "It's just me."

"Oh, stop it," she said. "Don't you see? If it's just stupid sex, that's fine. I'm talking about something else entirely. Listen, Mr. Wilkins—"

"Dent," he said. "Just call me Dent."

"What happens if it's fun?"

"It won't be fun, I can promise," he said. "I mean, if you're worried, I can—"

"Stop. Probably it'll just be fine. But what if it's more than that? What if it's great? What happens if I want to see you again?"

"We could do that," Wilkins said.

"Nah, we couldn't. Don't you see how fast it would get weird? It would be horrible. Some affair with a married man! See, I don't do that kind of thing."

"You're here now. You're doing that kind of thing right now."

Judith seemed stunned. "But I'm not really here," she said. "You paid me money."

"You can always give it back," he said.

"I can," she said, still slightly confused.

"And—and if you do give it back, then it will be exactly like you had an affair. Which means that you are the kind of person who would do such a thing. You are one right now."

"I am," she said.

He moved his fingers softly up and down the outside of her thigh. He moved gently towards her pubic hair, and caressed it with the back of his hand.

"I'm very confused," she whispered. "I think I have to work all this out on a piece of notebook paper."

"Okay," said Wilkins. "But . . . do you think you could think about it tomorrow? Please, Judith? Maybe you could just trust me for right now?"

"Trust you," Judith said. It was not a question. "Maybe I could trust you."

She reached under the covers and held him. She looked him in the eyes, and leaned and kissed the top of his head. "You're sweet," she said.

Then, just like that, it happened. Wilkins shuddered and moaned. "Yech," he said, smiling.

"Oh man," Judith said, jumping out of bed. She flicked her hand up and down as if it had some kind of poisonous glop on it. "Jesus Christ. I can't believe this. Oh, man. This is the worst. Maybe I'm going to vomit. Oh my god. This is something I can't believe." And, muttering in dismay, she ran into the bathroom.

Wilkins sat there in bed with a guilty smile on his face. He swallowed. From the next room he heard the sound of water running, and Judith making fretful and disgusted noises to herself. He felt badly. He really hadn't expected this to happen then. It had been a long time since he had been so filled with desire. What had just happened? He looked around. Powerful, nasty Wilkins was gone. Sympathetic, neurotic Wilkins was back. He looked down at the mattress. There was a tremendous stain on the sheets. And immediately, with a pang of guilt, he was besieged by images of Tawny. His darling. His own true love. He'd stood up in the church and in front of everybody said he'd love, honor, and obey her. Mother of his children. Heart of his family. And here he was, lying in their sacred bed, having goozed only seconds before into the hand of this young depraved woman with the shaved head. What the hell was wrong with him? What would happen if Miss Lenahan came back in here now, as grossed out as she should, by all means, be? What could he say to her? It was a disaster. How could he have lied to her? Had his viscous way with her? He sank beneath the covers.

Judith Lenahan came back. She was not taking things well. She snapped over to the bed and got in and pulled the blankets up to her chin. Wilkins watched her. She had moved through the room, bathed in that orange light once more, and once more he had seen the shadows dancing off her breasts and the dimples on her bottom.

"Judith—" he said.

"Just. Don't. Say. Anything," she said.

"I just wanted to say—"

"I know what you want to say," she said, "and believe me, I don't want to hear it."

"I'm sorry," he said.

"I know you are. I'm sure you are. I know you didn't even mean it. But what's done is done. I just want to go to sleep now. Can I do that?"

"Sure, of course," he said. "I just wanted to tell you I'm glad you're here."

"You what?" She sounded annoyed.

"I wanted to tell you I'm glad you're here." He rubbed her face. "Really."

"Well," she said, unforgivingly. "I'm glad you're here too."

"Come here," he said, and pulled her towards him. She wasn't happy about it, but she turned over and rested her head on his shoulder. "Just relax," he said. "We'll talk in the morning."

"Yeah, okay," Judith said. "By then I'll have made up my mind."

"Your mind?" he said. "About what?"

"About all this," she said. "I have to think. While I'm sleeping. 'Cause you know, Mr. Wilkins, I think something's going on."

"Please call me Dent."

"Dent?"

"It's short for Denton."

"Well, listen, Dent," she said. "Something's definitely going on, and it's not what I expected. There's a lot of facets going on here."

"Go to sleep, Judy. I'll see you in the morning."

"Judith."

"Go to sleep. Things will be clearer then."

"That's right. Tomorrow I'll have my mind all made up. That's the amazing thing about sleep. It's like all the molecules get boiled around."

"Yeah," said Wilkins. "They certainly do."

They lay there in bed for a while. Wilkins looked over at the bedside table and saw the wig sitting there, looking like a dead animal.

"You know, Mr. Wilkins, I never had a date like this one," she whispered.

"Thank you," he said.

"I didn't mean it as a compliment."

"I know," he said. "Good night."

And Wilkins closed his eyes, feeling Judith's soft head against his chest. Soon her breathing became regular, and it brought a sweet kind of majesty to the room. It was the same kind of breathing his little daughter made while she slept, the dream-breaths of a little girl. And as he slowly fell asleep, the soft warmth on his shoulder, he thought with affection of Judith Lenahan, this young, strange woman. But when he fell asleep, the head resting on his shoulder became the head of his wife. For his sleeping body recognized the old mattress, recognized the old springs beneath it, and in dream transformed the woman sleeping by his side into his wife as she had been, soft and young in dream, honeymoon eve, twenty-three years ago.

In the morning Wilkins awoke from a long and fragmented dream concerning the characters from Winnie the Pooh being embalmed and wrapped up in gauze dripping with a kind of mummification fluid as they were lowered into gold-covered Egyptian sarcophaguses shaped like bears and piglets and kangaroos. He found one of his hands tied to the bedpost with a kind of leather thong. Judith Lenahan was tying the other hand to the bedpost to his left. He looked around the room. The fire in the fireplace had gone out. The soft, pinkish glow of dawn fell on the hardwood floors.

"There," Judith said. "That oughta hold ya."

He was not quite awake. Judith Lenahan stood to his left, looking at the knots she had made. She was buck naked and wigless.

It was Easter Sunday.

"I guess you made up your mind," Wilkins said.

"Oh, yes indeed," Judith said. "It's all quite clear to me now."

She went down to his right foot, grabbed it, and began tying it to the bedpost with another leather thong.

"Does this mean you're not giving me the check back?"

"I think you should keep quiet," Judith said, and looked at him. "Slave," she said.

"Slave?" Wilkins said.

"Slave," Judith said.

"Holy cow," said Wilkins. He had read about stuff like this.

She pulled the thong on the right foot tight. She bent over and picked up a beer she was drinking. It appeared Judith had been awake for some time. Shaved her head again, anyway. She took a good long swig. Wilkins could see her Adam's apple pulsing. He was still trying to wake up.

"In eighteen-fourteen we took a little trip," Judith sang. He knew the song, but he couldn't quite figure out what it was.

"Along with Colonel Jackson down the mighty Mississip." He looked over to his left. The wig was still sitting there.

"We took a little bacon and we took a little beans," Judith sang. She grabbed his other leg and began tying it to the bedpost.

"And we fought the bloody British a-way down in New Orleans." That was it. The Battle of New Orleans. Judith took another swig of beer, then walked out of the room. It occurred to Wilkins at this point that he really was tied to the bed. Just like in the movies. He tried struggling a little bit but found he really was tied up. No question about it. Tawny had never tied him up. The thought had never crossed her mind, so far as he knew. At least she'd never said anything about it. Wilkins was a little bit scared. When he pulled on the thongs around his wrists they made reddish marks on his skin. This could become dangerous. But on the other hand, he had paid for danger. This was all well and good. He'd just have to trust Miss Lenahan. She seemed to know what she was doing. That is, she'd gotten as far as tying him up, which was an accomplishment. He wouldn't know how to go about tying somebody up. She'd even gotten one hand done while he was still sleeping. That showed a certain amount of finesse. For a moment he wondered if she had done this kind of thing before.

Miss Lenahan was still in the next room, fooling around with stuff in her black bag. She was still singing.

"We fired our guns but the British kept a-coming. Wasn't quite as many as there was a while ago."

"Are you all right out there?" Wilkins said. He was getting a little cold, all tied up by himself, wearing nothing but his white T-shirt. It was the same T-shirt he had put on yesterday morning, before he had left for the office. It seemed like twenty-five thousand years ago. "Judith?"

After a few minutes she appeared in the door. She was wearing a strange white makeup on her face, like the kind you see on circus clowns. She had painted her eyes with some sort of eye-liner, too, and put red stuff on her lips. She walked to the foot of the bed and looked at him as if from a great distance, as if she were gazing at him through a telescope.

Judith Lenahan stood at the foot of the bed, buck naked except for two white gloves. Mimeface makeup. Head shaved. It was quite a sight. She was holding a kind of pose. Wilkins noticed suddenly that she had strong arm and leg muscles, like a gymnast or a dancer.

She began to move. She was executing some form of dance. It was as if she were walking on a high wire. She seemed to be trying to balance between one thing and another. When she reached the wall, she turned around and began to walk again. For a moment it looked as if she might fall, but she regained her balance.

When she reached the opposite wall, she turned around and gazed out across the imaginary crevice that she had just traversed. Her face seemed lost in thought for a moment, then she stepped forward again, slowly, until she reached the exact foot of the bed again. She reached forward, but there was some kind of invisible barrier in the way. She felt all along the surface of this invisible plane, looking for a crack or crevice, but it was completely smooth. She stopped, looked around as if she were lost, let her hands fall to her sides. Her eyes closed. A look of sadness, an agony came across her face, a face that seemed to betray a vacuum that lay within. She raised her hands to her heart. It looked as if she were about to crack in two.

Her hands lay flat on her heart, then slowly moved outward so that each one came to rest on her breasts. She held herself for a minute, then moved her hands forward and hit the wall again. But this time Judith seemed to find a small opening in the wall, and she wiggled her hands inside, pulling the opening wider. She poked her head in. And there, inside, was Wilkins. She looked surprised.

"Hello there," he said.

She put her hands on her heart, then pointed towards Wilkins. Then she pointed back towards herself, and then towards him. It was as if she were indicating some kind of kinship. She smiled, withdrew through the hole, left the room. He could hear her rummaging around in her bag again.

"*Fired once more and they began a-runnin'*," Judith sang. "*Long the Mississippi to the Gulf of Mex-i-co.*"

She came back holding a pair of scissors.

"Hey hey hey," said Wilkins. "Whatcha gonna do with those, huh?"

She approached the bottom of the bed again, found the crack in the wall, climbed through, stepped onto the bed. The hinges of the old springs creaked underneath her. She walked forward, standing on her knees, so that Wilkins was underneath her. She sat down on his stomach. She grabbed his shirt at the bottom, and began to cut it off with the scissors.

"Hey, wait a minute," Wilkins said. "That's Fruit of the Loom."

She cut slowly, all the way up to the neck, then made two smaller cuts across his chest to the armholes. She dropped the scissors and pulled the pieces of shirt out from under him. Dent Wilkins was now buck naked.

She bent down and kissed his navel. The kisses were soft, and left a tiny trail of saliva and a whitish streak of face-paint on his chest. She moved up past his nipples, towards his collarbone, and sucked on the little hollow at the bottom of his throat. Quietly she kissed his neck, his ear, and at last, his lips. She was very gentle, Wilkins thought; it was like being licked by a kitten with a soft, abrasive tongue.

"Huh huh huh," Wilkins laughed. "Huh."

She reached up and grabbed his hair and cut off a big chunk from the left-hand side.

"Hey, wait just a cotton-pickin' moment," he said.

She threw a handful of his hair down onto the sheets. She grabbed another handful on the other side and cut it off too.

"What the fuck do you think you're doing?" Wilkins said, frightened now. "This was not part of the goddamn bargain. We never said a goddamn thing about this."

Judith put her finger over her mouth, to indicate that he should be quiet. She took one more good snip off the top, which was a difficult achievement considering the fact that Wilkins was now struggling. Wilkins didn't heed her suggestion about being quiet. He was pulling on the thongs and swearing. "Goddammit," he said. "You know what this is gonna look like? People are gonna know. You realize that? People are gonna fucking know now."

She stood up on her knees again, let the scissors fall onto the sheets. Wilkins looked at them, with tears raging through his eyes now. If he could have reached the scissors he would have threatened her with them. But, of course, as he well knew, he couldn't reach them. She was looking him in the eyes now; it was as if she'd dropped the scissors only to make him realize he couldn't hurt her.

"*Let me out of here,*" he said, but it came out funny. It took him a moment to realize that in his confusion he had spoken in the voice of Corky Chorkles. Judith just shook her head as if he were insane.

She made that same gesture she had made before, touching her own heart, then touching his. It was a sweet gesture, all things considered, that pantomime of kinship. She leaned forward and kissed him on the forehead, then walked on her knees back to the foot of the bed. She climbed back out through the hole in the invisible wall and left the room.

Wilkins lay in his honeymoon suite, surrounded by the tufts of his own hair. He still felt the tears in his eyes, but something within him surrendered. He knew he had crossed some border now, that there was no way back.

From the living room came the sound of an electric razor snapping to life.

"Oh God, no," Wilkins said. "Please, dear God in heaven, no. Deliver me from this please."

He had a sudden image of himself, bald as the full moon, clad in whiteface, dancing an invisible dance on the streetcorner in front of his own home.

And at that moment there came a tremendous crash, a sound of splintering wood and bodies falling onto the floor, and a sudden rush of cool air coming from the newly formed hole in the roof.

The body of Edith Schmertz, hurtling earthward through space and time and thoughts of Dwayne, crashed through the eaves of Wilkins' summer home, and fell, bull's-eye, upon Judith Lenahan. The two women collapsed on the floor in a cacophony of wood and shingles and falling moss, and the razor, still buzzing, flew out of Judith's hand and skittered onto the hardwood floor in the bedroom. It lay there vibrating, rocking back and forth, inches away from the bed upon which Dent Wilkins now lay captive, frightened and shivering on the far side of a long, invisible wall.

E A R T H

———————— ◑ ————————

The Provider of Home

The earth is conceived to consist of a series of molten shells.

Billings, hiding in the basement, ran his fingers through his thick black beard. Life outside the cellar was a mystery, an unfathomable sequence of frightening complications. First Mr. Wilkins was screaming, then there had been the hum of an electric razor, then the sound of something heavy crashing through the roof. Billings took off his Casey Jones hat and scratched his head. It sounded like he was going to have to wait down here for some time. Oh well, Billings thought, putting his cap back on his head, that's the way the scrapple crumbles. There's nothing so bad in the world you can't wait in the basement for it to go away. *With enough gum and a place to stand I can move the world.*

The gum industry had sure changed a lot since he had gone to Buchanan High School in the sixties. He thought of the Kennedy and Johnson administrations as the "Bazooka Joe" period of his life. Later, when he first got out of school and started doing maintenance work for the county, he'd gone through a kind of Bubble Yum thing. When Reagan got elected in 1980, they'd brought out liquid gum-in-a-tube. It was supposed to be a big deal, but like everything else it had blown over. The only thing he noticed was that liquid gum made him hairier. Which was saying something, since Billings was hairy to start with. In a way it was good liquid gum-in-a-tube had been canceled because he could have wound up looking like a show dog.

Billings looked in the front pocket of his denim overalls for another stick of Fruit Stripe. For the moment it was quiet upstairs. That crashing sound was really a new one. It had sounded like a bunch of meteors had come through the roof and landed in the living room. Of course meteors are usually covered with fire, so there were five or ten minutes there while he waited for the basement ceiling to burst into flames, but since it didn't Billings figured he could probably rule out meteors as one possibility of what had crashed through the ceiling. Maybe walnuts, but walnuts were too small, so either a big walnut or something else. Somebody's head. A cannonball.

The silence after the big crash was kind of scary, too. He wished he was Sherlock Fucking Holmes or something, then he'd be able to use detective logic. I can tell by the sound of the walnuts that they fell from a diseased tree, therefore you must be a lumberjack, and hence an accessory to the murder of the little woodchuck. That would show them. Now, Mr. Wilkins had started yelling *Judith*. "Judith?" he said, questioning. "Are you all right?" "Judith? Say something." And so on.

Billings scratched his beard. That Fruit Stripe sure was good. Of course you couldn't blow bubbles with it, but big deal, bubbles weren't in keeping with the situation. *Judith*. Mrs. Wilkins was named Tawny. Had Wilkins remarried? Seemed unlikely. Tawny herself had been up to the cottage just a month ago with some man named Shemp. He knew because that was one of the things she'd yelled in her sleep: *Shemp o yes Shemp*. He knew plenty of people with nicknames. Jonathan was called John or Johnny, James was called Jimbo, and Jimbo's wife Peg's real name was something like Margaret or Harriet. He knew a Dudley that was called Flippy. And he had a friend Doober whose Dalmatian dog had a special pedigreed name, Whispering Winds Ring of Clover. Holy cow! It was like the dog was the fucking Emperor of Japan or something.

Billings wished he had told Mr. Wilkins he was living in the basement earlier. If he had, then it wouldn't be necessary for him to keep hiding like this. He had moved in in 1981, after the house on Locust Street had been torn down. Carbon monoxide from the fire was seeping into the foundation. He hadn't meant to move into the Wilkins' cellar full-time; at first it was just a place to go until he got back on his feet. But it was such a nice house, and the cellar was cool and damp, just as Billings liked, and it was convenient to have your tools right next to the bed where you could get at them.

At the very least he should have let Mr. Wilkins know he was down here when the car pulled in last night. But, Billings thought, let's face it. I'm not the kind of person to put himself forward. Anyway, Mr. Wilkins was unlikely to come down into the basement. And as long as the deadbolt at the top of the cellar stairs was drawn, he couldn't get down here even if he wanted to. All Billings had to do was wait things out, and then he'd be on his own again.

Mr. Wilkins kept yelling for *Judith* upstairs. Judith must be the person who fell down in the living room. Maybe she was hurt. It sounded like it. But how had she done it? It sounded like something came through the ceiling. Maybe she bashed the roof in. It didn't make sense. She was probably pulling some kind of joke on Mr. Wilkins. Billings stuck out his tongue and pulled a large portion of his mustache inside his mouth. Somehow sucking on his own mustache always made Billings feel smarter. It was all that protein in the hair. He wished he could have gone upstairs into the kitchen to get a beer, but that would have been too much of a risk. Beer had even more protein than beard hair, and it tasted better.

"Help!" Mr. Wilkins started yelling. "Somebody help me!"

Billings chewed his Fruit Stripe. It tasted better than Bubble Yum, but somehow he was not able to enjoy the flavor. Sometimes that happened. The flavor just died out of it. Billings had this theory that it worked in reverse every once in a while—like you were the thing that had flavor, and the gum was what made you able to taste it. And times like this, when there was something upsetting going on upstairs that you didn't really want to know about, that was when the flavor went away, and it was like you were losing your own flavor, if you looked at it like that. Mr. Wilkins upstairs was yelling and screaming now. He sure was kicking up a fuss.

This was very, very bad. He was seriously tempted to go upstairs and find out what was going on. Why didn't Mr. Wilkins just go and help the woman who had jumped off of the ceiling? Was he unable to walk? Maybe somebody had gone and shot them. Some kook. There were all kinds of nuts in this world, and sometimes they did get loose and wipe people out. But if that were true, then the guy might still be upstairs, warming himself by the fire. No wonder Wilkins was screaming. Maybe some guy had pushed this Judith through the ceiling and then shot Mr. Wilkins. But no, he'd have heard a gun go off. Whatever was happening was happening as a result of the loud thump. And Mr. Wilkins was reacting to it. Well, he'd just have to get over it. Eventually he'd get in his car and drive away for help, and then maybe Billings could think of somewhere to go for a while. If it looked like they were going to come back, he'd go into town and have a few beers, wait until all this shit blew over, which it always did.

Mr. Wilkins kept it up, though, for ten minutes, twenty minutes. Billings wished he'd be quiet. Get over it. We all have things in life we don't like. Whatever this one was was one of them, and the sooner Wilkins came to terms with it, the happier Billings would be. *When life gives you lemons, go buy some lemonade.* It was ugly though, to sit downstairs and listen to Mr. Wilkins yell for help like that. Ugly especially because he should know nobody could hear him. The nearest living creatures, other than Billings, were the fish in the Catawissa River, and they didn't even have legs, except for the catfish.

Billings took out his Fruit Stripe. The flavor had just died. He couldn't think.

He thought about going up to help Mr. Wilkins. Maybe this was one of those times when you had to put certain things ahead of yourself. So what if he had been living in the cellar illegally. Mr. Wilkins would understand. Maybe he'd be grateful for him coming to the rescue. Give him a reward. Yeah, and what if part of the reward was being allowed to live in the cellar! His whole life could change on account of this moment. Here he was sitting down in the cellar by the oil burner and the pegboard for the tools when he could be coming to the rescue upstairs. And not just coming to the rescue of his employer's life, but in a way rescuing his own! He'd get his picture in the *Shamokin News-Item!* This could really be great!

Not that his life really needed rescuing. Wilkins was still sending him a check for two hundred and fifty bucks every month. All Billings had to do, in theory, was look in on the house once a week. The money would hardly have been enough to live on if he'd had to pay rent, but it was different since he had his house torn down. Now that he was living in Wilkins' basement, he had almost no expenses. Just gum and beer.

Intruding on whatever was going on upstairs could end up spoiling the good deal Billings had. What if Wilkins' yelling was all just part of some big game? On the other hand, the game might have gone wrong. Billings was going to have to come to the rescue, for better or worse. If only there was some way of disguising himself, he could go upstairs and just get a sense of what was going on. Scope out the situation. Make some decisions. Maybe get a beer while he was at it. And if it looked like his help was needed, then he'd do something and help out, and if his help was not needed, then he could go back to the cellar, and he'd at least have a beer. At two o'clock there was going to be a Phillies game and after that he'd have the whole afternoon all figured out.

A disguise then. What he needed, obviously, was a sheet. He could cover himself with a sheet and go up the goddamned stairs going *Awoo,* and if everything was under control he could flit away and they'd all figure it was just a ghost. He knew they all believed in ghosts. They had to, living in a dump like this. He looked around the basement, wondering where the sheets were, but he knew, even as he looked, that all the damn sheets were upstairs in the bedroom, the bedroom where even now Mr. Wilkins was yelling and screaming.

But look, right over here was a pile of old newspapers. Billings

put one of the sheets over his head. Fantastic. Now all he needed
was a lot more surface area. More newspapers. He had a big old
reel of masking tape there on the tool bench. That was it. Billings
was impressed by his own brilliance. He taped the newspapers
together, and made a few strategic cuts for the eyeholes, so people
couldn't look in and see who he was. He lifted the papers over
his head. Great, except he couldn't really move around. The
sheets kept slipping off. But Billings realized the answer to this,
as plain as day. He pulled the reel of tape a couple of times around
his waist, and made a little masking tape belt. Done. He stepped
towards the stairs. The papers crackled and rustled as he moved.

"Awooo, awooo," he said. Incredibly convincing.

He climbed the basement stairs and pulled back the deadbolt
at the top. A big risk. He knew he was taking his life into his
hands, but this was one of those times when crybabies had to just
sit down. He swung open the door.

"Awooo," he said. He was practically scaring himself.

It took him some time for Billings to figure out what it was
he was looking at. It wasn't the kind of thing you saw every day.
Of course there was the gaping hole in the ceiling, just as he had
expected, but there was no meteor. And on the floor of the living
room lay two people, collapsed on top of each other. Neither of
them was moving. One of them was a woman, at least he thought
so. She had breasts and stuff. It was the first time he had ever seen
a woman naked. But her head was bald. He figured it was a
department store mannequin, except that it was a little too life-
like. Maybe one had come to life and gone nuts, and the other
person, the one in the jeans with the backpack, had gotten stran-
gulated by it. That kind of stuff happened all the time.

The door to the bedroom was closed all but a crack. Fortunately. He could hear Mr. Wilkins thrashing around in there.
Billings figured he'd find out what was going on out here first,
before getting all tangled up with whatever was going on in the
bedroom. Billings had a bad feeling about this. Maybe Wilkins
had stumbled onto some kind of formula for bringing man-
nequins to life. It wasn't completely out of the question. And
now one of them had gone out of control.

Billings inched closer to the two crumpled forms. "Awooo," he whispered.

"Help! Save me!" Wilkins yelled from the bedroom.

It was not a mannequin. It was a young woman, no question about it. It was horrible to look at her, horrible to see someone you didn't know undressed. He wanted to throw something over her, but all he had was his newspapers and he needed them for disguise. She wasn't moving.

Billings pushed back the other person. Another woman. She had a big cut on her forehead. There was an odd-looking pack on her back. A parachute? Okay, a parachute. So then she was the one who made the hole in the ceiling. Why hadn't she pulled the ripcord? Or maybe she had pulled the ripcord and nothing had happened. The poor thing. Billings leaned over. "Come here," he whispered. "Come on. Wake up. Wake up."

He brushed the blood off of her forehead. He knew in an instant she was dead.

Jesus Christ. And this one had fallen on the other one. What were the odds of that happening? Not good. You don't suppose she'd been aiming at them? No, impossible. You can't aim yourself like a rocket. An accident. Billings had never seen a dead body before. He had always expected they would have a certain aura to them, like a glow or some kind of essence. But she was just there. Everyone always said that they just looked like they were sleeping. But this woman didn't look like she was asleep. She looked sad, like she carried a tremendous grief inside of her, in addition to the grief of being suddenly dead.

He reached out and touched the other one. This was even more terrible because she was naked. He reached over and took off the dead woman's gloves and placed them over the other one's private parts. It was nobody's damn business. But look—you could see her heart pounding away in her breast, although you had to look at her breast in order to see it, of course. But she was alive. Billings slapped her cheek. "Wake up," he said. "Wake up."

But she wouldn't wake up. He tried jostling her, prodding her in the ribs with his finger, but she just lay there. Something was wrong. She had gotten conked but good by the other one. At least that's the way he figured. The sky diver had come through the ceiling there, and had conked the other one on the head. Aw, that poor woman, Billings thought, looking at the dead one in her parachute gear. On Easter Sunday.

He stood up. Okay. This was a situation. Someone would have to take care of the hurt one. Someone else would have to take the dead one away. Tell her family and everything. The police would have to get involved. In fact there were probably people out looking for them right now. They'd notice that her parachute hadn't opened. They'd come looking for her. They'd see the hole in the roof. They were probably on their way.

But wait. If the police came, they'd search the place. They'd find Billings. They'd figure out that he lived in the basement. They'd throw him outside and in the winter he'd freeze to death. That was stupid. This other woman was already dead. Why should he have to wind up homeless just to make up for that? It wasn't his fault she'd come smashing through the ceiling. He was just sitting in his favorite chair in the basement, minding his own business. If it was anybody's fault, it was Mr. Wilkins'. Yeah! Mr. Wilkins! He'd forgotten about Mr. Wilkins. What was it he was yelling about?

Billings crept across the room, edging closer to the door. His newspapers rustled as he walked.

"Awooo," he said.

He peeked through the open door into the bedroom. There lay Mr. Wilkins, buck naked, his head partly shaved, and his arms and legs tied to the bedposts by leather thongs. An electric razor lay buzzing on the floor.

Billings turned around. You see! he thought to himself. This is what happens to you for trying to be nice. For trying to help people. He could have stayed in the basement, watched the Phillies game, kept out of this. But oh no. He had to come upstairs and help out. How this figured into it he didn't know. Mr. Wilkins in there, all tied up. Jesus H. Christ! Didn't he have any sense of self-respect? What was wrong with people, anyway? How could they get themselves into trouble like this?

Billings walked into the kitchen and got a beer. He had to rip open a little hole in the newspaper for his mouth. Now he was in for it. The police were going to come, were probably already on their way, and here he was halfway between two women, one of them dead, the other bald and naked, and Mr. Wilkins, who was—he stopped. Had he seen the scene correctly? Maybe his eyes had played some sort of trick on him. He crept back to the open door. Nope. That was Mr. Wilkins all right.

Let's think this thing through. Maybe the best thing here is just to leave for a couple hours. Go get a doughnut. Sure. Because the police are about to arrive, or somebody is, anyway, because they'll be out looking for the parachute woman, and when they arrive they'll find everything else, and they'll untie Mr. Wilkins and take the other woman to the hospital. Fine. And that way, nobody finds out that Billings lives in the basement, and life can go on per usual.

But what happens if there's a whole big scandal? Probably a whole lot of attention will get generated because of this. What if Wilkins has to sell the house? A whole lot of good that'll do him. Wait. Stop. It's time to think logically. He sucked on his beer for strength. It contained hops and barley and that would help. Hops were like the brains of yeast.

If nobody comes looking for the parachute woman, Billings thought, then things look bad for both the sick woman and for Mr. Wilkins. If only Mr. Wilkins could get himself free, then it'd be up to him to set things straight. After all, it was his mess. Billings didn't have the first goddamn thing to do with it. But those leather things looked pretty strong. He rustled over to the bedroom, and took another look. Yes, pretty strong indeed. But wait, there was a pair of scissors on the bed. Was Mr. Wilkins trying to cut himself loose? No, impossible. He needed a third hand to do it.

"Awoooo," Billings said.

"Who is it?" Mr. Wilkins said, suddenly, looking towards him. "Who's there? Judith?"

Billings opened the door. "Mr. Wilkins," he said. "I'm sorry—"

"Who are you?" Wilkins cried. "Good god. Judith? What's happened to you."

"I'm not Judith," Billings said. He remembered that he was supposed to be a ghost. It's just like me to forget I've taped newspapers on my head, Billings thought. I'd eat my own brain if it wasn't nailed down.

"Awoooo," he said.

"Spare me," Wilkins said. "Oh, spare me please."

Billings was fascinated. This wasn't exactly what he'd planned, but it was something.

"Okay, I'll spare you, already," Billings said. "Just stop whining."

Billings reached over and picked up the scissors.

"Oh no," Wilkins said. "Please don't. Please don't shave me bald like Kojak. I hate that show. Please have mercy."

"Shave you?" Billings said.

"Oh, mercy, mercy, mercy!"

"Stop it," Billings said. "I'm not kidding."

"I'm sorry," Wilkins said.

"Don't apologize, just don't whine like that. That's really annoying. I'm serious."

"Okay. Okay. Go ahead and shave me. You know what you're doing."

"I'm not going to fucking shave you," Billings snapped. He wished he'd never come in.

He reached forward with the scissors and cut one of Wilkins' leather thongs. His left hand was free.

"That'll get you started," Billings said. "Now I'm out of here." He put the scissors back on the bed and turned.

"Wait—" Wilkins cried. "Oh spirit, tell me, are these the shadows of things that must be, or are they only the shadows of things that, you know, might be?"

"What?" Billings said. "What are you talking about? Just pull yourself together. Jesus."

Billings swept out of the room.

He closed the door behind him. There in the living room were the two women. They looked so sad. He couldn't believe that Wilkins. The nerve of the guy. Well, he supposed there had to be an explanation but it was probably the kind of explanation he didn't want to hear.

People ought to know how to handle themselves better than that, Billings thought. He went into the kitchen, and got four beers and an opener. He took them to the basement steps, opened the cellar door, closed it behind him and pulled the deadbolt tight. He hoped Wilkins would clean things up and pull himself together. People should just live their lives. It was as plain as that. Live your life without screwing things up for other people. Otherwise he didn't want to know about it.

• • •

Wilkins sobbed for a few moments more before realizing that his hand was free. He'd gotten so used to howling his lungs out in the last twenty minutes, it was hard to break the habit. It wasn't until Wilkins found himself actually waving his free hand in front of his eyes that he came to believe that his release had come to be. He stared at his own hand as if it were some alien creature. There it was, floating in front of him, like some sort of pale starfish, a fugitive from the sea.

Wilkins cut the straps on his legs, swung them feet first onto the floor. He picked the buzzing razor up off the floor and turned it off. He reached down and put on his underpants, then pulled on his trousers. They were lying right where they had fallen last night. Last night! How tender he had felt then, he thought, remembering the riot of emotion. How much he had wanted to make love to her, and yet how afraid he had been! As if he were two people. Himself and someone else. But which one was the someone else? The one he was now? Had Judith split in half, too?

Judith. He went to the door, knowing that something terrible lurked behind it. She had gone bananas, then fallen silent. He was still confused from his twenty minutes of solitary confinement, but he knew enough to know that Judith's exit and the crashing sound had happened almost simultaneously. Please let her be all right, Wilkins found himself saying. Please.

There they lay—Judith Lenahan and the stranger, still folded on top of each other in front of the living room fireplace. Sunlight streamed through a hole in the ceiling, casting a soft spotlight on the dead. Judith was lying on her side, a pair of gloves covering her. Entwined around her, the stranger. Wilkins looked up at the hole in the roof, then down at the floor. The stranger lying there. Then he looked back up at the ceiling again. Impossible. And yet—there they lay, motionless, soundless. He moved closer. The one with the backpack. A woman, for crying out loud. Parachute gear. Her chute hadn't opened?

Wilkins moved forward. They weren't moving. The parachutist had blood on her forehead. Blood.

"Jesus Christ," Wilkins said.

He kneeled down beside the stranger. It was as he feared. She was dead, even cold. Her skin was the color of foam on a country river. Who was she? He felt as if he were meant to be receiving some sort of message, but its meaning completely eluded him. He felt Judith's body. Warmer. You wouldn't know she was dead just from feeling.

Wilkins kneeled beside the two women. Just a half hour ago he had been watching Judith do a dance for him, naked but for her gloves and the white paint on her face. That gesture she had made, touching her heart, and pointing to him. She was trying to tell him that they both belonged to the same family. That her fate was wrapped up in his.

He looked up at the hole in the roof. Thin clouds hung in a blue sky. From what strange place had this doom fallen? Everything seemed immaculate and silent up there, timeless. The clouds moved over the sun and the spotlight illuminating the women faded. Their faces looked up at Wilkins, sorrowful and exhausted.

Dead, then? he thought suddenly, and the reality of the situation hit him. She was really dead? The two of them, lying out here. All at once he was in a terrible jam.

For a moment he saw himself driving to the police with Judith's body in his car. Carrying her into the stationhouse and trying to explain. The cop, taking notes. Stories in the newspaper. Pictures of him. People in the hallway at Melon whispering.

Talking about how he'd gotten tied up. For a moment he saw Ken O'Donohugh, standing alone in Doc's Love Products wearing a look of surprise and fear. Wilkins' face was on the cover of the magazine he was reading. It was a nightmare. He had had this adventure on the single premise that no one would ever find out about it. What could he do now, faced with the prospect of public humiliation, maybe even jail?

His heart beat quickly. He looked at the bodies again. He was going to have to hide her. Take the body somewhere. He shook his head. To think that he was capable of such a thought, of dumping her by some roadside! He picked up Judith's gloved hand, held it for a moment. "I'm sorry," he said, and again he had the certainty that he was becoming an evil being. Again he had a desperate desire to hold on to himself, to keep from losing his sense of self.

As he held her white glove he realized the enormity of what he was going to have to do. There was no point in ruining his life on account of an accident. He couldn't bring her back to life by sacrificing everything. It was the only choice. To gather her up in his arms, and dispose of her. To carry her to some secret place, and bid her farewell.

Even as he made his decision he realized he had very little time in which to act on it. People would come looking for the sky diver. They did these things as a team. Probably knew right where she had fallen. They'd find her. It would be suspicious if he moved her, in fact. There wouldn't even be a crime in leaving her. That wasn't his responsibility. He wouldn't even have had anything to do with it if he hadn't been using the house that weekend. They'd find her, and it would be tragic, and the appropriate people could mourn. But she wasn't his responsibility. She would have fallen through his roof whether or not he had been home.

And yet, one thing causes another. Who knows what would have happened in some other world, a world in which he had never had the courage to ask Judith to run away with him? Maybe in that world, the effect of Wilkins staying home would have been enough to change this sky diver's fate. Perhaps in that other world, she was still falling free, floating on the wind above Centralia. He shook his head. This was how you made yourself insane, thinking about worlds other than this one.

He went back into the bedroom, and put on the rest of his clothes. He was going to have to make a quick getaway. He looked at the scissors lying on the bed, and suddenly remembered that ghost. He had been half out of his mind when the apparition appeared. But that voice was familiar. The smell of gum. Billings? The caretaker must have shown up in the middle of his tryst. Maybe he was too embarrassed to interrupt. But how had he gotten newspapers all over his head?

Wilkins walked back to the living room, opened the front door. There was no sign of Billings. For a moment Wilkins stood in the doorway, looking at the long weeds growing in the driveway. *Is it haunted?* Judith had asked, when she first saw the cottage. *Is it haunted?* Not then, honey, Wilkins thought, but it is now. Haunted by Judith and by another woman he did not even know.

He turned and looked into the house. There, once more in a shaft of sunlight, lay the two women. It was time to move. The others were probably already on their way.

He would just leave the sky diver where she was. When the others found her there, and the house deserted, they would deal with her in the proper manner, just as they would have if he hadn't come to Centralia this weekend. But Judith had to go. Her presence was evidence that the house had been occupied. On his way out of town, he would stop off at Billings' house, give him some money, make sure he kept his mouth shut about what he had seen. Wilkins felt his heart in this throat, suddenly aware of how fine the thread was by which his doom now hung.

Wilkins stood in the living room for a few minutes, licking his lips, feeling the air from overhead gushing into the room. He looked out the picture window at the Catawissa River. It was a warm day. The river rushed by, shushing over the rocks, the sun shining on the water.

Wilkins went into the bedroom and picked up all of Judith's things. The nightie she said had felt like a ball of string. The scissors. The pieces of leather thong. Her shoes and underwear. Her toothbrush from the bathroom. All of these he wrapped up in the nightie, dropped them in the black bag in the living room. He looked around, shook his head, came back. The wig, still sitting on the nightstand. He had almost forgotten.

He dropped all of her things into her black bag.

Wilkins went back into the bedroom and got some spare blankets out of the linen closet. He returned to the living room and spread two out on the floor, one atop the other. He lifted Judith onto the far edge, and began to roll her up into the blankets.

It was amazing: they'd always said some dead people looked just like they were sleeping, and Judith did. Not the other one, the one with the cut on her head. But Judith, yes. Like she was dreaming. He picked her up in his arms and walked out the front door. He walked around to the back of the house, and laid her down.

Wilkins looked underneath the deck. It was still there. He grabbed onto the bow and pulled, and with a kind of frozen, wooden groan, the old canoe lurched into the sunlight. The green paint he had covered it with almost seven years ago seemed gray now. There were old leaves on the bottom, but no holes. He grabbed the fraying rope and pushed the canoe into the water. The current caught the bow, and Wilkins felt the pull of the moving water against the hull. He tied the rope to the dock with a half hitch.

Wilkins turned back and picked up the rolled-up blankets with Judith inside. She seemed heavy now. He put her in the bottom of the boat. It drew more water with her in it. For a moment he was afraid it might tip, but it regained balance, the bow spinning out into the water away from the dock, almost as if anxious to join the current. He walked back to the house and got Judith's black bag, then went to the canoe and put it by her feet.

He wiped his hands against his pants and untied the rope. He threw the loose rope into the bow, but he missed, and it trailed in the water. The current was quick, and the canoe moved quickly into it. As he watched her sail away from him, Wilkins was filled with an overpowering sensation of grief. "I'm sorry," he said lamely. He raised his arms and held out his palms, watching her recede. "Dammit," he said. "Dammit, dammit, dammit."

Wilkins turned his back and started walking back up towards the house. He would just have to cut this whole nightmare out of his life. Pretend it had never happened. He had to get out of town. There was another person dead in his house still, and strangers were coming soon to find her. Wilkins was going to have to return to his own world.

· · ·

In the distance, the small gray canoe rounded a curve, its old rope trailing behind. Moving into the rapids, the boat began to move more quickly, following the current of the Catawissa River, which joined the Susquehanna at Catawissa, Pennsylvania, which joined the West Branch of the Susquehanna at Northumberland, which flowed past Sunbury and Harrisburg to join the Chesapeake Bay at Havre de Grace, which moved on past Baltimore, Annapolis, and the waters of the Potomac, until finally it passed Norfolk, Virginia, and joined the Atlantic Ocean, four hundred miles downstream.

Judith Lenahan, wrapped in gray blankets, breathed softly in dream, oblivious to the dawn of her long ocean voyage.

M A R S

○

The Bringer of War

The eccentricity of its orbit is greater than that of most of the other planets. Scientists once considered it a habitat of intelligent beings.

At the moment that the rabbit crashed through Phoebe Harrison's window, she had been dreaming of the pony she hoped to receive Easter morning. She would go downstairs and there it would be, covered in garlands, a wicker basket in its mouth. In her favorite story, *Misty of Chincoteague*, the wild ponies were driven from Chincoteague Island into the sea. The ones that survived the swim got to live in green clover. But the ones that didn't? It seemed wrong to let ponies die in the ocean. They weren't swimmers. Phoebe didn't understand why ponies floated in the first place. They were not buoyant creatures.

Phoebe could not float either. She tried it in the pool, but she sank like an anvil every time. Her older sister, Demmie, had just looked at her with her sarcastic Demmie expression and said: *You will.* Demmie wore black all the time and smoked cigarettes that smelled like decaying fruit. Demmie did not exactly have a levitating personality, and yet she possessed the very ability to float which eluded her little sister. Which typified the screwed-up universe, as far as Phoebe was concerned. The more you wanted to float, the more gravity got on your nerves.

Phoebe's birthday fell on Easter this year. The government moved Easter around; it had something to do with the moons and Lent. It wasn't very consistent. But at least this year she'd get presents and cake instead of having to put on a scratchy dress and sit in a pew at St. Luke's for two hours. Reverend Bickford said *Christ is risen,* and everyone else had to say *Christ is risen indeed.* It was like Reverend Bickford was the caller at a square dance. *Now promenade.* Phoebe found it hard to concentrate on the Messiah when the whole time she was thinking about bowing to her partner and suppressing the desire to itch.

In addition to the pony Phoebe had a vague hope that her mother would show up today. They'd only heard from her once since she'd left their father three years ago, when Phoebe was six. Mom had sent a postcard from Salt Lake City. It had a small bag of real salt stapled to it. The salt was supposed to have come from the Great Salt Lake. Phoebe had opened the bag and tasted it but it just tasted like regular salt you could get anyplace. The card just said: *Sorry, darlings. I love you, Mom. Please forgive.*

She had a pretty good idea the pony wouldn't be down there. She'd be lucky if there was anything at all. Dad had been out late last night and hadn't come in until eleven. He'd spent the whole week visiting their Uncle Pat, who lived in Devon, near Philadelphia. Uncle Pat had some kind of disease that was making him extinct. He claimed to have caught the same sickness that had killed off the dinosaurs. He had a temperature of a hundred and four and thought everything was funny, even stuff like knock-knock jokes. If you told him a knock-knock joke he'd laugh until tears came out of his eyes. He was not expected to last much longer.

While their father was away, Demmie was left in charge of Phoebe. Every night for the last week they'd had Pepsi for dinner. As an appetizer, Demmie said. Then she ground stuff up in the blender and mixed it with food coloring. She said that it was important to eat a balanced selection of colors if you didn't want to clog your guts. When Phoebe asked what was for dinner, Demmie would just shrug and say blue, or red, or purple. By Saturday, Phoebe wasn't even asking what it was she was drinking any more. She just stuck in her straw and got it over with.

In a way Phoebe didn't blame her mother for leaving them. It must have been upsetting to have a daughter like Demmie, and a husband like Phoebe's father. Wedley had worked for the coal company until the fire broke out. He was one of the first people laid off, and had spent the last five years going from one odd job to another. The most recent one was chimney sweep, which at least paid the rent. But there was something humiliating about it. It was odd to have a job where you had to wear a top hat and tails in order to get covered with soot. If Phoebe were her mother, she'd probably have headed for Salt Lake City herself.

It looked like a warm day outside, warmer than it ought to be in April. Mr. Plank in school said it was part of the hothouse effect. The oceans were melting. Big bits of the north and south poles were falling off, which made the oceans colder or something. Wedley talked sometimes about how they used to get spring snow in Centralia when he was a child, but this seemed like something that was no longer possible. Phoebe had gotten gypped. The adults had melted the oceans. Like thanks a lot, guys.

Outside Buddy barked a couple of times. That poor dog. Mom had gotten Buddy the year after Demmie was born. Which had to be almost sixteen years ago. Buddy was all beat up. He didn't know what to do without his mistress. Just hung around, waiting for something to happen. Which it never did. There wasn't a lot for Buddy to look forward to.

Phoebe closed her eyes. If only they would let you have a wish. Just once a year. She would have her mom pull up in her Mustang and open the door and usher her in, and the two of them would drive off into the horizon, perhaps as far as the sea. Ride along the beach wearing white. Phoebe had never seen the ocean first-hand but had seen photographs and had heard records.

The glass shattered as the rabbit crashed through the window. Phoebe screamed, even before she knew what it was. Sitting up in bed, Phoebe examined the projectile. Someone's sweater, filled with a warm, wet thing. Dead. She could see the blood, seeping from the neck of the rabbit into the yarn of the sweater, turning the white wool pink.

A few moments after Phoebe started screaming, her sister Demmie came into her room. She was wearing a black Danskin leotard and leather pants and had blue lipstick on and blackish blue eyeliner that made her look like a kind of sedated raccoon.

She looked at the blood on the sheets and on the sweater, and then at the broken window. She lifted a cigarette to her lips, held the smoke in her lungs, exhaled.

"Howdja do that, lame-brain?" she said.

Phoebe did not respond; she kept her eyes closed and continued to cry.

"Yo, lame," Demmie said. "What are you, stupid?" She oozed forward and picked up the rabbit in the sweater. "Oh gross," she said. "Gross me out raw." She dropped the sweater on the floor, recoiled, clasped one hand to her forehead. "I think I am going to puke. Seriously."

Phoebe opened her eyes. Demmie regained her composure. "You are gonna get whacked for this," she said, and picked up the rabbit again. Demmie slunk out of the room, holding the rabbit in the sweater. Phoebe listened to her steps in the hall. She could tell Demmie was trying to figure out what to do with it. It sounded like she went into the bathroom and put it in the hamper.

"Pa," Demmie called. "Pa. Wake up. Somethin's happening."

"Aw, no," Wedley said, half asleep. "Please no."

"I'm not kidding, Pa. Something's dead out here. I can't deal with this."

Outside Buddy was barking.

Someone started knocking on the door downstairs.

"Harrison," the voice said. It sounded like Dwayne from next door. Big dumb Dwayne. The Mighty Sequoia.

"Harrison," Dwayne said. It sounded as if he had opened the front door and was leaning into the house now. 'What's happening. Sounds like something's happening."

"Aw please, no," Wedley's voice said. "Not Dwayne." His feet padded around his bedroom floor, then accelerated into the hallway. Phoebe lay in her room, the wind blowing through the broken window, the red stains spreading on the bedsheet. She thought about that other world, the one where the ocean was, and felt it recede. It was as if it were being sucked out the window and blown away.

"What do you want?" Wedley said. "Don't you know it's Easter Sunday over here?"

"A rabbit came through the window, Pa," Demmie said.

"Shut up, sweetheart," Wedley said. "Let me deal with it."

"Buddy's barking," Dwayne said. He was climbing the stairs towards the bedrooms. "He doesn't bark like that unless something's going on."

"All right, Dwayne, just hold it." Wedley stood in his flannel nightshirt, his long black hair in a strange, tangled mess from sleep. His cheeks were raw and pink. "You've got no right to come storming over here. Just relax."

"I'm relaxed," Dwayne said. "I didn't say I wasn't relaxed. I said I thought something was going on. I thought—"

Dwayne held his enormous chin in his hands.

"You thought what, Dwayne?" Wedley said, tired and sad.

"He's thinking, Pa," Demmie explained.

Dwayne shrugged. "I thought I heard something go smash."

They all stared at each other without saying anything for a minute.

"Things don't go smash by accident," Dwayne added, embarrassed.

"Pa, there's a dead rabbit in Phoebe's room," Demmie said, impatient. "Somebody threw it through the window."

"What are you talking about?" Wedley said. He rubbed his eyes. There was still soot from someone's chimney on his cheeks. He looked at his eldest daughter, who even at this early hour was covered in black and purple and surrounded by cumulonimbus clouds. "Are you all right?" he asked.

"Like go see for yourself, Pa. Get off of my case already. You think I'm making stuff like this up? Believe me, Pa, I could really just as soon stay sleeping. I am so sure."

"What rabbit?" Dwayne said.

"It's in the hamper," Demmie said.

"I thought you said it was in Phoebe's room."

"I moved it."

"Is she all right? Dwayne, if you've touched a hair on my daughter's head, so help me God I'll—"

"You want I should get it?"

"What?"

"The rabbit, Pa. Like, duh."

"How could I have touched your daughter?" Dwayne said. "I just got here."

"Don't talk to me like that, Demmie," Wedley snapped.

"Oh, Pa, just get with it. Look, follow me." They all trailed Demmie down the hallway and watched as she swung open the bathroom door. She opened the hamper and held up the rabbit by the ears.

"See? I told you. A rabbit."

"Why's it in the hamper, sweetheart?"

"I put it there, Pa."

"That's Mister, uh—Mister, uh—" Dwayne moved his lips, trying to remember.

"Mister who, Dwayne?" Wedley said with a sigh. There was a painful silence while Dwayne thought his thoughts.

Demmie and Wedley looked at him, waiting for him to speak.

"Whiskers," Dwayne said finally. "That's Mr. Whiskers." He sniffed. It looked like there were tears forming in Dwayne's eyes. "You monsters," he muttered.

"Monsters?" Wedley repeated. He put his palm over his eyes, then moved it down his face, as if he were trying to wash the residue of Dwayne's existence from his being. "We don't know anything about this rabbit. We've never even *seen* it before."

"Well, how did it get here!" Dwayne shouted. "Rabbits don't grow on trees."

Demmie and Wedley thought about this.

"Dwayne, I think you ought to take your rabbit back and go home," Wedley said.

"Not until I get an explanation," Dwayne said. "Things have reasons."

"What, you think we threw it through our own window? Is that what you think, Dwayne?"

Dwayne was rubbing his jaw again.

"Tell me if that's what you think. I want to know if you think we're the kind of people who would break into your house, throw a rabbit through our own window, then come back here and lie about it. Is that your idea of who we are? I want to know, Dwayne. Honestly. Enlighten me."

Again there was silence as Dwayne thought. At last he blinked his eyes and said, softly, "I think it's possible."

"That does it," Wedley said. "Take your rabbit and go. Give him the rabbit, Demmie."

"Why should I?" Demmie said. "How do we even know it's his? Shouldn't we have him identify it first or something?"

"Give him the rabbit, Demmie," Wedley said. "Before I get angry."

Dwayne snatched it from her.

"Fuh-fuck you, man," Dwayne said. He swung Mr. Whiskers by the ears.

Harrison reached for Dwayne and shoved him up against the bathroom wall. "You don't talk that way in front of my family," he said. Dwayne dropped the rabbit, which then began to tumble down the steps.

"Oh Pa," Demmie said. "He's twice your size. Don't be a dufus."

For a moment Harrison held Dwayne against the wall. They stared at each other with hate. Then they heard Phoebe, as if for the first time. She was crying, sobbing in sadness in her little bedroom.

"Now look what you've done," Wedley said.

"What I've done—" Dwayne said.

"Stop it!" Demmie yelled. "Jesus. What a couple of morons."

"Don't you call me a moron, young lady," Wedley said. "I'm your father. We're going to get some answers."

Demmie started walking towards her sister's room. She stopped, turned around, looked at her father. He was still holding Dwayne against the wall with one arm.

"Moron," she said, and went in to see how Phoebe was doing.

Phoebe looked up at Demmie, standing in the doorway. She was biting one of her thumbnails.

"You are in for it," Demmie said. "You are going to get whacked."

"But I didn't do anything," Phoebe said. "I'm just minding my own business."

"That's why," Demmie said.

• • •

Meanwhile, next door, Vicki was still standing in the living room, one hand clasping the bracelet that had the inscription COCONUT.

Vicki held up her arm and slipped the bracelet on her wrist. The gold shone in the glow from the fireplace.

All right, she thought. Very well. I'm COCONUT.

Down the street you could hear the Dalmatians barking. Eerie. That had sure as hell looked like Edith just now. But what would Edith be doing back at Dwayne's house? She was the last person on earth Dwayne wanted to see.

Vicki went back inside and sat down on the sofa by the fireplace. The glow from the fire turned the lower jaw of Dwayne's mounted moosehead orange. Dwayne had hidden a stereo speaker in its mouth, so that when he turned his music up the moose itself seemed to be the source. If they kept going out, Vicki was going to have to try to get him to take it down. It didn't make a woman feel very relaxed, some moose watching you every second. Especially when heavy metal music came out its nostrils.

She got up and looked in the mirror. Her hair was piled in an attractive bun on her head, her makeup distinct but understated. An amethyst on a chain encircled her neck. She held up her wrist to watch the bracelet in the mirror. Vicki felt things were more real when you saw them in reflection.

This whole Dwayne thing just kept getting stranger and stranger, Vicki thought, overflowing with satisfaction. She went back to the couch and sat down, crossing her legs, then smoothed her wool skirt out with one hand. Seven years after graduation, six years after her family had left Centralia forever, she was living with the very man who had tried to seduce her in an old refrigerator at the Columbia County Dump. Life between that seduction and her present one had been good: she had moved out of

Centralia in seventy-eight and got a job at the Wurlitzer show-room in Reading. Now she was back, living in Dwayne's house.

On the day Dwayne reentered her life she had been dating a man named Ben Balbo for over three years. In fact, on the evening before she re-met Dwayne, Vicki and Ben had had a tremendous fight about whether or not they should get married. The gist of the fight was that neither of them wanted to get married, but each felt that the other one, by this time, ought to. For three years they had loved each other enough to want to be together, but not enough to commit themselves to marriage. So they had remained together, drifting, like a ship becalmed.

Vicki figured it was up to Ben, the man, to decide to propose, and if he were insane enough to do so, she'd be insane enough to accept. But Ben just got angry, said he thought they'd "been all through that," and the two of them wound up having an argument that concluded with Vicki smashing plates on the kitchen floor and Ben storming out. It was the first time since they started dating that they had not spent the night together.

Vicki couldn't believe what she had become. She had never pictured herself as the kind of woman who would smash plates on the floor. And yet, there she was, surrounded by broken dishes, hurled by her own hand. She looked in the mirror and for a second saw a complete and total stranger. She went into the bathroom, washed off her makeup, and went to sleep alone, leaving those fragments on the floor. Vicki was horrified by the suspicion that at some moment when she hadn't been paying attention she had accidentally become someone else.

The next day she couldn't bring herself to go out on the showroom floor. As long as she didn't know who she was, there was no way she could present herself to the world. The terrible thing about working at Wurlitzer's was that anyone off the street could just come in and start playing. In fact you were supposed to encourage people. Which was fine when there was only one customer, someone who had taken lessons. But usually you got five or six people out there at once, and none of them knew what they were doing. People picking out "Chopsticks" on the concert grand. Or "Heart and Soul," as a duet. More often than not there was one person playing "Chopsticks" in one corner and someone else playing "Heart and Soul" in another. In keys a half step apart. It was very hard to be helpful in this environment. More often than not she wanted to take a swing at the customers with her handbag.

The day after the fight with Ben Balbo, though, the place was deserted, and she sat in the office alone, crying into her fingers. The piano showroom had been a bank, and the manager's office was inside of what had once been the safe. Vicki had been thinking of swinging the door of the safe closed when the music began. Someone had entered the store without her knowing, had seated himself down at the baby grand, and started playing. It was *Clair de Lune.*

As Vicki listened to the music echoing through the vault, she started thinking of all the men she had ever slept with, counting them on her fingers. There were seven in all. The first had been Scott Eunichtz, "The Snail" in high school, who had managed to talk her into it the month after graduation. The weird part was that he had insisted on making her wear his glasses. On top of everything else, she couldn't even see anything. The actual physical experience hadn't been much like having sex. It was more like having someone attach suction cups to your body for about a minute and a half. Scott seemed to like it, though, and Vicki had felt an odd shame, primarily because what was supposed to be so pleasurable had been such a dud. She felt that there was something wrong with her. Two months later there had been Flip Carter, who called himself "The Love Starter." She met him at a square dance; he was the friend of her cousin Aglet. That was a dud, too, although it took him longer than a minute and a half to disappoint her. She wondered how he had gotten his inappropriate nickname. Fortunately, seven months later she had met Nick Lane, "The Perfect Man," who she not only had good sex with, but who wound up buying a piano. Nick was the one who first showed her what was possible. She felt those great rumbling waves, floating on invisible, vibrating tides. After that had been Patrick Dillehay, "The Honest Plumber," and Vladimir Chernyenkov, the classical musician. Patrick had come to get a clog out of her drain, and that was pretty much his attitude overall. Vladimir, on the other hand, had seemed to play her like a cello, which was both good and bad. It was nice to be treated like a person capable of music, but on the other hand there was something one-sided about being *played* like that.

So that was all seven. The Snail, The Love Starter, The Perfect Man, The Honest Plumber, The Russian, and Ben Balbo. No, that was only six. She'd forgotten someone. How was that possible? She knew there were seven, but she could only account for six. How was it possible to have someone enter your body, to hold you as tight as the universe would allow, and still forget his name? She felt as if she were losing little chunks of herself.

And as she had thought all this, the strains of *Clair de Lune* kept playing, and at last Vicki had stood up and gone out into the showroom, and there was Dwayne, playing by himself with his eyes shut tight. He played the whole thing with his eyes closed, and when he finished he opened his eyes and saw her and spoke her name.

That had been three months ago. In the evening Vicki had come back with him to the house in Centralia. He didn't tell her he was living with Edith, who was, conveniently enough, spending the weekend near Dorney Park in Allentown with some of her friends. She probably wouldn't have slept with him, Vicki told herself, if she had known he was involved with someone, especially her old friend Edith. But she hadn't known, and by the time she knew, it was too late.

This was the weekend Vicki had left her underpants under the bed. Somehow she had taken her own off and put Edith's back on. It wasn't that hard to do; clothes were lying all over the floor. But sleeping with one's high school sweetheart at age twenty-five was the strangest thing Vicki had ever experienced. It added a whole new verisimilitude to the concept of time travel. It was as if one were able to return to those lost years of adolescence with the knowledge and experience of an adult. To right all past wrongs and live one's life anew. She wished she had slept with Dwayne that night in the garbage dump, that night of the prom. Then he might never have been taken away from her. Still, if she had slept with him then, she probably would not have ended up sleeping with him now. And she would not have forgone the present at any cost.

Vicki moved her wrist a little bit and watched the gold bracelet that said COCONUT catch the light from the fire.

From next door came the sounds of voices being raised in anger. That dog was still barking. Vicki hoped Dwayne was not entering one of his states. Dwayne was much smarter than people realized. He simply thought more slowly. It was not wise to speed him up.

Again, Vicki saw that strange woman coming down the stairs, making eye contact, explaining that she was not herself. Had she imagined the whole thing? The shouting from next door was growing louder. Vicki stood up and went to the stairs. What was going on up there? She counted the steps; there were fourteen. As she ascended, she imagined that every other step was the upheld palm of a man she had slept with, until she reached Dwayne, right at the top. The strains of *Clair de Lune* hung in her imagination.

And hearing that soft piano music echoing in memory, Vicki turned and saw the empty hutch. She looked at the open window, and had a strange, odd premonition. Vicki had read in *How to Care for Your Rodent* about how rabbits sometimes got up on windowsills and jumped. There was a theory that they did it if they were sad. But what did Mr. Whiskers have to be sad about? Hadn't she given him plenty of cedar chips? Enough water? She let him hop around sometimes on his own when Dwayne was at work. What was there left to satisfy a rabbit with that she had not provided?

Vicki looked out the window. That sad dog looked up.

"Wuff," he said.

There was the sound of guitar music coming from the Harrisons' house. Vicki didn't like the idea of Dwayne getting involved in a struggle with Wedley Harrison. After all, Wedley, of all people, was the one Edith had turned to the night she found Vicki's underpants under the bed. She'd run out of the house in tears, and crossed over the lawn and thrown herself on Wedley's mercy.

"Save me," Edith had said to Wedley. His sarcastic daughters had watched this entire scene, and the older one, Demmie, had later told Dwayne the details, which was how Vicki got the story. Edith had waved the underpants in Wedley's face. "I found these," she said. "They aren't mine. Oh dear God, Wedley. Please save me."

He'd patted her on the back and given her some milk, and eventually walked her back to Dwayne's house and returned home alone. He had acted as if he hadn't understood, as if it were the underpants he had to save her from. Vicki wondered what he would have done, though, if his daughters hadn't been watching. Edith was so much like his ex-wife, the one that had disappeared. On the day that Edith came to move her stuff out, Wedley had sat on his front porch alone, drinking something out of a glass, watching Edith's every move. It was as if he wanted to go over and say something to her, provide some sort of salve for her pain. But by then it was too late. Edith had had to pack up her things and go.

"Wuff," Buddy said again. One of Vicki's black pumps was hanging from a rhododendron bush.

Vicki turned around. Her shoes were walking around by themselves, hurling themselves out of windows. That wasn't right. She left the room, walked back down the stairs, moved into the kitchen, determined to remain calm. Pick up the phone and make a call.

Except that there was something wrong with the kitchen, too. The blender. The toaster. The microwave oven. The mini-television. The Cusinart micro–chopper. The Kitchen-Aid Mix Master. Gone. All gone.

The Outcast. The one they kept warning people about on the radio. Some lunatic who had escaped from jail, went riding around on a burro, holding up hardware stores. Now he was stealing appliances. He was dangerous. It was time to get the cops in. Vicki felt herself growing dizzy, and raised her index and middle fingers to her temple.

Vicki Ambrasino picked up the phone. The Outcast hadn't taken that. She held it in her hand, worried, as if it might suddenly disappear. In a moment she was going to call the police, but for that second she just stared at the phone. Making it last.

•   •   •

Demmie, next door, was nervous. All this activity. It didn't make sense. Dwayne or somebody had thrown the rabbit through the window. All right, so, okay, that wasn't the kind of thing you expected on Easter morning, but on the other hand, they lived in Centralia, so it wasn't a surprise. Demmie and her friends had gotten used to this shit years ago. It seemed like that wasn't the issue anymore anyway. Now it was a matter of pride. Dwayne from next door—the Caveman—was pushing her father around and her father was pushing Dwayne around, and now it looked like Dwayne was going to hit her father with the rabbit.

Demmie was bored. Wanted just to get on with it. Opening up of the presents, having the big breakfast, and so on. Once the family stuff was out of the way she'd be free to go hang out with her friends. She wanted to see them one last time. Before she made her move.

Demmie left her sister's room, walked through the hallway past Dwayne and Wedley, still at odds over the rabbit and god knows what else, and walked up the circular stairs to her room in the attic. She locked the door. On one wall was a big picture of Ozzy Osbourne. He was a rock musician who had been in Black Sabbath and later in his own band. Ozzy had a song about being a Bad Bad Boy. Demmie knew all about it, being bad that is. In fact, if they ever met, which Demmie hoped they would, she figured she could tell him a thing or two.

Demmie went over to her bureau and opened the sock drawer. Underneath was the can of Gillette Foamy. She took it out and shook it up and down. You wanted to get it all shaken up first. She brushed back her black hair, went to the closet, and took out the fringe jacket, the one with the artificial ostrich-leather lapels. She put it on. Perfect. She put one hand out flat, palm up. With the other she depressed the button on the top of the Foamy and made a little mountain in the middle of her hand. She put the can down. Slowly, with the delicacy of ritual, she drew the foamy white cream all over her cheeks, her upper lip, her chin. She looked at herself. Perfect.

Demmie had invented this look herself. It was so simple she was sure some other person was going to steal it from her before she was famous. In the seventies Mick Jagger and David Bowie and all of them had started wearing lipstick and eye shadow and all that. Glitter rock, they called it, and all the heavy metal groups still had that same look, more or less. But what about women? Demmie wondered. What was the big deal if Demmie wore makeup? In fact, when Demmie wore makeup, she looked like somebody who went to work in an office. Not right. So she figured, okay, what's the opposite of that for me? Answer: shave cream. So simple, you'd think someone else would have already thought of it. But no one had, not that she'd heard of. And the twist was, she didn't take it off. It just sat on her cheeks, foaming. Like she said, it was her own look. The kind of look that would really make the bastards think twice.

She went over to her amp and flicked the switch. She picked up her Stratocaster and fastened the strap and checked the tuning on the guitar. It was close enough. She hit an E chord. Bam. Grabbed the whammy bar. *Boiinng—ooiinng—ooiing.* She walked up to a lampstand that she pretended was a microphone and began to sing. Blobs of shave cream separated from her chin and dripped onto the floor. *Wild Thing.*

•   •   •

Meanwhile, several miles away, the telephone at Officer James Calcagno's house started to ring. Calcagno held his head and watched the phone. It was not a good Easter Sunday. He'd been woken up in the middle of the night by the ghost of a plastic rain hat which was haunting his house.

"Huh. Huh. Huh," Calcagno said, testing his voice before he actually answered the phone. He didn't want whoever it was to think he'd just woken up. "Huh. Huh. Huh."

"Hello?" he said again, picking up the phone. Officer Calcagno listened to Vicki's voice. She spoke for some time before Cal-cagno could get a word in.

"All right," he said at last. "All right. I'll be right over." He hung up.

Calcagno had hoped that this might, perhaps, be a quiet day, but it looked as if the few remaining residents of Centralia were thinking otherwise. He didn't even understand what this woman was talking about. Something about rabbits and pianos and shoes. But she sounded upset. She might be having some kind of break-down. He was going to have to drive over there, see what was going on.

As he pulled his pants on, Calcagno looked at the radiator, still hissing in the corner of his bedroom. If you looked carefully, you could still see the place where the rain hat had melted. It was just about all that was left of his wife. She had left that rain hat there by accident one day, and the next thing you knew the heat came on and melted it onto the pipes. There was no way to get it off. The rain hat and the radiator had fused on the sub-atomic level.

He looked in the mirror. He needed a shave. After he smoothed things out on Almond Avenue, he would come back and clean himself up, maybe sit in the tub and read the Sunday *Inquirer*. Go through the comics in the tub. That Garfield really cracked him up. It was a shame they didn't have Dondi anymore, though, or Little Iodine. Terry and the Pirates. Little Nemo in the Kingdom of Ice. There Oughta Be a Law.

His wife had died in her sleep two autumns previous. Simply went to bed one night and never arose again. Calcagno didn't know she was dead at first; he just figured she wanted to sleep late. But then the heat came on and that rain hat started to melt again and the room filled up with the terrible smell of burning plastic. That's what woke him up, and that's how he knew she was gone, when she didn't react. Usually when anything smelled funny, she was the first one to start hooting and hollering. That morning, though, the rain hat filled the air with its rubber and plastic smell, and Elizabeth just lay there, still.

It had been over two years ago, but Calcagno still missed her.

The red flush in her cheeks when she was laughing. The way she collected shoes. Her special sauce for eggplant.

Calcagno remembered the problem with the squad car as soon as he reached his driveway. He was the only officer on duty in the county this weekend, on account of the holiday. And they'd taken the police cruisers in to get their oil changed. Indeed, the only vehicle left was what the officers in Columbia County called the "ice cream truck," which was really a Chevrolet van that had been refitted so that nine or ten prisoners could be locked up in the back at once. In all his years on the force, he had never had to arrest more than one person at a time. Shaking his head, Calcagno started the van and began to drive towards Almond Avenue.

Calcagno's head hurt. It had been a long night. He'd gone over to his sister's house to help assemble a wagon for his nephew. She wanted to fill it with Easter treats. It had sounded simple. Just put the wheels on and there you'd be. He had no idea how complex it would get. The hours went by, still he couldn't figure it out. Finally around two he managed to fake it. He wasn't sure the wheels would stay on, but the hell with it. He'd check it out in the morning.

Unfortunately, two hours after he got home and went to bed, that rain hat had started stinking up the house again. He sat bolt upright in bed and said his wife's name out loud.

"Elizabeth," he said. "What is it?"

He sat there, almost expecting her to give him instructions, but the only sound was the steam hissing in the radiator. He lay back in bed. Was she trying to tell him something? Maybe she wanted to tell him to get over her. To try to fall in love again. Calcagno was only forty-three. He still had time to be someone's sweetheart. Was that it, then? Elizabeth was trying to let him go?

A plane went by overhead; Calcagno watched as a red streamer soared out of the fuselage, unreeled, and slowly drifted towards the earth.

•   •   •

"Just leave," Wedley was saying to Dwayne. "If you don't leave you're going to be sorry."

"I already am sorry," Dwayne said.

"Not as sorry as you ought to be," Wedley said.

"How sorry am I supposed to be?" Dwayne said. "You tell me that."

"Sorrier than you are, Dwayne."

"How do you know how sorry I am?"

"I can tell things about people," Wedley said. "I'm not stupid."

"Are you saying I'm stupid?" Dwayne said.

Wedley looked at him.

"It's *your* rabbit," Wedley said.

"I know whose rabbit it is. Don't act like I don't know whose rabbit it is."

"Whose rabbit is it, then?"

Dwayne shrugged. "It's Vicki's."

Wedley seemed to shudder. "Oh yeah," he said. "Her. Well, no wonder."

Dwayne started clenching and unclenching his jaw again.

"No wonder what?" he said.

"No wonder her rabbit committed hari-kari."

Dwayne made a fist with one hand. "If you were a rabbit that belonged to Vicki," he said, "I'd throw you out a window myself."

"If I were something that belonged to Vicki," said Wedley, "I'd jump."

• • •

Meanwhile, Phoebe had quietly gotten out of bed, gone to the window, and looked out. Buddy looked up at her. Buddy looked sad. He had seen the whole thing. If only he could explain it. Wasn't there some drug, some truth serum, that could allow dogs to talk, just for a little while? They had done it with other animals. Like whales, for one. They slowed whales down and they made these groaning noises. And porpoises, too. Except it was harder to slow them down. There had been this episode of

"Nova" in which they got these chimpanzees to use sign language. Which was fine except that it turned out they didn't have much to say. *We would like some more bananas please.* Why not make dogs talk? They were thinkers. The problem was the lips. No wonder they just arf. Not the same kinds of lips. If dogs had the right kind of lips the world would be different. You couldn't shut them up, probably.

Phoebe went out into the hallway where her father and Dwayne from next door were gesturing at each other. Dwayne was swinging the rabbit around by its ears. It was ugly to watch. Wedley was usually so restrained. He kept his sadness inside somewhere. It was awful to watch it spill over like that, like some molten magma or something. Worse to see Dwayne step in it. She went past the men, unnoticed, and descended the stairs into the living room, to look at the Easter baskets.

She picked up the eggs. Demmie had dyed them all black and blue. Several of them had little skulls and crossbones on them. Another one was labeled POISON.

There was something odd about the way they felt, too, as if Demmie hadn't boiled the eggs first. She shook one of the eggs marked POISON. It was true. Demmie had decorated a bunch of raw eggs.

Phoebe stood up and went to the front door. She opened it up and looked out at Centralia. A police van was pulling up next door. A tired, unshaven man got out of the van and started walking towards Dwayne's house.

Suddenly, Buddy raced towards her, put his paws up on her shoulders. She had forgotten about Buddy. He had brown junk oozing out of his eyes. Good old Buddy. He couldn't stand on his hindquarters very long, though. Legs too weak. Phoebe and the dog bounded back into the house. Buddy was glad to be inside. He leaped about the living room, sniffing things.

From upstairs came the sound of her father yelling at Dwayne.

Phoebe decided she would open her presents then and there. Demmie wasn't going to be coming down for a while. She was doing the shaving cream thing again, probably. From upstairs came the sound of Demmie playing electric guitar. *Wild Thing.*

Phoebe took one of her presents and put it in her lap. Buddy sat down next to her. It was her main present from her father. It was small, light, rectangular. A box containing a new martingale? Something like that? She wasn't sure. She shook it, heard a soft rustling. Of course Pa hadn't bought it himself. Demmie got it and wrote *For Phoebe from Dad* on it. But that was close enough. With excitement and joy she tore open the package.

It was a carton of Winstons.

At this moment, two things seemed to happen simultaneously. First, the front door opened and an attractive woman stepped in with that policeman. Phoebe recognized her as the woman who had been living at Dwayne's for the last couple of months. The policeman looked tired. They were both looking up the stairs.

Coming down the stairs, at that same moment, were Dwayne and Phoebe's father. Dwayne was in front, being chased. Dwayne reached the bottom of the stairs, came face-to-face with Officer Calcagno, and made a fast left into the living room. Wedley grabbed the back of Dwayne's shirt, which ripped. The policeman got out his billy club. Vicki grabbed onto the billy club to keep Calcagno from hitting Dwayne with it. Calcagno started yelling at Vicki, and she started kicking him in the shins with her high-heeled shoes. Wedley had a hold of Dwayne's neck, strangling him.

Which was when Buddy became upset. He bounded towards the interlocking forms of Dwayne and Wedley and put his paws up on their shoulders. He bared his teeth and started snapping at the air between the fighting men.

Phoebe, standing, crying, let the box of Winstons fall to the floor. She picked up one of the black eggs and threw it across the room. It shattered and began to ooze down the wall.

"You hate me!" she yelled, her voice choked with sobs. "Why do you hate me?"

She picked up more eggs and started hurling them across the room. One of them hit Officer Calcagno in the head. There was a little blood, mixed with raw egg, on his forehead. He was still being kicked in the shins by Vicki. He kicked her back.

"Police brutality!" Vicki shouted. "My rights are being violated!"

Another egg soared overhead and smashed on the wall next to where Vicki and Calcagno were standing.

"Jesusgod!" Calcagno shouted. "The whole family's gone berserk!" He had heard about situations like this. Mass hysteria.

He swung his billy club through the air, knocking Dwayne to the ground.

"Dwayne!" Vicki shouted, going over to him. "Moron!" she said to Calcagno. "Jerk!"

"Aw, knock it off," Calcagno said, getting out the handcuffs. "Gee whiz." He quickly shackled Vicki and Dwayne's wrists together. Buddy was still barking. Another egg shattered against the wall.

"You hate me!" little Phoebe was saying. "Why does everyone hate me?"

"Mister, call off your dog," Calcagno said to Wedley.

"It's my daughter's dog," Wedley said. "I don't have any influence with that dog."

"Well, tell your daughter to call off the dog."

Phoebe looked at them and yelled, "Why does everyone hate me?"

"Oh, never mind," Calcagno said, and hit the dog with the billy club. Buddy fell to the floor.

"You hit the dog!" Vicki yelled. "I can't believe this. Mister Law Enforcement comes into people's homes and billy-clubs their animals!"

"You just keep quiet, ma'am," Calcagno said. "Everything's under control."

Still yelling, Phoebe picked up her Easter basket, and began to spin around. It looked like she was going to do shot put.

"Sweetheart," Wedley said. "Phoebe, darling—"

With a bloodcurdling scream, Phoebe let go of the basket. Jelly beans and raw black eggs flew through the air like shrapnel.

"All right, that's it," Calcagno said, walking across the room towards her.

"You're not going to hurt her, are you?" Wedley said.

"What do you care?" Phoebe said.

Calcagno put the cuffs on the little girl, pulled her back across the room towards the adults.

"Of course I care," Wedley said. Calcagno handcuffed the father and daughter together. "I love you, darling."

"If you love me so much how come you give me cigarettes for my birthday?"

"What?" Vicki said.

"He gave me a carton of cigarettes," Phoebe said, sniffing. "Winstons. Can you believe that?"

"Winstons!" Vicki said, unimpressed.

"Do you know how much a carton of cigarettes costs these days?" Wedley said. "A lot."

"Why didn't you just give her cancer straight off," Vicki said, "if that's your idea of love."

"Aw listen, Phoebe," Wedley said. "Demmie must have bought those. I'm sorry, sweetheart."

"Just be quiet," Phoebe said.

"Don't tell me to be quiet," said Wedley.

"Oh, do what she says," Vicki muttered.

"I'm her father!" Wedley said.

"You're a jerk," Vicki said.

"Shut up!" Calcagno yelled. "All of you. You—can you stand?"

Dwayne groaned.

"If you were so concerned about his health maybe you shouldn't have clobbered him," Vicki said.

"He killed Buddy." Phoebe sniffed softly.

"I'll have your badge for this," Wedley said.

"The dog is fine," Calcagno said. "He's just resting."

"He's dead," Phoebe whispered.

"Listen," Calcagno said. "You are all in a lot of trouble. I don't know what's going on here, but I'm throwing the book at you. Assaulting an officer. Resisting arrest. Disturbing the peace. You want to hear your rights?"

"Oh, just take us in," Vicki said. "We don't need for you to read us our stupid rights."

"He has to read us our goddamn rights," Wedley said. "It's the law."

"You always talk that way around your daughter?" Vicki said.

"Shut up," Wedley said. "Why can't everyone just shut up?"

"We're letting you set the example," Dwayne said.

"Don't even talk to me, Dwayne," Wedley said. "You and I are at war."

"This is kind of exciting," Phoebe said. "Is Buddy at war with Dwayne, too?"

Buddy was still breathing, and his eyes were still open, but he didn't seem to be present in the same universe as everyone else. His eyes followed the movements of things unseen, watching the shapes of the invisible galaxies expand and explode around him. Buddy's purple tongue hung loosely from his moist and spotted mouth.

"I can't speak for your mother's dog, sweetheart," Wedley said. "Buddy's going to have to speak for himself."

•　　•　　•

Demmie Harrison, her cheeks covered with Gillette Foamy, played a few chords on her guitar as she stood before the window. The policeman was taking everyone away and leading them towards the paddy wagon. Her father, handcuffed to her sister. You had to give Phoebe credit. She had something. And Dwayne from next door, handcuffed to Vicki. Even took the dog. The cop turned back towards the house. Well, Demmie thought. I'm next.

Demmie was not next. For the moment she had been forgotten. In a minute the cop was outside again, holding something fluffy. Vicki's rabbit. Poor Dwayne: he still didn't have a clue. The cop threw the rabbit in the back of the van, then started it up and drove away. Made a big deal out of it. Flashers going around, even the siren.

Demmie smiled. They were all gone. *Wild Thing.* Everything was going according to plan, even better than the plan. *You make everything.* She threw her head back and sang. *Groovy.* Soon she would be free.

A S T E R O I D S

◖

*One attempt to account for the presence of the
asteroids is the theory that they are fragments of
a planet which exploded. Some scientists hold that
this theory lacks supporting evidence.*

Emily Harrison, Wedley's estranged wife, walked by the
ocean in her white dress. The evening stars were beginning
to come out above the city now. The sea plunged and receded,
the foam enveloping her wide toes. She placed a hand at the
bottom of her throat and felt her necklace, a crucifix. She thought
of her daughters, of Centralia, and the sea.

•   •   •

Billings let the saw fall to the floor. Once he had heard
someone play the saw on "The Ed Sullivan Show." Was that
possible, to make a saw into a musical instrument? It would be
painful at square dances.

He stood and looked up the stairs towards his unknown future,
his love, and distant space. What he needed was some rosin and
a bow. Above Centralia thin smoke hung in the dying spring air.
Footsteps were approaching. The house filled with the sound of
strangers, women, crossing the unseen threshold in horror and
yearning sadness.

•   •   •

The orbits of most asteroids lie at least partially between Mars
and Jupiter. The largest is *Ceres,* with a diameter of c. 480 miles.

Other asteroids include *Pallas, Juno, Astrea, Adonis,* and *Hermes.* Many believe that their origin can be blamed on the planetesimal hypothesis.

• • •

PALINDROME FOR UNHAPPY MARRIAGE

as performed by Wedley and his wife Emily

—Well, sometimes that's how I feel.

—That's just like you. Acting like someone else.

—I don't want you going over there, Wedley. That girl is in love with you.

—You're crazy. I'm just being friendly.

—What about me? Doesn't charity begin at home?

—I haven't forgotten. It's not as if I've forgotten, is it?

—Yes. You made a promise then.

—When, at our marriage?

—What did you say?

—I do.

—I thought you loved me.

—I do.

—What did you say?

—When, at our marriage?

—Yes, you made a promise then.

—I haven't forgotten. It's not as if I've forgotten, is it?

—What about me? Doesn't charity begin at home?

—You're crazy. I'm just being friendly.

—I don't want you going over there, Wedley. That girl is in love with you.

—That's just like you. Acting like someone else.

—Well, sometimes that's how I feel.

• • •

HOUSTON: Okay, Neil, we can see you coming down the ladder now.

ARMSTRONG (Apollo 11): Okay, I just checked—getting back up to that first step, Buzz, it's not even collapsed too far, but it's

adequate to get back up. It takes a pretty good little jump
. . . I'm at the foot of the ladder. The LM footpads are only
depressed in the moon's surface about one or two inches.
Although the surface appears to be very, very fine-grained, as
you get close to it, it's almost like a powder. Now and then,
it's very fine.

I'm going to step off the ladder now.

●　　●　　●

Buddy looked out the window of the paddy wagon. There
were these things called Snausages he hoped he'd get a chance to
enjoy. Sort of like Play-Doh intestines. Shoes hung suspended in
midflight. There was the scent of something tragic in the air,
something nearly as tragic as Snausages. The ineluctable escaping
skunklike stench of things unhinged.

●　　●　　●

Demmie packed her things into an athletic bag and looked in
the mirror one last time. There. It was done. Her name was
henceforth changed to Scabbaxx. Demmie looked in the reflection. Scabbaxx looked back.

"Look out, world, I'm not fucking kidding," Scabbaxx said.

Aspects of Various Characters on the Surface of the Asteroids:

NAME	WEIGHT	CEREAL	TRANSMOGRIFICATION
PHOEBE	13 lbs.	Lucky Charms	"Lucky" the Lark
EDITH	21 lbs.	Quisp	"Laura" the Swan
WEDLEY	28 lbs.	Kix	"Ned" the Bear
DEMMIE	20 lbs.	Frankenberry	"Ozzy" the Screech Owl
JUDITH	21 lbs.	Kaboom	"Jimmy Stewart" the Gazelle
WILKINS	30 lbs.	Coco Krispies	"Mumbles" the Snake

●　　●　　●

Pinkeye is prevalent among horses and is fatal if not properly
treated. In humans it is also called Mr. Phartley's Syndrome and

characterized by an angry redness of the membranous sheathing of the eye and a distaste for puppets.

* * *

Uncle Pat lay, loveless and perspiring, in his hospital bed. "Knock knock," he thought. "Who's there?" He looked out the window towards the moon. A dog howled somewhere in the distance.

"Nobody," he said.

* * *

It was assumed that nebulous matter acted upon by forces of gravity already had some degree of rotation and that as it condensed it would whirl faster and faster, changing shape from a globular mass to a spheroid with flattened poles.

* * *

The evening stars were beginning to come out about the city now. *I thought you loved me.* It would be painful at square dances. *About to lose my balance in one direction . . .* The ineluctable escaping skunklike stench of things unhinged. *Look out, world, I'm not fucking kidding.* "Nobody," he said. *In humans it is also called Mr. Phartley's Syndrome.* She thought of her daughters, of Centralia, and the sea.

* * *

Scientists at last became convinced by their own calculations that their explanations do not fit our own solar system, although they may hold true somewhere else.

JUPITER

◐

The Bringer of Joy

*Most noticeable among the changing spots of the
surface is a great red patch, carefully studied since
1878, when it became obnoxious.*

Phoebe looked out the window of the paddy wagon, watching the houses go by. On the left was the Odd Fellows'
graveyard where the fire had begun, all those years ago, before
she was even born. Phoebe knew a girl at school named Mindy
whose mother was buried there. Her mother had died on the same
day as Anwar Sadat.

Phoebe was handcuffed to her father. Wedley was looking at
the steeple of the Greek Orthodox church, towering above them
at the top of the hill. He had been married in that church twenty
years ago. Emily's brother Pat had been the best man. The organ-
ist was his friend George Moogus. Now Moogus had moved to
Anchorage. Emily had vanished. Pat had that laughing sickness.
The police van moved up and around the hill; there was a quick,
last view of Centralia down in the valley on their right. They
passed through a thin cloud of smoke and left the town behind.

Vicki was sitting across from Wedley. She was trying to avoid
looking him in the eye. This was an unacceptable situation. A
woman of her background ought not to be susceptible to such
situations. When they got through with whatever this ordeal was
going to entail she was going to let Dwayne have it. Going back
in time with him had not included the agreement to wear handcuffs on Easter. And it was Dwayne's fault for stirring up these
Harrisons. The entire family was out of plumb. The way that

Phoebe had lost control like that. It was clear Wedley was letting his girls grow up to be maniacs. It was because he let them run wild, because they had no positive female role models. This Phoebe was going to wind up worse than her sister. Anyone who had an attachment to a dog like that had to be deranged.

Dwayne was handcuffed to Vicki. He was looking to his right, out the back of the van, watching Centralia recede. In the air above the town four people hanging from parachutes were drifting towards the earth. That would be fun, Dwayne thought. Drifting like that. You could see things from a different perspective. That was how you learned things.

He rubbed his wrist, feeling the chafing from the cuff that joined him to Vicki. His wrist was chained to hers, the one that was wearing Edith's bracelet. Dwayne felt a sudden blackness at having given it to her. At this moment he felt a great dislike for Vicki. Look at her there, sitting with her legs crossed and her hair up like that; she thinks she is the Queen of Sweden or something. She didn't have the slightest understanding of Dwayne's special thinking. The only person who did was probably Edith, but that was only because Edith had a special kind of thinking herself.

He had never really been able to describe the way his brain worked. Dwayne was aware that it was different from most other brains. Other people had one thought at a time. Whereas with Dwayne there was a great multitude of cacophonous and contradictory ideas present in his head at any given moment. If he concentrated it was possible to move linearly, like normal people, and thus move forward from one idea to the next. But often it made more sense to move laterally, so that any one idea might lead into new and unknown territory. It was very interesting, like having a multiplex movie theatre in your skull all the time, but it made it hard to follow a conversation, or to take part in one. Everything was a distraction from everything else.

If he could have found Edith at that moment he might have tried to explain things to her. If he could get six or seven tape recorders and tape a set of feelings onto each one, then he could play them all simultaneously, and sit in the midst and say to Edith, you see, this is what my mind is like exactly. All those words would be like a kind of music. The low notes would be his darkest, most pessimistic thoughts. Like how his presence in a room seemed to make light bulbs blow out. Or maybe his memories of his grandmother when he was a kid, how she used to make him eat cream sauces and chicken à la king against his will. His fear of Sno-cones. Then the middle part could be four or five voices that explained just what a normal day was like. The main theme would be the complexity of waking and blinking and sleeping. One strain for driving the car. Another for worrying about whether it was going to rain or not. A third to monitor whether you were getting sick. A fourth for God and Jesus. Then the high notes might be the kind of optimistic, romantic things that he hoped were true. Oat bran makes you live longer. Love conquers all. If you hold your breath near a graveyard the people in purgatory get your oxygen.

If he had been able to provide this music for Edith then she might have had some sympathy for what it was like to be Dwayne. Women assumed that being a man was easy. They thought that you were filled with a sense of power, that the world was at your command on account of being a couple inches taller than they were and getting paid more. Being a man, in fact, meant that you were responsible for things that you had no control over whatsoever. He knew all about fidelity and monogamy and the righteousness of trusting people. But Edith didn't know what it was like to look up and see the face of a woman like Vicki. He regretted his inability to make himself understood. Sometimes he felt trapped inside his own mouth. There must be a language of the heart that would enable him to explain all of the things he felt at once, a language that would enable him to speak with the sense of music that burned inside of him. But in the absence of such a language he'd lost Edith and now he was handcuffed to Vicki in a police van with a dead rabbit and a gelatinous dog.

It was funny how much Vicki had changed since high school. She had become so much more refined and elegant. Dwayne didn't know where she had learned all that, Scranton maybe. She looked like the kind of woman you'd see playing the harp in an orchestra. In high school she just looked like anyone else, except maybe taller and more bosomy. The only reason he had started being friends with Vicki in high school was so he could get to know Edith. Yet the more he hung out with Vicki, the farther away Edith got. She wound up going to the prom with Scott Eunichtz, The Snail. The last time he saw Edith before graduation she was desperately trying to get his glasses off her face.

And yet, after Vicki moved to Reading, Dwayne had the rare feeling of returning to himself. That he had been some other Dwayne the entire time he had been going out with Vicki, and only now was able to come home, like a wheel coming into true. When Edith called him after Hurricane Hildegarde, and they became lovers at last, he felt that he had recovered himself completely. For the first time in his life he was able to be both outside of himself, in love with someone, and true to his insides, too. He was in tune.

They were coming into Buchanan now, a small mill town west of Centralia. Most of the stores downtown were closed for the holiday. A few couples wearing their fine church clothes walked hand in hand down the sidewalk. Bells were tolling from steeples. A statue of James Buchanan, Pennsylvania's only president—and the only presidential bachelor—stood in the middle of a small green square. He held one hand outstretched, pointing east in the direction of Centralia.

Dwayne still didn't know how he had lost Edith. Things had been so good for the first year it was as if he took their harmony for granted. Maybe it was the harmony itself that had gotten on his nerves, like too-beautiful music when you're not in the mood. She grew jealous, demanding. She wanted things to be remarkable every minute of the day. It wasn't possible for him to be himself and to be consistent. That's when he'd first thought about getting all those tape recorders and playing them all at once. But the longer they stayed together, the more it was clear that Edith would never understand. It was right around then that he had almost hit her with the shovel by accident and given her the tag that said JOCKO.

He'd been wondering what the devil he was going to do about

Edith that day he'd stopped at the piano store in Reading. Everyone always thought Dwayne was incapable of art. On account of how slowly he moved. But he had taken lessons all those years and he sat down in the store and played the baby grand. He closed his eyes, and thought about Edith. He was filled with his sense of love for her, as well as with his fear that things were slipping away. Wherever she was, he hoped she would hear what he was playing and that the two of them could be healed. He tried to express all the inarticulate emotions which raged within him through a song. If she heard the vibrations in the air, somehow, she would understand him. That was when he opened his eyes and saw Vicki.

That whole time he had been playing, he had been mistaken. His song was not for Edith. It was for Vicki, whom he thought he had lost.

"Vicki," he'd said. She smiled, and came to meet him.

"What?" Vicki said. They were still handcuffed together.

Dwayne looked around. They were passing through Buchanan.

"Nothing," Dwayne said. He shrugged. "I thought I saw something."

"What?" Vicki said, insistently. "What did you see?"

At that moment Dwayne hated her. He couldn't explain. "Weather balloon," he muttered.

They passed by the Buchanan Hardware and Appliance. A small burro was tied up in front of the store. The glass in the front door was broken.

"Look," Vicki said. "The Outcast! He's struck again! Sure as you're born. Officer? Aren't you going to stop?"

"What?" Calcagno said from the front of the van. "I can't hear you."

"Didn't you see that? Someone's breaking into that hardware store. There was a burro out front. Isn't that the maniac they've been talking about on the radio? The lunatic?"

Calcagno stopped the van. He turned around and looked at the burro, standing in the road.

"Ah, jeez," Calcagno said.

"I think we should just keep moving," Wedley said. "We don't want to get involved in anything."

"Keep quiet," Calcagno said, putting the van in reverse. "Let me just see what's going on."

He backed up until he was adjacent to the burro. It was tied to a parking meter with a length of twine.

"You all wait here," Calcagno said, getting out of the van.

"As if we have a choice," Vicki said. "Really."

"What's he doing, Pa?" Phoebe said.

"I don't know," Wedley said. "I think he's looking for the Outcast."

"What happens if he gets shot?" Phoebe said. "Does that mean we can go?"

"Shush, honey."

Everyone looked at the hardware store except for Dwayne, who was looking at Buddy. Calcagno drew his gun and went into the store.

Buddy watched the progress of the elements in his own universe. He blinked as meteors and asteroids passed him by. He saw a smiling god at the center of the galaxies and he wagged his tail. He moved towards the empty blackness at the edge of infinity and whimpered quietly. Buddy licked his jowls with his dry, purple tongue.

If you could understand the universe the way Buddy understands it, Dwayne thought, you could explain things. If he had the insights that Buddy had, he might still be going out with Edith.

Two shots rang out from inside the hardware store. There was silence, then another shot.

"Oh my God," Vicki said. "Dwayne, save me."

"Save you?" Dwayne said.

Vicki burrowed her face into Dwayne's neck. "Oh God, please. Save me, Dwayne."

"I'm trying," Dwayne said.

"What's happening, Pa?" Phoebe said. "Who was that shooting?"

"Stay with me, Phoebe," Wedley said, holding his daughter's handcuffed hand in his.

Buddy stood up and shook. He walked towards the rear of the van and put his front paws up on the glass, so he could look back at where he had been. But his hind legs were too weak, and Buddy fell over. He lay on his side and groaned.

"That dog is pathetic," Vicki said. "You ought to have it put down."

"Vicki," Dwayne said, holding her. He hated her.

"We ought to have you put down," Phoebe said.

"Phoebe," Wedley said. "Mind your manners."

The door of the hardware store flew open and a fat man walked out, his hands on his head. Calcagno shoved him up against the wall, then frisked him. He handcuffed the stranger, then led him towards the van.

"Move over, folks," Calcagno said. "You've got company."

"You're kidding," Vicki said. "You're not putting him in here with us, are you?"

The fat man shrugged. "I don't mind," he said.

Calcagno shoved him into the van, then got out his radio. He was having an animated conversation with someone on his walkie-talkie. He put his radio back in his belt and got back in the front of the van.

"Now you all just sit tight. It's just a couple miles to the stationhouse in Mount Carmel."

"What about my donkey?" the fat man said. He had a deep, loud voice. "You planning on just leaving him there?"

"I'll come back for your donkey," Calcagno said, annoyed.

"Oh no you don't," the Outcast said. "You leave him there, anybody that wants can just come up and take him."

"No one's going to steal a burro," Vicki said, shaking her head.

"I would," the fat man said. "As a matter a fact, I did! That's how I got him in the first place!"

Calcagno got out of the van again. He untied the donkey, then started tying the rope to the rear door handle of the van.

"What's he doing?"

"Hey, Ironsides! What's up?" the Outcast said.

Calcagno got back in the van. "Everyone relax." He started the engine.

"Hey! Little Gomez can't move too fast! He's got a sprained ankle! You're gonna kill him!"

"I'm not going to kill your donkey," Calcagno said. "We're going to drive nice and slow until we get to the stationhouse. Like I said, it's only a couple miles."

The van started moving forward. Gomez planted his feet in the ground and strained against the rope.

"You're going to pull his head off!" Phoebe said. "Daddy!" She covered her eyes with her free hand and leaned into her father's chest.

Calcagno looked in the rearview mirror. "I'm not going to pull his goddamn head off," he said. He started muttering to himself.

The donkey started to trot behind the van. Calcagno accelerated. The stores and houses of Buchanan slowly moved past them.

"Hey!" the Outcast said. "This is really something, isn't it."

No one spoke. Buddy got up again and tried to look out the rear window at Gomez.

"Awful quiet back here," said the Outcast. "Yes indeed. Mighty quiet." He cleared his throat. "Scuse me. I got something in my throat. *Eenh enh enh enh.*"

"Do you have a cold?" Vicki said.

"Yeah," the Outcast said. "I got me some a that postnasal drip. You know what that's like?"

"Certainly," Vicki said. "I've had that. It's quite annoying. You should take some Dristan."

"Dristan, huh? I think I tried that once and got nothing. You don't know what they put in those things. Capsules. Could be chalk, you know?"

"Oh, I don't think it's chalk," Vicki said. "I think there's a law. Federal Medicine Testing Authority or something. They'd know if it was chalk."

"Sometimes I use some a that whatdoyoucall it. The caplets."

"Tylenol?"

"Nah."

"Anacin?"

"Nah."

"Ecotrin?"

"Nah."

"Contac?"

"Nah."

"Well, I don't know," Vicki said. "A caplet, you say?"

"Yeah," said the Outcast. "It's stuff like I don't know what you call it. Dries you right up."

He sniffed.

"Dries you up?" Dwayne said, looking at the Outcast.

"Yeah." The fat man sighed.

Phoebe was still looking out the window. Wedley stared into space, off above Dwayne and Vicki's heads. He wanted no part of this emerging friendliness. If Dwayne and Vicki wanted to get all palsy-walsy with this Outcast by talking about Dristan, that was their business, but he and his daughter were still wrongfully imprisoned. All of this cheeriness could only serve to obscure the fact that a miscarriage of justice was continuing.

"Sudafed?" Dwayne said quietly. "That dries you out."

"Yeah, yeah, yeah," the fat man said. "That's the stuff. Sudafed. Boy oh boy, now that stuff is not just chalk. Let me tell you. That's like practically having a vacuum cleaner in your brain. You know what I mean. I mean you go to bed with your head just brimming over with snot, you know what I'm saying? Just *brimming over with snot,* and the next morning, schlooop, all gone, like they just vacuumed the inside of your brains out."

"Do you mind?" Wedley said.

"Hah?"

"Do you mind?"

"Do I mind what?"

"Do you mind talking in that way?"

"What way?"

"I mean is it really necessary to talk about your snot and everything in front of a child?"

"I don't mind, Pa!" Phoebe said, suddenly cheery.

"You see? She don't mind," the fat man said.

"Well, I mind," Wedley said.

"Now you see you shoulda said that right off. See, I don't mind people speaking their own brain. That's fine. But don't pawn it off on your kid. You gotta speak your brain like it was your own."

"Fine," Wedley snapped. "I'll bear that in mind."

They drove on in silence for a while.

"Sure wish I had some of that Sudafed right now," the fat man muttered.

"I had some Bufferin in my purse," Vicki said. "But the officer has my purse. He said I'd get it back later, but I'll believe that when I see it."

"Yeah, you get it back when they let you out," the Outcast said. "I been through all this before."

"You've been in jail, then?" Wedley said, tired and sad.

"Oh, yeah. Sure. Lotsa times."

"He just escaped from jail," Vicki said. "Didn't you?"

"Huh?"

"You just escaped from jail. It was on the news. How you hold up hardware stores and everything? Isn't that you?"

The fat man did not reply. Vicki seemed embarrassed. "I mean, I just assumed that was you. On account of the burro. On the news they said you had a burro, but maybe I wasn't listening carefully. I could have sworn they said you had a burro."

The fat man looked like he was going to explode for a moment, and Wedley was afraid. It was as if he was going to throw up on all of them at once. Then he started to laugh. He had a huge, deep laugh that made your eardrums rattle. He turned red in the face and shook.

"Haw haw haw! Yeah, yeah, that's me! The Outcast! Hey! Get a load of me! I'm world famous!"

"I *thought* that was you!" Vicki said, smiling. It was as if she had run into an old friend.

"Yeah. That's me. Went into Cheyney last October, out by Christmas! Back in by Easter Sunday! But hey! That's life in the fast lane, you know what I'm talking about!"

"Dwayne, isn't this interesting?" Vicki said. "He's the Outcast, and we're riding right here with him!"

"I'm pleased to meet you," Dwayne said. He put his hand out to shake, but forgot that it was manacled to Vicki.

"Ouch," she said.

"Fine. I'm fine. Listen, you call me Morty. Everybody does. Who are you supposed to be then?"

"I'm Vicki Ambrasino, and this is Dwayne."

"You all married?

"Not yet!" Vicki sang. "But maybe!"

Dwayne glowered. "Yeah maybe." He twitched. "When like muh-maybe hell freezes over!"

The fat man exploded again, and he and Dwayne both laughed their haw-haw-haw laughs and exchanged significant glances.

"He zinged you there, little lady!" Morty said. "Yes, sir, that was a real zinger!"

"Yeah," Vicki said, hurt. "He sure zinged me."

"You stick with him, you be laughing all the time." He looked over at Phoebe and Wedley. "And who are you, little lady?"

"Phoebe Harrison," she said.

"Phoebe!" Morty said. "Now that's a name you don't hear much."

"It means 'shining' in Greek," Phoebe said.

"Does it now! You're a regular Einstein there," Morty said. "Uh-huh, a regular Einstein. This your dog here, and uh, rabbit?"

"That's my dog," Phoebe said. "But that's not my rabbit." Phoebe sighed. "Dead anyway."

"But your dog's okay?"

"He's okay."

"What's that stuff on his nose?"

"He's just old," Phoebe said.

"The rabbit's mine," Vicki said. "Or was. Somebody threw it out of our house through the Harrisons' window."

"Who?"

"I don't know who. Probably the same person who stole all our appliances. Frankly, I thought it was you."

"Me? Nah. I don't do that shit. That's just stupid. What'd you say? It went through a window?"

"It came in my window," Phoebe said. "I was thinking about something else."

"Dwayne went over to find out what happened and he and Wedley got in a fight like a couple of morons," Vicki said.

"I'm Wedley," said Wedley.

"Wedley. What kind of name is that?"

"It's my name," said Wedley.

"Jeezo-peezo," said the Outcast. "I don't envy ya, that's for sure. What do people call you for short? What's your wife call you when she's mad at you?"

There was silence in the back of the van for a moment. The only sound was the hum of the engine and the clopping of Gomez's hooves against the pavement.

"Whatsa matter, cat got your tongue?"

"My mommy left us," Phoebe said, still looking out the window. "She's out there somewhere. Driving. She's got the car."

There was more silence.

"Well now, I'm sorry about that. Honest I am. Didn't mean to pry there, Wedley."

"That's all right," Wedley said icily.

"You raising this girl all by yourself?"

"I try," he said.

"Yeah, you do a good job, too," said the Outcast. "That little girl's gonna realize what you done for her someday. She's a little button and no mistake. That little Phoebe of yours. She's a regular pipsqueak."

"Thank you," Wedley said.

"Yeah, a man's gotta do his best for his wife and kids. Now take me. I got married. Haven't seen the wife for five years. Couldn't hack it. I got a boy somewhere too. Must be almost seven or eight now. If I was someone else, I'd be looking out for 'em. Wish I was someone else sometimes too. But what are you going to do? Man's gotta eat."

"Is that why you hold up hardware stores?" Vicki said contemptuously. "So you can eat?"

"Yeah, maybe it is. What the fuck do you know about it?" He shut one of his eyes. "Goddammit."

"Is something wrong, mister?" Phoebe said.

"It's nothing, sweetheart," he said. "I got a little of that conjunctivitis. You know what that's like?"

"Pinkeye," Vicki said. "You get it from germs."

Phoebe looked carefully at the Outcast. One of his eyes was an unpleasant shade of red.

"You don't know what it's like. I feel like scratching out my own eyes sometimes."

"I know what that's like," Dwayne said suddenly.

Vicki looked at Dwayne uncomfortably.

The fat man shook his head. "I don't know. I shoulda quit while I was ahead. I figured nobody would be looking on Easter Sunday. I figured I'd make one more hit, then take it easy for a while."

He shrugged. "You got to admit it's a fine life. All things considered. Even this. Getting arrested. I don't mind. You got to enjoy life. Can't waste your time being a crybaby. When things are good, they can't be beat." He shook. "God! I love to hold up hardware stores! It's just so satisfying!"

He looked from face to face, hoping that his enthusiasm was spreading.

"The smell of them! All that sawdust and plastic and fertilizer! Just makes me feel so damn alive, you know what I mean? All those lengths of pipe, and the circular saws, and the drill bits! It's just so fine!"

"Maybe you should *own* a hardware store," Phoebe said softly. "Instead of trying to rob them all the time."

The Outcast's face went blank. "You know, she's right," he said, awestruck. "I never thought of that."

The police van suddenly took a hard jolt. The brakes squealed. The prisoners in back were buffeted from side to side. Officer Calcagno pulled to a stop. There was a thump as Gomez hit the rear door.

"Sorry about that, folks," Calcagno said.

"Gomez!" the Outcast shouted. "Is he all right?"

The donkey brayed.

"I think he's mad," Dwayne said.

"What happened?" Vicki said.

"I think we hit something," Calcagno said, getting out of the van.

"Why don't you be more careful?" Vicki said. "Tsk."

Officer Calcagno, though, didn't hear. He had already gotten out of the van, left the engine running. He knew in his heart what had happened, ran back hoping his senses would be contradicted. But there it was, someone's cat, dead by the side of the road. Poor thing. Calcagno kneeled over, stroked the still-warm fur. Calcagno looked up and down the street, saw the shadows on the lawns cast by the pines and beeches.

This poor cat had suddenly darted out of the bushes. He hadn't even seen her coming. The van couldn't have been going more than fifteen miles an hour at most, on account of the donkey tied to the rear door. Poor dumb thing. Calcagno found tears welling up in his eyes. It wasn't fair, damn it! He picked up the cat in his arms. She didn't have a collar.

"Listen, folks," Calcagno said. "We've had a little accident. I'm going to notify the family, then I'll be right back. You all behave yourselves back there, you understand?"

"What is that?" Phoebe said. Buddy was swaying back and forth.

"Don't look, sweetheart," Wedley said.

"You klutz!" Phoebe said. "Imbecile! Goon!"

"Sweetheart," Wedley said.

"Moron!"

"I said, you all behave. I'll be back in a moment."

Calcagno turned his back, afraid to look at his prisoners. The girl was right. He was a klutz. He was having a terrible day. It had all begun with that rain hat, and things had gone downhill from there. Now he was really in for it. But he had no choice but to find the owners and apologize. It wasn't his fault.

In front of him was a large stone house. He walked up the driveway, over the flagstones, and knocked on the door. An elderly woman in a flowered dress answered the door.

"Yes?"

"Sorry to bother you, ma'am, but is this your cat? She's had a little accident. I'm so sorry."

"My cat?"

"Yes, ma'am. Like I said, I'm sorry. She just darted in front of the squad car."

"That's not my cat."

They stared at each other.

"Are you sure?"

"Of course I'm sure. Do you think I don't know my own cat when I see her?"

"Have you ever seen this cat before? Do you know whose it is?"

"Yes. I've seen her around. Maybe the people next door. I'm not sure. Did you check for a tag?"

"I did. You say maybe the folks next door?"

"Yes."

"Thank you, ma'am. Sorry to bother you."

"I'm not bothered. Did I say I was bothered?"

"No, ma'am."

The door slammed in his face.

He left the house, walked across the lawn to the house next door. The van with the prisoners was still idling out in the street.

"Yes, Officer, what is it?" A large man in a flannel shirt stood on the threshold, smoking a short cigar.

"I'm sorry to disturb you, sir, but this cat's been run over."

"Well, I didn't do it. I've never even seen that cat before. I was right here with my family the whole time."

"No, sir, I'm the one who hit it. With the squad car. I'm sorry."

"Don't apologize to me. I don't give a darn about it. It's none of my business."

"Well, have you ever seen it before? Does it belong to anyone?"

"It's gotta belong to someone."

"I realize that, sir, but to who? Do you know whose cat it is? I thought I could leave a note."

"Maybe next door. Over there. They've got kids." He puffed on the cigar.

"All right. Thank you, sir. Happy Easter."

The door closed.

Calcagno went to the next house over, but no one answered. Maybe they were out having a pancake breakfast or something. The next house after that, though, a young woman answered. She was holding a glass of milk and seemed to have chocolate cookies all over her upper lip.

"Yes, Officer?" She looked guilty of something. Calcagno knew this look. You saw it all the time. People are always up to something. It's in their nature. The moment a policeman shows up unexpectedly it's as if they think they've been caught.

"Do you know who owns this cat?" Calcagno said.

"That cat?"

"Yes," Calcagno said. "It's dead."

"That's Pinky," the woman said.

"Pinky? Is he yours?"

"No. No, he belongs to the Jacobsons. Next door. He belonged to their youngest. The crippled boy. Binny."

Calcagno felt himself stabbed. "The—the crippled boy?"

"Yes. Binny. Pinky was his. Just about all he lived for. Who did it, Officer? Those bastards! Are you after them?"

Calcagno hung his head.

"I did it," he said. "With the police van. I didn't mean to. She just ran in front of the car."

"You should be more careful," the woman said.

"I know."

Calcagno stood there holding Pinky, thinking about little Binny.

"This Binny—you say he's crippled?"

"Yes."

"Badly?"

"Oh, he's crippled all right. Can't even talk. Just blinks one eyelash for yes, twice for no. He blinks it three times to say I love you. He used to say that to Pinky all the time. Guess not anymore, though."

Calcagno's lower lip started trembling.

"Well," he said. "I guess I ought to go over and tell them."

"Yes," the young woman said. "I guess you'd better. I don't envy you right now, though, no sir."

"Happy Easter, ma'am."

"Thank you, Officer."

Calcagno walked across the lawn holding little Pinky. He knocked on the front door of Binny's house.

No answer came from within. The house seemed dark. Was Binny at home? The woman said Binny was the youngest, but how old might the youngest be? He might be fifty years old. What if he's home alone by himself and can't come to the door?

Calcagno knocked again. There was no sound from within.

Well, he'd just have to leave Pinky there. Put him on the doorstep. They'd figure it out. You come home, your cat is dead, you figure it out quick, somebody ran it over and tried to find you and say they were sorry. You weren't home. What was Calcagno to do? But still, it seemed like a rather gruesome way to tie things up. How could he just leave it there? What if the Jacobsons were away for a week or two? Some dog might come along. Then it would get really ugly.

Maybe he could just leave it in the street. People did that all the time. There wasn't any law. You had to try to find the owners, and he'd done that. He'd call them later. That was all the law required. More than required, even. But no. The woman next door would tell. He'd just have to leave it. He put Pinky down on the welcome mat. Was that that, then?

He turned away and started walking towards the street. He pictured Binny coming home from the ski resort. He hadn't minded just sitting by the fire while all the other children were out on the slopes. Such a good boy. So mild. He hobbles up to the front door. Suddenly a scream rents the air. No, Binny. Please. I'm sorry. But it's too late, Officer Calcagno. The damage is done.

Calcagno turned around, walked back up to the house next to the Jacobsons'. He rang the bell. That young woman with the glass of milk answered again. She had wiped off her mouth, but she still looked guilty.

"Yes, Officer? Did you find them?"

"They weren't home," Calcagno said. "They're out."

"Oh. What did you do with the cat?"

"I left it there," he said. "On the mat. Where they'll find it. I was wondering, though, if you had a notepad and a pencil I could borrow. So I could leave a note."

˙ She looked at him. "Don't you have anything to write on?" she asked. "You're a policeman."

Calcagno shrugged. "Just tickets. I didn't think I should ... You know, it being the nature of the thing. Use a parking ticket to write my regards on. If you follow."

"Oh yes. I understand. Wait." She left and went in search of the things he needed. He stood there, staring into her house. Funny how you get to peer into people's lives this way. She's got a cuckoo clock on one wall and an old-fashioned mirror. I wonder if she lives with anyone. I don't see anybody.

"Here's the things, Officer."

He thanked her. He tried to look in her eye, but she just closed the door. Why did she have a cuckoo clock? Didn't it drive her nuts? Well, anyway. Back to the Jacobsons' again. There was Pinky, asleep on the mat that said WELCOME.

Calcagno wrote a note on the pad: *I'm sorry.* He signed his name and his telephone number and put it on Pinky's body. Covering it. But that was no good. It was going to blow away. He put Pinky on top. Like a paperweight. Still no good. She'd leak. So he opened up Pinky's mouth, already growing rigid, and made her bite down on the edge of the paper. That did it. When you first looked, it was as if Pinky was the one who was sorry. Which maybe she was.

Calcagno walked back to the young woman's house and rang the bell.

"Yes?" she said.

"I got the pad and pencil," he said.

"Are you done with them?"

"Yes. I left them a note."

"Okay." She took the things from him.

"Thanks for the loan."

"No problem. I'm sorry you had to do what you had to do."

"Me too." He cleared his throat. "Say, miss. That cuckoo clock."

"What?"

"That cuckoo clock. The one you got."

She looked around. "Oh yes. What about it? I almost forget it's there sometimes."

"It broken?"

"Yeah. It's broken all right. It was my mother's. It broke a long time ago."

"Those things usually do. Hard to get 'em fixed, too."

"Yes. I tried once but they said it couldn't be fixed. So I just keep it broken."

"Hey, it's right twice a day, though, huh?" Officer Calcagno smiled.

"What?"

"That clock. Even though it's broken, it's right twice a day! Ha ha ha."

"I don't understand."

"It's right twice a day. You know, twice a day it's the time on the clock, even though it doesn't work."

"Oh, yes, I see. That's very interesting."

"Well, I guess I gotta go."

"All right, goodbye, Officer."

"You think you'll be seeing the Jacobsons?"

"Excuse me?"

"I said, you think you'll be seeing them? The Jacobsons?"

"Maybe. Eventually. I don't know. We run in different directions, if you know what I mean."

"Well. You tell 'em I'm sorry. Tell that boy to call me if he wants. I don't mind. I'll take him down, show him the stationhouse. Kids love that sort of thing."

"I suppose they do."

"You ever want to see a stationhouse, miss?"

"Me?"

"Yeah. Like I said, I show people around sometimes. I could show you the jail."

"I don't want to see the jail! Why should I want to see a jail?"

"I don't know. Some people find it interesting, that's all. No offense."

"Officer, are you all right?"

"I'm fine. I'm just a little shaken up. That poor kid."

"You say the cat just ran out of the bushes?"

"Yeah. Out of the blue. I tried to swerve but I couldn't."

"That's a shame. You must be upset."

"I don't know. I'm just having one hell of a day. I got woken up at four o'clock in the morning, by this plastic rain hat my wife used to have, and it's been one thing after another since then."

The woman looked him up and down. She dug into her mouth to get something out of one of her molars, then licked her lips.

"What do you mean, a rain hat," she said.

"Oh, I don't want to bother you with it. I just gotta get over it. My wife died a couple years ago. I still miss her, I guess."

"Officer—what is it—Calk-uh-*gah*-no?" she said, reading his name tag.

"Cal-*cag*-no," he said.

"I'm Wendy Walisko."

"I'm pleased to meet you, Wendy," Calcagno said.

They shook hands.

"Do you want to come in and have some cookies?" she said. "I was eating some and maybe you'd want to have some too and talk."

"Naw," Calcagno said. "I gotta get back to my squad car. I got some people I'm taking to jail."

The woman smiled, embarrassed. "Suit yourself," she said.

He looked towards the squad car. From this angle you couldn't see the burro. He'd forgotten about the burro.

"On the other hand, what the heck. Maybe I could come in for just a second," Calcagno said. "Since you're being so nice." The woman turned, and he followed her over the threshold. The front door closed behind him.

"Oh, I know what that's like, to run over someone's pet," the woman said. "I once punctured a life raft with my shoe." She shook her head. "Boy, were the other passengers mad at me!"

They sat down in a small but elegant kitchen. Wendy poured Calcagno a glass of milk. "Double-stuff or regular?" she said.

"Excuse me?"

"Double-stuff or regular? Oreos."

"Oh, uh, regular, I guess. Regular is fine." Calcagno drank some milk. "Mm-hm," he said. "Good old milk."

"I've got Fig Newtons too, if you'd rather."

"Oreos are fine."

"Good. They're my favorite, too."

Wendy sat down in a chair next to him and unscrewed an Oreo. She dug the creamy filling off the cookie with her teeth, then threw the cookie into a trash can she had placed next to the table.

Calcagno looked at her in wonder.

She smiled. "I only like the stuffing," she said, running one hand through her wavy brown hair.

Calcagno unscrewed an Oreo and scraped the creamy filling off the cookie with his teeth. He drank some milk. He threw the cookie away. He was beginning to feel dangerous. It was the same feeling he had had the night before, when the rain hat woke him up. As if anything might be possible.

In one corner of her kitchen, he noticed a green, conical hat with a scarf coming out of the top.

"What's that?" he said.

"Oh, that," Wendy said, standing up. "It's part of a costume." She put it on her head. "Maid Marion."

She struck a theatrical pose. "Oh Robin Hood, Robin Hood, let down your hair!"

"I don't think that's how it goes," Calcagno said.

"Hah?"

"I mean, that's something else, the thing where they let down their hair. Rapunzel, is what that is."

Wendy looked sad. She took off the conical hat and put it back down on the counter.

"I'm such a loser," Wendy said. "Always have been. Always will be."

"I could be wrong," Calcagno said. It looked like Wendy was going to cry.

"No, you're right," she said. "I don't know what I was thinking of." She looked at the hat. "Sometimes I get so confused!" she said, a little too loudly.

"Where's the rest of it?" Calcagno said. "Is there more to it than that?"

"Upstairs." Wendy came back to the table and sat down. She unscrewed another Oreo. "I collect costumes."

"Do you?" Calcagno said. His heart was beginning to beat wildly in his chest.

"I have what you could call a very active fantasy life," Wendy said, drinking more milk.

Calcagno displayed an agitated smile and nodded his head. "That's good," he said.

"*Very* active," Wendy said. She looked sad, and shook her head. "Hoo boy."

"Huh," Calcagno whispered. The rest of the world had disappeared.

"Well, you know. A person can't just keep things bottled up inside," Wendy said. "You have to live out your dreams." She scraped another Oreo against her teeth, and threw out the cookie. "Isn't that right?"

"Of course that's right," Calcagno said, intrigued and alarmed. "Can't just save 'em for a rainy day. That's not living."

"Oh Officer Calcagno!" Wendy said, standing up. "I'm so glad you agree. Do you really mean that?" She drew near him.

Calcagno thought it over. "Well, sure," he said. "You have to live your own life and not someone else's."

"Will you do me a favor?" she said. "Wait right here. I have a surprise for you!"

Wendy almost ran out the door. He heard her going upstairs, and then the sound of her going through her closets. His heart was pounding insanely.

She was gone for some time. He wondered what she was doing up there. Whatever it was she was up to, it sounded like it needed a lot of preparation.

Calcagno ate another Oreo. He finished his glass of milk, and smacked the empty glass down upon the table. He licked his lips.

He had a creamy milk mustache.

He heard the sound of her coming down the stairs.

"Here I am," Wendy said, reentering the room. She was wearing a leopardskin skirt. In one hand she was holding a club. Wendy was not wearing a top; her breasts swayed gently in the harsh fluorescent light of the kitchen.

"Bam, bam," she said. "Bam bam bam." She smiled. "Wild, huh?"

Calcagno nodded. "Wild," he said softly.

"Okay, listen. From now on, I want you to call me Oona."

"Okay," he said. "Oona."

"And why don't we call you Unk. You like that? Unk?"

"Unk," Unk said.

"Here," she said, holding up a tiny pair of men's underpants made of the same leopard-spotted material.

Unk took the underpants from her.

"I'm sure they'll fit you, Unk," Oona said. "You're the same exact size as my dead husband."

• • •

"You'd think he'd have at least locked the door," Phoebe said, watching the scenery wheel past them at fifty miles an hour.

"You'd have thought a lot of stuff," the Outcast said. "You okay driving, Miss Vicki?"

"I'm fine," she said.

"She says she's fine," Dwayne said, sitting between them in the front seat. Vicki was driving with her free left hand. Her right hand was handcuffed to Dwayne.

"I heard her," said the Outcast.

"For the last time," Wedley said from the back of the van, "turn this thing around. We're going to be in serious trouble."

Gomez made an unpleasant braying sound from the seat next to Wedley.

"I think he might be right," Vicki said. "That policeman's going to be angry."

"Aw, just keep driving," the Outcast said. "I'd do it myself, except I got both hands cuffed. You guys are lucky you all got a hand free. I'm about to go outa my skull."

"I still don't see why it was necessary to take your donkey with us."

"Sorry, babe. Where I go, Gomez goes. And at the speeds we're traveling I don't want him running behind. He might get hurt."

"Where are we going, Pa?" Phoebe said.

"You're asking me?" Wedley said. "Ask the Outcast."

"Where are we going?" Phoebe said again.

"I told ya. We're going to my mom's house. That's where I keep all my stuff. We gotta use the band saw to cut these cuffs off."

"And then we can go?" Vicki said.

"And then you can go," the Outcast said. "Unless you want to hang out at my ma's. She makes one hell of a meatloaf, I'm not kidding. Whole slices of onion in there, the size of a human eye!"

"And then what?" Vicki said. "Are you going to go hold up some more hardware stores?"

"No, no, no, man. I'm gonna live! I got all of life spread out in front of me! I got stuff to do! Get me! I'm gonna do the hotsy-totsy!"

"You're insane," Wedley said.

"What do you know about it?" the Outcast said.

"Yeah," Dwayne said. "What do you know about it? Being sane is all the same to you."

Wedley sighed. The day was getting on now. He wondered for a moment about Demmie, at home alone. She hadn't even known they were getting arrested. For all Demmie knew they had gone off and left her. Poor girl. Underneath all that black smudge she was starting to look like her mother now, just like Emily had looked years ago. He thought about the day he and Emily were married. On their wedding night he had given her a pearl necklace that had belonged to his mother. She gave him a kaleidoscope.

"Don't worry, Pa," Phoebe said, not looking at him. She held his handcuffed hand in hers. "We're having an adventure."

SATURN

◐

The Bringer of Age

*Some rings are not circular, and at least two rings
are intertwined, or "braided."*

The canoe bearing Judith Lenahan drifted around a soft bend
in the Catawissa River at one o'clock in the afternoon. The
bow of the boat brushed against the reeds as the hull scraped the
mud on the riverbed and came to rest in the shallows. She lay
like that for some time, shipwrecked and unconscious, as min-
nows swam back and forth in the still water and leaves from last
autumn slowly floated past. Water striders balanced on the surface.

Judith came to consciousness from a great and mysterious
distance. Her last memory was of waking in Wilkins' house that
morning, with Wilkins still asleep by her side. She had lain next
to him for an hour or so, thinking about the situation, listening
to his soft breathing. Then at last her path had become clear, and
she performed her pantomime. She had held out her hands, trying
to teach him a lesson, but he wouldn't listen. The man was
tone-deaf.

But hadn't there been something, a flash in the air, a single
moment before she had been extinguished, the sight of some
airborne being impending above her? For a fraction of a second
there had been a human face, speeding downward, the mouth
open. She could see the fillings on the molars, the gold crowns
and gums speeding earthward, looming like an unanswered question.

Her head ached from a strange ringing blow, as if her entire skull had been rung like a bell. *Proclaim liberty throughout all the land and unto all the inhabitants thereof.* She swept back the gray blankets that enshrouded her. There was an exhaustion in her veins, as if she had been stung by a spider, drained of blood, encompassed by coils of silk.

Judith Lenahan stared up into the blue sky with shock and wonder, returning to the world. Birds were singing. There was the soft sound of water moving. She was wearing her white mime gloves, and her clothes were gone. *They rolled back the stone from the tomb, but there was nothing there. Just some towels.*

She sat up, trying to understand the situation. The fact that she was in a boat accounted for the strangeness of gravity. But there was no explanation for her sense of place. She was not the kind of person to set sail in a canoe naked and not remember it. Had she run away to sea while dreaming?

Her sense of balance was uneven and waterlogged as she unrolled the blanket, tried to stand, and put one foot on the riverbank. The canoe, freed of its cargo, spun free from the mud, and Judith lost her footing. There was a loud splash.

"Goddammit," she said, sitting waist-deep in the river. "Goddammit to hell."

Dripping the waters of the Catawissa, she sloshed to the riverbank, covered by the soaked gray blankets. The canoe spun buoyantly out into the stream and began to float downriver. For a moment Judith Lenahan stood on the banks of the Catawissa, watching the canoe sail away from her. She noticed the black lump near the stern of the boat, vaguely recognizing it as a bag that contained her possessions. No impulse came over her, however, to retrieve her lost belongings. She stood there, shivering in her damp blankets, and watched her things recede.

Judith turned her back on the river and climbed up the bank.

That was the moment she first confronted the abandoned, depraved remains of the James Buchanan Memorial High School.

Never before had she seen putrescence sustained on such a large scale. An old, collapsing mansion stood at the center, with various and grotesque additions haphazardly and inefficiently joined on to it. The central section had stupendous dormer windows and a circular stone tower. To the left was a flat, utilitarian addition with tennis courts on the roof as well as the fractured dome of a miniature observatory. Another wing off to the right was a threatening, windowless box of cinder blocks painted a repulsive vomitlike tint. On the roof of this was a dented antenna, a warped satellite dish, and a broken flagpole. A massive, monstrous smokestack towered above the school and cast its shadow towards the river. In leering, lime-colored paint along one side of the smokestack was written the phrase JAMES BUCHANAN HIGH SCHOOL, and on the other side, the legend LET's GO WEASELS.

Between Judith and the school lay a kind of open sewer filled with greenish liquid. Pink chunks of matter floated on top, resembling a kind of viscous cupcake Judith remembered from childhood called Snowballs. The air was filled with a faint smell of burning hair and ammonia and the entrails of gutted fish.

For an instant, in a high window, Judith thought she saw a human figure, looking down on her. The shadow fell behind a curtain.

Judith took a step to the left, to avoid the pit of green water, and walked across the kickball field towards the school. No matter how despicable the building appeared, she was going to have to go inside for help. Get some clothes, dry off, use the phone. If she could call Wilkins in Centralia, he might be able to come for her. Otherwise, she would be stranded, shipwrecked, hysterical, naked.

Before her, at the head of some broken granite steps, loomed the front door of James Buchanan High School. To her right was a curving driveway, and beyond that a small garage. There the remains of a yellow school bus stood on cinder blocks. Ivy was growing over the emergency exit.

Judith walked up the stone steps and swung open the old oak door. A damp, burnt smell wafted from the darkness. She took a step forward, and the door closed softly behind her.

She was in a dim, paneled hallway. There were a few security lights on, faintly illuminating the cobwebs on the ceiling. Doors to empty offices stood half closed. Floor tiles cracked beneath her feet.

Before her was a paneled room. Flags that she did not recognize stood on crooked poles. There were a few worn-out couches, a fireplace filled with empty cans of birch beer, and portraits of former principals on the wall. A man with pince-nez and an odd, breathless expression stared back at Judith from above the fireplace. FENTON WEEMS, the portrait said. FIRST PRINCIPAL 1889–1892.

She walked back out into the hallway and practically knocked over a plaster statue of a plump man in a long coat. He had high Wizard-of-Oz cheekbones and a kind of leering, alcoholic cast to his face.

JAMES BUCHANAN, read the inscription on the pedestal. 15TH PRESIDENT. His arms were outstretched, as if he were about to catch a basketball. IF YOU SEEK HIS LEGACY, LOOK AROUND YOU.

"Yuck," Judith said, and shook her head. Buchanan? Wasn't he one of those presidents before Lincoln? They all merged into each other, Buchanan, Polk, Pierce. Her memory of history was dim. William Jennings Bryan, and the cross of gold. The French and Indian War. Chester Alan Arthur. The Dred Scott Decision. The Battle of Wounded Knee. The Monkey Trial. Patty Hearst. Jimmy Carter and the swimming rabbit. Arbor Day.

She walked down the hall, muttering and shaking her head. There was a bad smell to James Buchanan High School; it was the kind of place that made you wonder how people ever made it past age fourteen. You could sense how much the students here had hated it. It was the kind of place that took innocent Columbia County children and turned them into hooligans and maniacs and gorillas. Mushrooms were growing through the floor.

"Hello?" Judith said, remembering the silhouette of the person she had seen on the upper story. She hoped that this shadow had belonged to a caretaker, someone who could help her out of her predicament. But with her luck, it would turn out to be some lunatic, someone who had about as much to do with Buchanan High School as Judith did herself. She would walk into the old

German classroom and there would be this other woman, naked and soaked, wrapped up in wet blankets.

"That would be just my luck, to get divided in half between two people," Judith muttered.

She picked up a piece of yellow paper from the floor. It was a copy of the *Buchanan Bugle,* dateline March 1982. There was a big headline about how the school was closing. Judith moved towards one of the security lights so she could read the paper. The newspaper, in broken, illiterate language, explained the story. How an offshoot of the Centralia fire had traveled all the way underground to Buchanan, how the school had been shut down, right in the middle of the year. A new school, the Gerald Ford High in Shapp City, was going to take up the slack; apparently the closing of Buchanan had been anticipated for some time. There was another story about a phonics teacher named Miss Costello, who had gotten hiccups that had never stopped. At the time of the article she had been in the hospital for two years. She was in a special clinic where they shot her up with chemicals and psychoanalyzed her and forced her to hold her breath and tried to frighten her by popping paper bags in her face, but the hiccups persisted. That was in 1982. She was probably still going.

At the bottom of the front page of the *Buchanan Bugle* was a note about how the Science Fair was going to close immediately, and anyone that wanted to take their project home had to pick it up before Friday, March 12, 1982, after which time all the science projects were going to be dismantled and incinerated.

It wasn't the kind of high school Judith could see people getting all teary-eyed about.

Judith walked to the end of the hallway and pushed open a door.

Before her was a vast spiral staircase, with banisters carved from cherry. One wall of the staircase was a great stained glass window that stretched several stories. Thousands of tiny panes of glass created a mosaic of a three-masted ship, sailing on a gray ocean.

An enormous pendulum was suspended from the ceiling above the stairwell. The tremendous weight at the bottom had a tiny pointer that was supposed to knock over small tiles on the floor. To demonstrate scientifically that the earth revolved. A plaque on the landing read FOUCAULT'S PENDULUM. Foucault had invented one that worked. There was something wrong with the one in Buchanan High School, though; it refused to demonstrate that the earth spun on an axis. The plaque went on to try to explain the pendulum's malfunction. It had something to do with magnetic rocks below the surface. Lodestone. Even now the pendulum was swinging back and forth, along a black line that had been painted on the floor. Judith shook her head. If she were a young, impressionable scientist, she would have found this all very disconcerting.

She went downstairs, still hoping to find a phone or some dry clothes. Now she had a distinct desire to get the hell out of Buchanan High School. There was something unambiguously dreadful about it. The farther in she went, the more she was filled with a sense of loathing, as if she were becoming tainted by its very atmosphere. Could breathing the air in a place such as this make you begin to resemble it, in some sense, just as pet owners, in time, come to resemble their pets? Judith shivered. The waters of the Catawissa had soaked into her bones.

"Hello?" Judith said again. Her voice echoed unpleasantly in the empty stairwell. At the bottom of the stairs the enormous weight of the pendulum swung back and forth. There was something frightening about a force that heavy moving in silence. She looked up towards the distant ceiling, three or four stories overhead, where the top of the pendulum was moored, but there was only darkness.

And for that moment she had the certainty she was being watched. She waited for the shadow to lean over the top of the stairs and introduce itself, waited until she became unnerved by the sound of her own breathing.

"Hello?" she cried again. Judith shook her head, ran her fingers over the bare surface of her scalp. Her head seemed excessively skullish to her at that moment. She turned her back on the swinging pendulum and opened the door to the basement. It was better to just keep moving.

She entered what had once been the girls' locker room, and found some foul fragments of uniforms from the high school sports teams. Judith dropped her gray blankets on the floor and tried on some of the clothes. The only things that really fit were a basketball jersey marked MESSALONSKEE, a plaid skirt for field hockey, and a silk robe for judo. She went into the bathroom and looked at her own reflection. Judith smiled; she looked like the captain of some sport that had not yet been invented. Turning on the water from the spigot, she ran warm liquid over her face and scalp. It was just beginning to get a little prickly up there. She dried her face with a disgusting towel.

In a bathroom stall, the girls had left hieroglyphics for Judith to contemplate. Things about teachers, about boys, about other girls. *I Want It Bad,* someone had written. Above the roll for paper was the legend *Buchanan Diplomas, Take One. Ha-ha.* And there were initials in hearts run through with arrows.

Judith left the girls' locker room via a back door. She wasn't quite sure where she was now—she saw a long hallway with a series of small doors built into the wall, like condos for dwarves. A broken squash racquet lay on the floor.

In the hallway beyond was a kind of public space, and a stairway coming down on the right. She followed this up a story and entered a large auditorium, well lit by a set of glass blocks set in one wall. The sun was shining through the glass, casting orange pools of light upon the floor. A banner overhead read SCIENCE FAIR 1982.

Hundreds of dusty, homely science projects still stood there, taking up half a dozen plywood tables on sawhorses.

There was a jar of formaldehyde with a pair of bovine lungs and a heart floating in it. There was another exhibit showing a cross section of Skylab, the space station that crashed in Australia. There was a Play-Doh structure in the shape of a car engine called MOTER that had toothpicks in the Play-Doh indicating what each part of the engine was. Apparently it had been very hot in the auditorium at one point because the Play-Doh MOTER was somewhat melted. They put salt in Play-Doh to keep kids from eating it. You couldn't blame them. Even as Judith looked at the MOTER something in her wanted to pick it up and eat it. Suck on the spark plugs. The radiator. The fan belt.

There was a skeleton hanging from a hook. It was wired together, bone by bone. Somebody's job, wiring it up. Whose skeleton? Some homeless person, some benevolent soul who had dedicated her body to science? People did that. Instead of being buried. They donated themselves. And medical students did experiments. Gave you nicknames, after you were dead, they gave you some screwy grad school nickname like Skeezix or Hooter. Horrible, if you thought about it. You thought you were helping science but some sophomore is calling you Skeezix and yanking out your spleen. Later they cleaned you off and someone else wired your bones together and before you knew it you were hanging from a hook in the abandoned Science Fair in James Buchanan High School. What had gone wrong for this person, Judith thought, looking at her hanging there. What was the decision she had made in life that had brought her to this end?

She reached out with one hand and touched the face of the skeleton. She traced the orbital bones where the eyes had been, moved her hands up along the cheekbone, which was labeled *zygomatic arch,* then felt the tiny ridges along the top of the skull where the bones were fused together. The coronal suture, joining the parietal bone, the frontal bone, and occipital bone. How very strange, Judith thought, that everything should have a name.

Hanging from the ribs was a faded blue ribbon, and the words *First Prize.*

Judith turned her back quickly, suddenly afraid, and walked away from the Science Fair. She felt as if she were going to scream. She made an agreement with herself that if she didn't find a telephone soon she would just leave the place. Now that she had clothes there was no reason she had to stay here. She could walk down the street and see if the next people down would help her out. She was going to have to call someone. Wilkins, if she could get him. If not Wilkins, then someone else. For a moment, Judith thought about all the people that she knew, realizing that there was no one left that she could turn to for help.

The next room over contained the remains of the school

lunchroom. Brown bags erupted from a gray trash can. Long industrial tables were lined up in geometric fashion. At the head of these was one slightly less ugly table, where the teachers sat. Beyond that was a set of stainless steel corrals where the old sourpuss punched your lunch ticket. And beyond all this, in stainless steel magnificence, the innards of the James Buchanan High School Cafeteria Kitchen. It was awe-inspiring. All those rows and rows of ovens and refrigerators and fifty-gallon sinks. Tremendous cauldrons and pans and spoons hanging from hooks. There was an eerie and complex assortment of long knives and cleavers. On a sign was posted the menu for the week of March 8, 1982: *Monday:* Steakums, Tossed Salad, French Fries, Peach Pudding; *Tuesday:* Spaghetti, Cabbage Salad, Pineapple Chunks, and a Roll; *Wednesday:* Hot Dogs, Mashed Potatoes, Buttered Corn, and Jello. *Thursday:* Turkey Sandwich, Green Beans, and Pickles. *Friday:* Fish Sticks, Succotash, Grapefruit Halves, Marshmallow Octagons, Scrapple.

At the head of the teachers' table, a glass of white wine stood next to a half-empty bottle. Judith looked at it: *Chassagne-Montrachet 1980.* The wine had been chilled.

She picked up the goblet, rolled the wine around in the glass, then raised it to her lips.

She blinked. "Nice," she said.

She was tempted to polish off the bottle. It was almost as if it had been left for her. Go ahead and do it, she thought, sitting down in the chair. *It is always better to apologize later than to ask permission.*

She took a few more sips of the fine wine. *What is scrapple?* she heard herself asking, when she'd first moved to Philadelphia. She was at the home of her ex-boyfriend Muggs, trying to make a good impression. *Everything but the squeal, dear,* Muggs' mother said, miserably. Judith was afraid she was going to grow dizzy and flop headfirst into her soup.

Pouring herself another glass of the Chassagne-Montrachet, Judith thought about poor Muggs. She'd had him on the brain for some reason the night before, when she was wrapped up in her nightie, lying beside Wilkins. The strangeness of the situation struck her. She had gotten herself into trouble with this Wilkins because she'd been trying to teach him something, trying to give him an example for living a life unlike his own. And yet that's exactly what Muggs had tried to do to Judith. Colonized her, as if she were a backward country in need of development.

For a while it had been grand to receive that kind of attention. To feel that she was worthy of being remade. But the charm of this conceit had not lasted long. It was impossible for her to be the person Muggs was trying to invent, since Muggs himself had no precise blueprints; all he knew was that Judith herself was in need of alteration. How terrible sex had become in the end, to be held that close and encircled by someone who only thought of you as a rough draft. One day he told her he didn't like her laugh. Why don't you laugh more like this, he said, and then he demonstrated the kind of laugh he preferred. Now you try, he suggested.

That was the end of Muggs, and the end of meeting the world halfway.

So she had started up the Purifier, and everything else had fallen into place. No more goon boyfriends who told you how to laugh. No more smiling and asking how people were when you didn't care. No more kowtowing to fashion or the whims of the vampire culture. For three years now she had lived the truth.

She lifted her glass and toasted her new life. Judith wanted this to be a victorious moment, but somehow it seemed sad, there in the empty cafeteria of an abandoned high school, with her head shaved, wearing Messalonskee's basketball jersey and a skirt from field hockey. She put her glass down. Okay, sure: it had to be admitted that on occasion a pure life was a little odd. It wasn't always as pleasurable as she wished. It was hard not to feel nostalgia, sometimes, for the exquisite elaboration of the world of deception.

That's what had started her weeping in Wilkins' bed last night. She remembered Muggs giving her that sexy nightgown on Valentine's Day. He might have been a creep, but on occasion he was capable of kindness. Did forgoing creepiness mean forgoing all kindness, living the rest of her life alone? It was nice to be with people sometimes, to be wanted. Surely there had to be a way of dwelling in the world without becoming contaminated by it?

She felt a sudden gasp within her suddenly, as if something had come out of alignment, and once again she felt the urge to cry. She saw the face of Muggs before her, telling her not to come crying to him. She saw the face of her father, walking her around Independence Hall. And her mother, trying to cope with his loss, letting Judith stay up late and grow wild. Then her mother's death had followed, five years after her father. She used to serve Judith crème de menthe in a tiny aperitif glass. Judith had thought it was the elixir of some secret race of people, that fiery taste coming from that strange green liquid, filling her up with evergreen and flame. Calling her Bunny Rabbit. Where were they now, those parents of hers, those people who had abandoned her? Where where they, those people that had loved her, and that small green glass?

I'm coming to pieces, Judith thought. That's the long and the short of it.

She finished off the wine, wiped her face with the napkin, and stood up again. It was time to find the phone, or be gone.

The hallway outside the cafeteria led past dozens of old class-rooms. There were maps of Europe and Southeast Asia; erasers stood in dusty chalk trays; old wooden desks with holes for inkwells stood in rows, nailed to the warped oak floor. One room had a bust of John Keats sitting on the windowsill. On the blackboard someone had written, *O weep for Adonais he is dead!* In the next room an enormous slide rule hung from a wall. Judith followed the hallway back to the staircase, where the pendulum was still swinging back and forth along the painted line upon the floor. Sunlight filtered through the brilliant glass mosaic of the ship upon the sea.

This time she followed the stairs up to the third floor. There had to be an office or something somewhere in the building. But the first room Judith came to was some sort of old science laboratory. There were a dozen black desks with shiny silver gas jets built into them. A chart of the periodic table of the elements hung from a nail. There were lots of empty cages, one of which was marked KINKAJOU: *Potos caudivolvulus.* Someone had added a note at the bottom of the plaque, which read: *Note the lustrous eyes.*

Leaving the science lab, she walked to the end of the hallway, where a window faced the river. She saw the lawn of the school stretching out before her, saw the broken sewer line filled with green liquid and Snowballs, saw the Catawissa River snaking off into the hills beyond the horizon.

She realized it was the same window she'd seen from the ground, where the figure had been standing. On the windowsill before her there were fingerprints in the dust. Who was it that lived in this old school, leaving glasses of wine for her, spying from behind old and tattered curtains?

To her right was a door that led towards the roof. Judith went outside, glad to feel fresh air on her face again. On the flat blacktop before her stood some athletic equipment—some weight machines, a tennis court, a bench press, a trampoline. Judith looked towards the river again, searching the horizon for the sight of the boat that carried the things that had belonged to her.

Judith looked again at the trampoline, and remembered bouncing on one at Rehoboth Beach, when she was ten. The sound of the ocean nearby as she rose and fell. The one here on the roof of Buchanan seemed pretty beaten up, but still, it lured her. How can I refuse, Judith thought, after the events of today? She took off the silk judo robe, field-hockey skirt, and jersey until she was buck naked and climbed onto the canvas. The old springs groaned and flaked off bits of rust.

Judith Lenahan bounced into the air, was held motionless for a second, then fell, plummeting down into the depths. She soared into the air once more, slowed, then again was held at apogee. That was the best part. Not the upward motion, or the falling, but the moment when the two were in balance. If only there were a way of sustaining that single moment, Judith thought, caught between gravity and momentum. That would be heaven.

It was impossible to make a dissonant motion, she found, bouncing up and down on the roof of James Buchanan High

School. Only meters away was the tremendous aching bulk of the school's monstrous smokestack, covered with the letters that spelled out LET'S GO WEASELS. Judith just laughed. She did complete body flips, somersaults, jackknives, pirouettes, flying higher and higher each time, until at last she shot up into the air, held her arms wide as if gathering the universe into herself, then fell. She landed on her back, bounced up and down a few times, and then, at last, came to rest. Her heart was pounding in her breast.

And at that moment she thought of Wilkins. That dog.

How had she gotten from that place to this? Had she finished the process of teaching him a lesson? The pantomime. The question mark. This she had given to Denton Wilkins. Never before had she offered anything so personal to a stranger.

She stood up and put her things back on. It was time to leave, past time in fact. She opened the door to the hallway and walked past the music room and the geography class and the slide rule and the bust of Keats and the blackboard that said *O weep for Adonais he is dead!* back to the main stairwell. Foucault's Pendulum had not progressed.

I have got to get out of here, she thought, beginning to feel panic.

But at this moment, she noticed a light coming from a room at the end of the hall. She walked quickly towards it, and found what she had been hoping for—a room with a bookcase and some file cabinets and a desk with a telephone on it. Judith sat down behind the desk and picked up the phone. A Tiffany lamp hung down from the ceiling.

A dial tone rang in the silent room.

"Excellent," she said out loud.

She dialed information and got the number for Wilkins' summer house in Centralia. She wrote it down on a large desk calendar, and realized, after she hung up, that the calendar was from the current year.

Her heart beating quickly, she picked up the phone again and dialed Wilkins' number.

The phones out here in Columbia County sounded funny when they rang. Not like the sound you heard on the line when you were in the city. They sounded like the phones in a distant nation.

"Hello? Mr. Wilkins? Dent? It's Judith."

The person on the other end of the phone said, "Judith?"

"It's me. You know. Judith Lenahan. Listen. I'm sorry about this morning. There's so much I want to say."

"You're confused."

"You're right. I am. Of course I am, why on earth would I try to shave a person I barely know? I was trying to make a statement. I screwed up. I'm sorry."

"Who did you shave? Could you repeat that?"

"Is this Mr. Wilkins?"

"The people who live here aren't home."

"Is he coming back? Mr. Wilkins I mean? I have to give him a message. It's terribly important."

"I can try to have him call you. That's all I can tell you."

"I'm calling from James Buchanan High School. I don't think it's far away. But I don't know. I don't know where I am. Can't you have him call me? I can leave the number."

At that moment, Judith looked up and saw an elderly woman looking at her. She was bent with age, and something in her eyes burned with a queer fire.

She was standing in the doorway of the office, holding a double-barreled shotgun. She wore a black dress and stockings; a braid of black hair fell nearly to her waist.

"Hang up," she said, pointing the gun at Judith's head.

"Let me just give them the number," Judith said.

The shotgun went off. The cradle for the phone flew across the room and clattered, in many pieces, on to the floor. Judith was still holding on to the receiver, the end of the now-severed cord swinging back and forth.

"I said hang up," the woman said, moving rapidly towards her. "Are you deaf or what?"

"Well, I didn't know you were going to—"

"Stand up."

"Listen, I'm sorry to have barged in here, ma'am, but I was in trouble, and I—"

"Stand up. God–damn! You're stupid, is that it?"

Judith stood up.

The woman in black shoved the gun into Judith's stomach.

"You drank my wine," she said.

"I thought you put it out for me," Judith said.

"You?" the woman said. "You? I don't even know you!"

"I'm Judith Lenahan."

"Quiet. What are you doing here? What's that you're wearing?"

"I lost my clothes. I came to you for help."

"You lost your clothes?" the woman said. She shook her head, and lowered the gun. She clasped one hand to her face as if in mortal pain.

"Oh, God!" she moaned. "How I *dislike* people! How I loathe and *despise* them! Goddammit to hell!"

She picked up her gun by the barrel, and swung the butt–end of the rifle at the Tiffany lamp. The shards of blue and green glass fell upon the desktop

"Oh God in heaven," the woman muttered. "How I *hate* things!"

She looked at Judith again, her teeth clenched in malice.

"How can you lose your clothes? How is that even possible!"

Judith opened her mouth to explain.

"Stop! I don't want to hear it! Not a word out of you! Your lies will give me goiter!"

Judith opened her mouth again.

"Quiet! God! Before I have to listen to you! Oh, what a day! What a putrid existence! My wine consumed! My privacy destroyed! It's all ruined! Everything is wrecked beyond repair!"

"Jesus, lady, what is your problem?" Judith said, turning red. It would almost be better to be shot by this woman than to have to listen to her any longer. "I came to you for help! Pardon me for being alive! I was half drowned when I got here. I've been walking around in the dark for half an hour now and all you can do is rant and rave at me!"

"Ranting?" the woman screamed. "Raving!"

"Look at yourself," Judith said.

The woman made an odd chewing gesture with her mouth, licking her lips and tightening her jaw muscles.

"That's my robe, too," she said.

Judith took it off. "Here," she said. "Take it. A lot of difference it makes now."

Judith threw it on the floor.

"Pick it up nicely," the woman said. "It's silk. Haven't you ever had nice things? You can't just throw things on the floor."

Judith picked up the robe and folded it, then placed it on the desk. "No, I never had nice things," Judith said. "Not in a long time, anyway."

"My heart bleeds for you," the woman said.

Judith clenched her teeth.

"How'd you lose your clothes?" the woman said. "You tell me that."

"I don't know how I lost them," Judith said. "I was in a fight with some man."

"A fight?" the woman said. She huddled forward, clutching the rifle to her breast. "A man?"

"Yeah. I think I got hit on the head by something."

"Did he hit you?"

"I don't know."

"He probably did. They always want to hit you. Either they hit you, or they want to. Same thing. You hit him back?"

"I don't remember. Next thing I knew I was floating down the river in a canoe. I must have blacked out. I woke up in the canoe. Out there."

"I saw that," the woman said. "I seen that canoe come down the river, with something in it. I said to myself, that's unusual. I watched it for some time. Then you got out of it."

She lowered the rifle, rubbing her chin, thinking. She almost seemed to forget that Judith was in the room.

"This is interesting. Yes, interesting. She misplaced her clothes, then she got lost at sea. She wound up here. Yes, I can see that actually happening."

She looked back at Judith again. Suspicion clouded her face. "Who are you calling? Are you bringing people here?"

"No," Judith said. "I was calling him back. I hoped he could help rescue me."

"Rescue you?" the woman yelled. *"Rescue* you!" She screamed, dropping the rifle on the floor. "No! No! No! What you want to do is call the police! The National Guard! Get that son of a bitch in jail! Don't call him up, asking him for favors! What's wrong with you?"

Judith looked at her, confused and frightened, but not unconvinced. "Who are you?" she said.

"Me?" the woman said. "Me? I'm Mrs. Hackles. Who are you again?"

"Judith Lenahan. I'm pleased to meet you, Mrs. Hackles."

"Don't say that!" Mrs. Hackles moaned, clutching her hands together at her breast. She shook her head. "You aren't pleased to meet me! You hate me! You despise me!"

"I barely know you," Judith said.

"Why would you like me? No reason."

"I didn't mean to presume."

"Ah, no one *means* to presume, do they? They just come lollypopping in here, drinking your wine, wearing your clothes, talking their talk." She stopped suddenly. "What's wrong with your hair, girl? You do that to yourself?"

"Yes," Judith said. "I got it done last week."

"You look like some sort of mannequin or something. You look like you're nuts."

"You don't know anything about me," Judith said.

"I know more than you think. You're in love with some guy who hits you on the head, you drink other people's Burgundy, you got terrible taste in clothes."

"Well, so what?" Judith said. "What's the difference? Who cares?"

"You don't know who you are," Mrs. Hackles said, shaking her head.

"And you do?"

"At least I respect myself," Mrs. Hackles said. "I got a sense of personal style. Look at you. You're a mess. See, you don't respect yourself. If you did, you wouldn't be standing here wearing Messalonskee's uniform. God, especially Messalonskee. What a moron. I swear that boy could make a *goat* stupid. Just by being in the same room with it."

"I told you I lost my clothes."

"Well, look, I'll give you some clothes. I got closets and closets of 'em."

Mrs. Hackles rubbed her chin some more, and moved it up and down as if chewing. "If I give you some clothes, then, will you promise to listen to me? You won't go back to that bastard who's trying to bash you on the head?"

"Why should I promise you anything? A second ago you were going to shoot me."

"I ought to," Mrs. Hackles said. "I don't know why I even *bother* with people. Still, you've got something, Lenahan. You don't quiver and quake. I could make something out of you."

"I don't want you to make anything out of me. I can do that by myself."

"Oh yeah, sure. You're a mess. Face it, so far, you've screwed up. I've never seen such a case. You let me get you outa them clothes and into something nice. I'll talk and you'll listen. I want to get something into your head." She picked up her rifle, then extended a hand to Judith.

Judith shrank back from the woman, afraid that her touch would turn her to stone.

Mrs. Hackles reached forward, took Judith's hand. "I said come on. We've got work to do. You stay with me, I'll show you how the world works. I know secrets. Terrible things. You stay with me I'll tell them to you. If you can stand it. They're horrible things, *horrible.* Hurry."

Mrs. Hackles pulled Judith out into the hallway, then walked towards the spiral staircase. "Have you seen much of the school? Do you want me to walk you around?"

"I've seen a lot of it," Judith said. She reached out to hold the banister.

"Isn't it wonderful?" Mrs. Hackles said.

"It's disgusting," Judith said.

"Exactly," Mrs. Hackles said.

"Why haven't they torn it down?" Judith said. "What's it doing here? It's an abomination."

"An abomination!" Mrs. Hackles said cheerily. "That's it exactly! It's a disgusting abomination! Oh, you're a smart one. We're going to get along fine! You're just like one of my babies!"

She looked at Judith's head again.

"You know, once you get used to that, it's really very attractive," she said. "Your not having any hair, I mean. Different."

"I'm glad you like it," Judith said.

"No you're not," Mrs. Hackles said. "You think I'm a kook. Don't lie to me." She stopped suddenly on the stairs, clutching one hand to her head. Judith noticed suddenly that Mrs. Hackles had a silver ring on every finger. "God! I hate it when people lie! How I despise that!" She pointed the rifle at Judith's head again.

"You lie to me again I'll blow your head off," she said. "Don't make me blow you all to bits. That would be truly repulsive. I can see you rolling down the stairs already, your head blown off. You're making me choke just thinking about it!"

"I'm sorry," Judith said. "I'm just a little nervous. If you want to get the truth out of people you shouldn't threaten them."

"Well, I know what I know," Mrs. Hackles said, moving down the staircase again. "If you knew what I know you'd be edgy yourself. I know horrible things. Horrible! I forget if I mentioned that."

"What's the story on this pendulum?" Judith said. "How come it's broken?"

"I don't know," Mrs. Hackles said. "Magnets, I think."

There was a distant sound, a car moving on a country road. She looked up suddenly. "Oh no," she said. "Dear God in heaven, no."

"What's the matter?" Judith said.

"Oh no," Mrs. Hackles said, beginning to run down the stairs. "Tell me I'm wrong, please."

Judith followed the woman down the steps, racing towards the first floor. From outside came the sound of the car approaching, then the crunch of gravel as it lumbered up the drive.

"No!" Mrs. Hackles screamed. "Oh, what a day I'm having!"

Car doors slammed outside. Footsteps approached.

"Oh God please, spare me, spare me, *spare* me!"

The front door opened, and five people, a dog, and a small donkey entered the school. There was a tall man with pale eyes, handcuffed to an attractive blonde woman. There was a tired-looking man with long black hair, handcuffed to a little girl. There was an old Dalmatian, limping behind them.

A fat man led them up the stairs, pulling the burro by a rope. He looked at Mrs. Hackles with fondness, leaned towards her, and kissed her cheek.

"Hiya, Ma," the Outcast said. "I'm back."

URANUS

◑

The Magician

The planet is believed to consist of hydrogen slush.

Mr. Dent Wilkins, heartsick, fearful, his head half-shaven, looked out a car window at the brown earth. Lawn ornaments stood in what had once been the Billings' front lawn, paddles rotating in the wind: Tweety chasing Sylvester, Canadian geese with counterclockwise-spiraling wings. Wilkins remembered the shape of the missing house: the dormer windows on the second story, the rotting old porch. A water pump out front. Italian opera playing from the kitchen. Alfalfa: *I'm the barber of Se-ville.* Boxer shorts with hearts, hanging on the clothesline. *Fig-a-ro, Fig-a-ro, Fig-a-ro.* Driving down this street with Tawny in the early days of their marriage, the top of the convertible open, music playing on the AM radio. He had read somewhere that Alfalfa had died in Vietnam, which was just about what you'd expect. Some angry boot camp sergeant, yelling into the kid's freckled face, the head shaved Marine-style except for the enormous, vertical cowlick. *From now on your name is not Private Alfalfa, you understand me, Private? From now on your name is Private Cowlick. You hear me?* Sir, yes sir.

He put his car back into gear, left the Billings' house behind. It was time to leave Centralia. It was going to take a massive effort of suppression to keep Judith's loss from overwhelming him. That look she had given him just before she vanished, suggesting kinship. That was going to be a hard thing to forget.

He drove back up to Locust. *I'm the barber of Se-ville.* His mother used to take him into that place in Kennett Square. The barbers' names were in neon in back of the mirror by the chairs. Three guys in a row, three chairs, three mirrors. *Fig-a-ro, Fig-a-ro, Fig-a-ro.* The one in the middle was Kenny. He had black glasses and a silver flattop. The one with the jokes. On the right was Link. Bald with bifocals. The businessmen all got Link. He was fast. On the left was Johann. The German one. He didn't understand English. They gave you Johann if you were just a kid and it didn't matter. Wilkins' mother would take him in there, and Kenny, who was the boss, would say, "Who you want," and she'd say it didn't matter, and he'd get Johann. Mrs. Wilkins would explain what she wanted done, and Johann would say, "*Ja, ja,* votevah you say," and then he'd give you a crew cut. Sometimes he cried. Wilkins, that is. Johann didn't give a shit.

Downtown Ashland was closed, all the stores shut down for Easter. There was even a barber shop with a pole outside, just like the place in Kennett Square. Wilkins slowed down, looking through the plate glass. An old leather chair sat in the midst of the shop, combs soaking in a jar of blue liquid on a long table, hair on the floor, magazines piled up in a corner. In the Dark Ages they'd take out your appendix, too.

A friend of his in the air force had had his appendix out. "Boomer" Goodman. He had them put it in a jar and he'd wish on it. Whenever they went out on a mission, he'd wish on that jar with the appendix in it for luck, say his wife's name. Where was Boomer now? Did he still have his appendix in a jar? What had he done with it if not? Thrown it away? Maybe he had it buried in a plot, wherever he figured the rest of him would go when he died. How much of a person made a person? Like when you clipped your fingernails, nobody got sentimental over that. But if you lost your foot, say, or a whole leg, or even your entire body below the waist. That happened. You couldn't just throw it out. No, you'd have it buried, put up maybe half a tombstone there, then when the rest of you came along, they'd finish it.

He'd heard about people that were just heads, the rest of them controlled by machine. Surely they'd buried the rest. Treat the body with respect. That body was more the body than that head was. Some head strapped up to a bunch of wires, a mouth chattering away, issuing orders, the idea was enough to make you want to take a swing at something. Once the wife of that head had kissed the chest and held the arms and stood in the ocean with the water just rolling around the knees. Why did the head get to hang around when the body was abandoned? Was it only because that's where the mouth and brains were?

The Ship of Theseus. Professor Beckwith had explained it in school. Theseus has a ship, he loves his ship, but over a period of years he replaces the boards as they warp, the masts as they crack, the sails when they tear. But all the while somebody, some slave or something, is saving the pieces they take off. After ten years, the slave puts together a ship made out of all the pieces. There's two ships now, identical, one with all new parts and one with all the old. Which is the true Ship of Theseus?

It's like the story of the farmer who says, "This shovel has lasted me forever. I've replaced the handle four times and the blade three."

So what about people then, he thought, driving through Ashland back towards civilization. You had relationships with people all the time, told them things, made them promises. And yet all the time you were changing. Your cells were reproducing and dying. Pieces of skin flaking off. Food going in and coming out, rebuilding you all the time. Were you the same person you were ten years ago? Were you committed to the things you'd said? Or were you a new person altogether? What of the people you'd known? Were they the same persons as before?

The Marriage of Theseus is what you'd call it. You stood there in all your innocent wonder and promised to love someone until the day you died. And yet, ten years later, where were those lovers who had looked each other in the eyes? Where was that husband? Where was that wife? They had seen the sights of ten years, had experienced the changes of ten years of history, had stood out in the blistering sun and had had children wake them in the night and lost bits of skin and eaten tons and tons of potatoes. Same people? Same agreement?

He thought of Tawny, sitting in her parents' house in Michigan. What now for him? Had this transgression in Centralia ruined his promise? Did the promise still count if he'd already broken it? Did the promise still count if the person he'd made it with had vanished?

Wilkins again thought about the barbershop. He remembered a barber telling him once, "All barbers are alcoholics." He didn't want to talk to the barber, but the barber didn't mind. He was just chattering away. And now he was explaining how all barbers were alcoholics. Why? *I'm the*— "Because they got their scissors next to your eye." *I'm the barber of*— At that moment, the barber happened to be snipping his scissors less than an inch from Wilkins' eye. Wilkins said something like, "Huh," and the guy kept clipping. *Fig-a-ro*— "Yes sir," he said again. "We got our scissors right next to your eye."

Damn stupid business they've got having to talk to anybody who just walks in. He took a left on Route 61. Barbershop, some guy sits down, you have to take care of him. Keep the conversation going. Dentists the same way. You got to look down someone's throat, pick all the corn on the cob off of their molars, the whole time they're chattering about their kids. Yeah, Homer's in chiropractor school now. Learning how to crack people. Okay, spit. And Penny's in San Francisco. Making homes for bees. Spit. She was home for Thanksgiving, she built a beehive out of some shoes. Incredible the way bees work together, isn't it? If only human beings had some a that spirit. Okay, spit.

Wilkins had this dentist who was slightly insane. Wouldn't drill. If he was going to be insane at least he was insane on the side of not drilling instead of drilling. That much was all right. But every now and then Wilkins wondered if his teeth were falling apart anyway. "The mouth is not a perfect place," Dr. Fronefield said. "You got a lot of little potholes here, but I'm not gonna fill 'em. You got to make a big hole just to cover up that little hole, and then the rest of your life you're plugging fillings. Dentists got a saying, you know what it is? 'When business gets slow, sharpen your explorer.'" The explorer was that little probe they picked your teeth with. Fronefield said dentists plugged your cavities when it wasn't necessary, because they were charlatans. But Fronefield wasn't doing fillings unless he had to. "See, all the problems started with that Kennedy. Spit. JFK he encouraged all the colleges to start dental schools. So it's the late sixties and suddenly we got ten thousand dentists loose in the country. Not only that, at the same time we got fluoride in the water, so kids aren't really getting cavities anymore. What do you get? You got a lot of wise guys trying to give people fillings they don't need. Personally I haven't filled a cavity in a year and a half. Sure you got a few dents in there. *But The Mouth Is Not a Perfect Place*. These things happen. It's not worth drilling your teeth over. It's not worth charging you for."

I'm going to have to balance the checkbook, Wilkins thought, before Tawny comes home. Have to look over all the checks and see what's what.

Dent Wilkins hit the brakes of his car, hard. He pulled over into the breakdown lane. Cars honked at him and whizzed by, shaking his car from side to side as they passed. He sat there, dumbstruck, amazed and horrified at his own life.

That check. The one he wrote Judith Lenahan. He hadn't taken it out of her bag. He'd thought of everything but not that. Wrapping her up in the blanket. Putting her in the boat. Watching her ease into the distance. It seemed like years ago. He'd watched the bag with her things in it float into the distance. As if he were giving her a Viking funeral. Wherever she washed up, they were going to find her purse, with his check still in it. His signature. That was how they would trace her to him. The phone would ring, and Tawny would answer, and he'd have to explain the whole thing. Dent Wilkins watched his entire life disappearing downstream.

He was going to have to go back there. Rethink the scheme entirely. Go down the river, try to find the boat, swim out to her, and redo things. It might attract attention, but it was a risk he had to take. How far downstream would she be by now? All the way to Baltimore? What if she had gotten waylaid somewhere, washed up on some deserted island?

He turned the car around. No matter where she was, he was

going to have to find her. That check in her purse was like a calling card, asking for people to connect him with her. No matter where she was, or how long it took for people to find her, it would surely happen some day, and then his phone would ring. He was going to have to find her once again, and get rid of Judith in a manner that was permanent, a manner so final that even his own memory would not be haunted by her.

That was going to be a more difficult matter than he had first imagined. She was everywhere. Her smell on his fingertips, her words still echoing in his brain. Would he ever be able to look at Tawny again? The very thought of his wife made Wilkins shudder. Those teeth of hers. He imagined their bedroom in Bryn Mawr, the suet for the grackles on a string outside the window, her binoculars at rest upon the sill.

That moment when Judith had taken off her nightgown. Said it felt like wearing a ball of string. Her beautiful breasts, full there in the shadows and light from the fireplace. And that smooth head of hers. It filled him with a sense of aching mystery, with the shock of things beyond his understanding.

Well, she was gone now. The mouth is not a perfect place. He tried to slap himself, to force himself back to his senses. He had work to do, and thinking sad thoughts about Judith was not going to make his work less serious. He was in big trouble. Dent Wilkins gave himself a good talking to, driving through Ashland, climbing up the big hill into the place where Centralia had once been. But the memory of the night before, the wonder, the mystery and the sweet horror, remained.

The image of Judith Lenahan, the feel of her body against his, each minute red hair brushing against his skin, stayed with him all the way up the hill and then down again. It stayed with him as he passed through the cloud of smoke and steam that marked the progress of the mine fire underground. Down there. Burning away, just as it had been for twenty-two years. Relentlessly proceeding, erasing, forgetting. Entering town.

He had a sudden misgiving that he would not be returning to the world.

• • •

It was not even much of a surprise, then, a few moments later, when Wilkins saw the Death Angel, dressed in black robes, sweeping out from behind a boarded-up house and stopping in the center of the road. He watched the figure as it turned to face the oncoming car. The skeletal hands raised into the air and gestured for Wilkins to cease. To bring his whole depraved being to a halt.

Wilkins slammed on his brakes. The dark shape, sailing towards him, filled Wilkins with fear and regret. He almost ran it over. That would be typical, Wilkins thought. To run over Death with the car. They would probably take away his license.

"I'm sorry," the shadow said, coming over to the window. "You're my last chance. You gotta help me."

Officer Calcagno threw back the hood. He looked up and down the street to see if anyone was watching. "Jesus, I don't even have any pants."

"Who are you?" Wilkins said. "Do I know you?"

"Sir," he said, "I'm a police officer. I'm in a bit of a jam."

Wilkins looked at the bewildered, urgent face of Calcagno. The man seemed thoroughly disoriented.

"You're a cop?" Wilkins said.

Calcagno nodded, miserably.

"What happened?" Wilkins said. "Why are you dressed like that?"

"Oh brother," Calcagno said. "You don't want to know about it."

"Sure I do," Wilkins said. "You look like Merlin the magician. Like somebody you'd see on television."

"I've never been on television," Calcagno said sadly.

"Sawing a girl in half," Wilkins said. "That kind of thing. You know what I'm talking about?"

"I know what you're talking about," Calcagno said.

"Is that what you're doing? Sawing a girl in half?"

"I told you. I'm a *police* officer. I don't know anything about sawing people."

Wilkins shook his head, trying to remain calm. Now he was in for it. This cop could send him to jail, if he found out about Judith. "Where's your badge then," Wilkins said, "if you're a cop."

Calcagno shrugged.

"My badge was in my pants."

There was an uncomfortable silence.

"What happened to your pants?" Wilkins said.

"Oh, I don't even know," Calcagno wailed. "I'll probably never even *see* them again." It sounded like Calcagno was about to weep.

"What do you want from me?" Wilkins asked. His voice broke. He was on the edge of apoplexy.

"A ride, as far as the Mount Carmel stationhouse. I gotta get another squad car." He looked down the road again. "Some more pants, too. Some shoes."

"Mount Carmel? Where's that?"

"Two towns west. You go through Centralia, then Buchanan, then Mount Carmel."

Wilkins shook his head fearfully. "All right," he said. "Get in, if you have to."

"Thank you, thank you, thank you," Calcagno said. "You don't know what this means to me." He walked over to the passenger door and pulled on the handle.

"It's locked," Calcagno said, knocking on the window glass.

"Sorry," said Wilkins, leaning over to unlock the door.

Calcagno lifted his robes and sat down. He sighed.

"Man," he said. "The day I've had. I'm so depressed."

Wilkins drove on, nervously eyeing his passenger. He was trying to think of a way to get Calcagno out of his car. Maybe he could pretend to have a heart attack, or a stroke. With my luck, Wilkins thought, it would backfire. Calcagno would just try to give him mouth-to-mouth resuscitation and pound on Wilkins' chest with his fist.

Officer Calcagno looked out the window. He should have known it would end like this. Unk and Oona. Maybe he should just have played along. She hadn't meant any harm. That Wendy was trying to let him into her world. He should have just put on those leopardskin underpants and have done with it.

But he'd stood up, afraid, wanting only to leave. What did she mean, he was the same size as her dead husband. There was something about the way she said it, as if those leopardskin underpants had had something to do with the fact that Wendy's husband wasn't around anymore. Maybe they were too small. They looked like they'd be a pretty tight fit. Perhaps that was the idea.

Anyway, he'd rushed to his feet, wiping Oreo cookies off of his lip, explaining that he had to leave. His embarrassment was plain to see. And that was when Wendy realized the enormity of her miscalculation. Her face had turned white and her lower lip had trembled, and she'd let first the underpants and then the club drop to the floor and then she collapsed in her chair and began to weep.

"Oh, what a fool I am," she moaned. "I'm so sorry."

Calcagno had turned his back, fully intending to flee the house and get back to his prisoners outside, but the intensity of emotion in Wendy's voice held him. He couldn't just leave her there, sobbing, topless in her kitchen, wearing her leopardskin skirt. He had encouraged her, in his own way, into trusting him. It was his own fault for egging her on. It wasn't fair for him to urge her into sharing her secrets with him, only to flee at the first signs of oddity. "You have to live your own life and not someone else's," he'd said. That was why she was before him now, in jungle clothes and tears. She had trusted him.

"I'm sorry," he said, going to her.

"Get away," she said, not looking up, but pushing him with one arm.

"No," he said. "I am. I encouraged you."

"Just go," Oona cried. "You think I'm weird."

"No I don't," he said, putting his hand on her shoulder blade. "You just took me by surprise. You have to admit this is unexpected."

She sobbed. "I thought you'd like it! Oh, I guess I'm just insane. That's all. You should just go."

"I want to stay," he said.

"No you don't," she said. "You're just saying that." She still wasn't looking at him.

"No, I'm not," Calcagno said. "Please let me stay. I want to stay."

She sniffed.

"Ask nicely," she said.

"Ask you nicely?"

"That's right."

"Okay, can I stay please?"

"That's not nice enough."

For a second he wanted to take the club and conk her with it. Instead he said, softly, "May I please stay with you?"

"Oona," she suggested.

"May I please stay with you, Oona?"

She looked up and smiled.

"Okay," she said. She stood up, got her club back, retrieved the underpants. She looked down at them, as if they were a bouquet of flowers that had wilted.

"But these are ruined now," she said. She shook her head sadly. "We'll have to start over, with new characters."

"Okay," Calcagno said. "We'll start over."

Wendy turned her back and started to go up the stairs again. Halfway up, she stopped, turned, and came back into the kitchen. She leaned over and kissed Calcagno on the cheek.

"I love you, Unk," she said.

"I love you, uh, Oona," Calcagno said.

Wendy beamed. She turned and went back up the stairs.

Again there had been the sounds of boxes opening, hangers falling to the floor, tissue paper rustling in hurried fingers. Calcagno remembered standing there, listening to her moving upstairs, knowing that the next time Wendy descended it would be worse. Worse than Unk and Oona, if that was possible. *I have a very active fantasy life*. No kidding.

He wanted so desperately to be up to his own adventure. If only it were possible to have the kind of courage that would enable him to enjoy this sense of the unknown, to feel that sailing into uncharted territory was a fine and wonderful thing. But he only felt fear and embarrassment. All that kept him there was a sense of honor; he had made her cry the first time and now he had to undo that. But there was nothing in his blood that seethed as he desired. Last night the ghost of his wife had given him permission to try to find romance again. And now he stood on the threshold of that romance, listening to Oona combing her closets, feeling wonder and dismay.

When she came down the second time, it was just as he feared. She was wearing a long pointed witch's hat, a broomstick between her legs. A long tattered black skirt swirled around her legs. A black lace bodice barely held back her bosom. She had painted her lips blood red, and covered her eyes with some kind of deep blue shadow.

In her arms she was carrying a black robe.

"Behold, I am Svenda! Witch of the South-southwest," she said, moving towards him on the broomstick. "Who are you?"

"I'm Officer Calcagno," he said shyly. "From the Columbia County Department of Law Enforcement."

"No, no, no!" Svenda said. She stamped one foot. "You are making me angry! Very angry!"

"I'm sorry."

"Who are you?" she said again, impatiently.

"I'm, uh—" he shrugged. "I don't know who I am."

"What?" Svenda said.

"I don't know who I am," Calcagno said. "Maybe you should tell me."

She held open the folds of the black robe, and helped Calcagno step into it. She gave him a little wand that had a twinkling star on the end of it. Svenda took the witch's hat off her head and placed it on Calcagno's, coronating him.

"There," she said, and smiled.

She looked at him with thin eyes, probing his soul. Her mouth opened suddenly, and she gasped.

She held out one hand to him, and felt his cheek.

"Is it you?" she said. "Oh my goodness, can it really be you?"

"Who?"

"You!"

"It's me all right," Calcagno said, embarrassed.

"Zoron!" she said. "King of Darkness! Lord of the Despicable!"

"Yup," Calcagno said, swinging his arms. "I guess so."

"Say it," Svenda said.

Calcagno blushed.

"Say it, say it," she rasped.

"Okay," he said. "I am Zoron."

"Lord—"

"—of the Despicable."

"O my master," Svenda said, raising her hands to her bust. "O Lord of Irritation! Master of Unpleasantness!"

Her fingers reached into her bodice, tightly grasping the material.

No, Calcagno thought. Please please no. What would have been so wrong with simply having milk and cookies together? Talking. What had happened to the world that situations like this seemed so inevitable?

Svenda pulled on the material, ripping the lace, letting her breasts burst out of the material. *"Take me, Zoron!"* she screamed. *"Make me your Nether-wife from Hades!"*

Calcagno yelled, turned and ran. As he rushed through the hallway, the cuckoo clock began chiming. The bird popped out from behind its little doors, hooted, and disappeared.

She lied to me, Calcagno thought. She said it was broken.

Zoron, Master of the Despicable, ran out into the spring sunshine. To his left was the Jacobsons' house. There was a group of people standing on the front porch around Pinky. It looked like an angry mob.

He ran out onto the street, trying to attract as little attention as possible in the wizard outfit, and that was when he found the van missing. In his mind's eye he saw himself closing the back door and neglecting to lock it. It hadn't taken them very long to figure it out. Probably that Outcast had watched the whole thing, waiting for his moment to escape.

The crowd of people on the Jacobsons' front porch turned to look at him. Someone pointed at Calcagno and said something. The mob started coming towards him.

He ran through the backyards of Buchanan, dogs barking, citizens in pursuit.

He ran for five minutes or more, believing that the crowd behind him was growing in size, getting nearer and nearer, until at last, out of breath, Calcagno turned to face them. To make one last stand. To look his accusers in the eye and show them he was an honest man.

There was no one there.

Zoron, Master of the Despicable, walked along the country road, back towards Centralia, carrying his magic wand.

He walked for some time, wondering what would happen next. Everything was silent. Smoke from the mine fire drifted in the air.

It was some time before Wilkins had driven up. It hadn't been as difficult to explain his situation as he'd thought. This Wilkins didn't seem to care. He had problems of his own, Calcagno figured. Something was on his mind. That didn't make him a criminal. For all Zoron, Lord of the Despicable, knew, the man behind the wheel was a man after his own heart.

"So. Where you headed, then?" Calcagno asked.

"North," Wilkins said. "Following the river."

"How come?"

Wilkins still seemed nervous. "I don't know," he said. "No reason."

"Seein' the sights?" Calcagno said. "Is that it?"

"Yeah," Wilkins lied. "Anyway, I, uh, know some people around here. Thought I might stop in and see them."

"You mean like a party?" Calcagno said.

"Yeah, like that."

They drove on in silence. Up ahead was the entrance to Wilkins' driveway. There were half a dozen cars there, and many people moving about. An ambulance came down the drive, its beacons flashing, and tore out into the street.

"Jesus," Calcagno said. "Something's happening here." He shook his head. "I hope it's not old Tawny at it again. Jesus, that would just about make this day complete."

"What?" Wilkins said, slowing the car down. "You know Tawny? Tawny Wilkins?"

"Wilkins? Is that her last name? Never knew it. That poor old broad. Thinks she's Marilyn Monroe or something. Every month and a half it's the same old story. Half of the vice squad arrests in the county happen right here in this driveway."

Wilkins felt as if he had left his body.

Calcagno looked over at him. "Sorry to do this, pal, but I gotta ask you to stop. I better check and see what this is all about."

"Okay," Wilkins heard himself say. He pulled the car into the drive, turned off the engine. The men got out of the car. Calcagno put the pointed hat on his head.

"You forgot your magic wand," Wilkins said, miserably.

"Oh yeah," Calcagno said, reaching in for it. "Thanks."

They walked towards the house. Wilkins looked at Calcagno. "This isn't where you were headed, was it? That party you mentioned?"

Wilkins shrugged. He was looking at the hole in the roof.

"You know ol' Tawny yourself," Calcagno said, "don't you!"

"She's my wife," Wilkins said softly.

"Yeah, right," Calcagno said.

A group of women, standing by the door of Wilkins' house, looked up at the two approaching men. They were wearing jumpsuits emblazoned with the legend CENTRALIA AERHARTS. They fell silent, watching the approaching men with suspicion and distrust.

"What's going on here?" Calcagno said.

"An accident," Jane Peabody said. "Who are you?"

"Police officer," Calcagno said.

"Yeah, right," Jane Peabody said.

"I'm Dent Wilkins." He extended his hand. Jane Peabody didn't shake it. "I live here."

"Don't lie to me," Jane Peabody said. "No one lives here anymore. Not for years and years."

"You do live here, don't you," Calcagno said, astonished. "You're her husband."

"Whose husband?" Jane Peabody said.

"We've never seen him before," Jody said.

"I'm not even married," Jenny added.

"Listen," Calcagno said, "I'd like to ask some questions."

"Oh, do you have to?" Jane Peabody said. "We've been through so much already and we don't even know anything."

From inside the house came the sound of the phone ringing. A woman answered.

Wilkins was completely confused. Something in him wanted to blurt out the whole story. To begin with Doc's Love Products and carry on from there. The drive to Centralia with Judith. Their night together. Waking up to her derangement. Getting trapped. Putting her in the canoe. Would it make sense if he tried to explain?

"Is Tawny here?" Officer Calcagno said, hopefully.

"Tawny who? We've never heard of her."

"Wait," Jody said. "Tawny Wilkins, the old sexpot? I've heard of her! This is her house?"

"She's not here," Wilkins said softly.

"What's going on," Calcagno said. "Where was that ambulance going?"

"To the hospital," Jenny said. "Like, duh."

Calcagno looked angry. "I'm a police officer," he said. "I'd appreciate your cooperation."

Jenny just shook her head. "Pitiful," she said. "A police officer, he says."

"Listen, you all just disregard this outfit I'm wearing. It's not your concern." He took off the pointed hat, handed it to Wilkins.

"Here," he said. Wilkins held the hat.

"Oh, Officer," Jenny said. "Don't take off the hat. You're ruining the entire effect!"

All of the women smiled at him sarcastically.

"Better hand me the magic wand, too," Wilkins whispered, out of the side of his mouth. "They aren't buying this."

Calcagno gave him the magic wand.

There was silence for a moment as they all looked at each other. Wilkins held the wand in his hands.

"He really is a police officer," Wilkins said at last.

"You coming from a party together? Is that it? Where's your costume?"

"This is it," Wilkins said. "I'm wearing it."

"Huh," Jane Peabody said. "You don't look like anybody."

"That's right."

Jane Peabody didn't believe Calcagno was anything other than some local eccentric, but she told him their story—all of it: meeting the woman who said her name was Brenda Schmertz at the airfield that morning, taking off, doing the jump, watching the stranger fall and fall, her chute never opening. They went inside and looked at the hole in the ceiling. There were gray clouds in the blue sky.

"She did it on purpose," Jenny said.

"You mean, what? She took her own life?" Calcagno said.

"Yeah," Jenny said. "She sure had something on her mind."

"We should have paid attention," Jody said. "Maybe we could have helped."

"Well, I *tried* to talk to her," Jane Peabody said. "Whatever was bothering her, though, she didn't want to talk about it. If only I'd tried harder!"

"I'm sure you did the best you could," Calcagno said.

"It's all my fault!" Jane Peabody said.

"Now, now," Jody said, rubbing Jane on the back. "You couldn't stop her. She'd made up her mind before she even woke up this morning, probably."

"We found this in her pocket," Jane Peabody said, holding up the laundry ticket Edith had written on in the plane. Officer Calcagno took it from her.

"Two shirts, starch," Calcagno read. "One dress."

"The other side," Jane Peabody said, annoyed.

On the back of the ticket was written the words: *I just wanted people to like me.* At the bottom it was signed: *Edith Schmertz.*

Dent Wilkins and Officer Calcagno stood in the living room, watching the faces of the Aerharts, as wind from outside blew through the hole in the roof.

"Is one of you Dent Wilkins?" Rosalee said, approaching the group.

"I am." He turned to look at her.

"I'm sorry, you just got a phone call. I didn't think you lived here."

"A phone call? Here? For me? Who was it?"

"Said her name was Judith."

"Judith?" Wilkins turned pale. "Judith!"

Everyone looked at him.

"What did she say? Did she leave a message?"

"Sort of. We kind of got cut off."

"Please," Wilkins said, moving towards Rosalee. "You have to remember!" He was shouting.

"There was a lot of stuff I didn't understand. Oh yeah, she said she was sorry she tried to shave you bald."

Everyone stared at Wilkins' head, especially the part on the left-hand side where a majority of his haircut was absent.

"And she said she was at the Buchanan School. If you wanted to reach her, she's there."

"The Buchanan School?" Wilkins said.

"Yuck," said Jenny. "P.U."

"That old place is closed," Calcagno said. "Been closed for years."

"Well, that's where she said she was."

Wilkins ran towards the telephone, picked it up, and dialed information. The Aerharts talked among themselves. Calcagno walked around the house, taking notes, lifting things up and putting them down.

Wilkins dialed the number for the school and waited for his connection to be completed. But he only got a high-pitched squealing sound, and a recording that the number was out of service.

"Damn," Wilkins said, slamming down the phone.

"We can drive there," Calcagno said. "It's on the way to the stationhouse."

"We have to go there," Wilkins said urgently. "This Buchanan School. We have to get there right away."

"All right," Calcagno said, surprised at Wilkins' insistence. "We can go. Looks like everything's under control here anyway."

"It's over," Jane Peabody said. "At least I hope so." She looked up at the hole in the ceiling again. "Poor thing."

"You've done a good job," Calcagno said.

"Yeah, well, not good enough," she said. She started to sniff, blinking back tears. "Dang it, here go the waterworks again."

Jenny gave Jane Peabody a hug. "It's okay," she said. "You're allowed to cry. It's sad."

"When they found that note," Jane Peabody said. "Dang it, when they found that note . . ."

She was unable to finish.

"It's all right," Calcagno said. "You did your best."

"What the hell did she have to join us for?" Jane Peabody said. "What did we do? We never even saw her before."

"You can't worry about it," Rosalee said. "You're not some mind-reader."

"Didn't even know what she was doing," Jane Peabody said. "Probably had never even been in a plane before. Stupid girl."

"Come on, let's go," Jody said. "Let's go get a drink."

"Maybe Wilkins here has something for you," Calcagno said. "Hey, you got something in the fridge we can all drink? It's been a rough day so far."

Wilkins sighed. "Sure," he said. "I got some beer in the kitchen. Help yourselves. Everybody take two. Three if you want."

He handed the beers around, noticing that there were fewer bottles than there had been this morning. Was it Billings again? As the Aerharts drank their beers, Wilkins thought about the unexpected events: Tawny, cheating on him in their old house, just as he was cheating on her. These strange skydiving women, mourning their lost companion. And Judith, alive! How could he have mistaken life for death? Had he been that anxious to do away with her?

Soon the Aerharts had finished their beers, and it was time for them to return to their homes. Everyone thanked Wilkins for his hospitality, and Jane Peabody apologized to Officer Calcagno for making fun of his wizard costume.

"It's cute, actually," Jane Peabody said.

Calcagno grimaced, still humiliated.

"Thank you," he growled.

Rosalee was the last one to leave.

"If you learn anything about Edith, let me know," she said. "It's such a shame. She was nice."

"We will," Calcagno said.

"Even though I thought she was somebody else, I still liked her."

She closed the door. From outside came the sounds of the women starting up their cars.

Calcagno looked up at the hole in the ceiling.

"Jeez, that's a big one," he said. "Bats could fly in."

"Yeah, I gotta get that taken care of," Wilkins said. He looked through the hole at the sky. Just imagine her traveling all the way down, twisting and falling, watching the tiny house grow nearer and nearer. Imagine that. What a restful feeling that must have been, falling free, right up until the last.

"So," Calcagno said. "You want to go?"

"Yes, let's get out of here. You won't mind if we go to that school and pick up my friend Judith? I have to see her. It's important."

"Fine by me," Calcagno said. "Longer we take to get to Mount Carmel, longer it is before Stroke chews me out."

"Stroke?"

"Lieutenant Stroke. My boss. Jeez, is he gonna rake me through the coals."

"Let's go then. I'll come back here later and deal with the roof. Talk to Billings. Billings is the caretaker."

"He is? He lives here in Centralia?"

"Yeah."

"Never heard of him."

They walked back out to Wilkins' car.

"There used to be a Billings family out on Locust, but they moved."

"That's the ones. George Billings. He looks after the place."

"George Billings. Yeah, they had a son named George. I haven't seen him since their house got torn down. Didn't know he was still around. You're sure about him?"

"Yes, yes," Wilkins said, starting the car. "He's in charge here. I send him a check every month to make sure the house is okay."

"Well," Calcagno said, "like I said, your wife comes out pretty regular. I know she's taking care of things."

There was an awkward silence for a moment.

"Listen, I'm sorry for that crack I made," Calcagno said. "About your wife. Wouldn't be the first time someone said such a thing, though."

They reached the end of the driveway and turned north. "Why don't you tell me what you know," Wilkins said. "About the house, about Tawny, about that costume you're wearing. I'd like to hear it."

"Everything?"

"Everything."

Calcagno didn't know where to begin. There was so much to describe. He figured he might as well start with the rain hat, though. He tried to describe the smell of it, as the glistening rubber melted down the old iron baffles. That smell was where things began, the first step that led away from home.

The car passed out of the driveway. The sounds of Calcagno and Wilkins died away down Route 61. Then the house was silent. Wind rushed softly through the hole in the roof. The Catawissa trickled over the rocks.

Then, at last, the footsteps came up the stairs. The basement door was unbolted. Billings peeked out into the house. The coast was clear.

Everything Billings owned was contained in a paper bag, clutched tenderly to his chest. He'd taken a small saw with him, too, just in case, and a chisel. You never knew when you'd stumble onto some boards that were just too long, or need to make a hole.

He lifted his last beer to his lips, let the last few drops of the amber liquid swirl down his throat. He put the empty in the trash in the kitchen, then walked to the front door. Billings looked out on the spring.

He reached into his pocket and got out a stick of Fruit Stripe. Everything was full of flavor, pulsing with gum.

George Billings crossed the threshold, chewing, and entered the world.

·   ·   ·

"Well," Wilkins said, some time later, "that's about the size of it." They were driving through Buchanan, just west of Centralia, passing the hardware store with the broken plate glass out front, where hours earlier Officer Calcagno had apprehended the Outcast and his burro. It was three o'clock. Wilkins had been talking about the events of the last twenty-four hours. After Calcagno had told his story, it had been impossible not to reply in kind.

So he told Calcagno what being married to Tawny was like. How he had lost his passion. How he had found Judith. He described their night together, had even confessed the events of the morning, including the dance Judith had performed for him, wearing only her white gloves and the white makeup for mime.

But he hadn't been able to do it justice. He felt like a fool, explaining what he had done. "It sounds shameful," he said. "I'm trying to tell you what I've been doing, but I only feel ashamed."

"I feel ashamed, too," Calcagno said.

"Why is that?" Wilkins said. "Are we bad men? Is something wrong with us?"

"You make a left up here to get to the high school," Calcagno said. "No, there's nothing wrong with us. We took some risks. That's nothing to be ashamed of."

"I still feel like I've betrayed my wife and my kids. I feel like I've let everybody down, like I'm not the person they thought I was."

"Well," Calcagno said, "you weren't the first."

Wilkins sighed. "You better tell me about my wife. What she's been doing out here."

"Aw, I don't want to go into it. You don't need to know. It's bad stuff, Dent. As bad as you'd imagine."

"How bad can I imagine?"

"Well—" Calcagno shifted uncomfortably in his seat. He was spinning his wand around in his hand, making the star transparent. "There was this barbershop quartet. The Singing Farmers. One time I went out to the house they were all there. Your wife was indisposed."

"Why'd you go out there?"

"Neighbors complained."

"But the nearest neighbors are a quarter of a mile away."

Calcagno shook his head sadly. "That's right."

"Jesus," Wilkins said. "And Tawny was—indisposed with one of these—Singing Farmers?"

Calcagno nodded again. "With all of 'em." He grimaced. "This was some Sunday morning, about a year ago. She was drunk, Dent. And the tenor was smoking marijuana. When I got there she was lying in bed with those four Singing Farmers, eating pancakes off a paper plate."

"Don't tell me any more," Wilkins said.

"One of them had a baby piglet."

"I said I didn't want to know—"

"Eating flapjacks, right out of her hand."

"Stop," Wilkins said. "I don't want to know."

"Disgusting."

"Enough! I get the picture! Oh, I've been such a fool."

"You've been a man," Calcagno said.

"Same difference. Only reason we're here is so women have something to cheer them up."

"Well," Calcagno said, "it's a hell of a world. I'll give you that."

"When I think of how long I've been holding back, remaining true to her. When I knew things weren't working. I stayed true, out of commitment. Obligation. When all else failed, I figured at least I was keeping my promises."

"That's good, Dent," Calcagno said. "That's nothing to be ashamed of."

"Of course it is," Wilkins said. "If life was going to be so stupid, it might at least have been enjoyable."

"The high school's right up here on your left."

"It's impossible to know the right thing in this world," Wilkins said.

The repulsive outline of James Buchanan Memorial High School came into view. Wilkins felt a shudder of distaste as he looked at the collapsing eaves, the cracked dome of the observatory, the tall smokestack with the messy lettering.

"Man oh man," Wilkins said. "Looks like a bomb went off."

"Jesus," Calcagno cried out suddenly. "There's my van! Right out front! You see that? That's my van!"

They pulled into the driveway right behind the empty police wagon.

"Don't see any signs of that burro," Calcagno muttered. "I hope they didn't pull its head off."

Wilkins looked at the officer. They were getting out of the car.

"Don't forget your magic wand and hat."

"The hell I will," Calcagno said. "You saw what happened last time. People just laughed."

"Well, suit yourself. How do we get in here? Right through the front door, I guess."

"Yeah, but be careful. There are felons inside."

From the distance came the sound of a donkey braying.

Calcagno and Wilkins looked at each other.

"Burro," Calcagno muttered.

He pulled on the front door, but it was locked.

"Jesus," Calcagno said. "I'll bet they saw us coming. Maybe we can get in through a window."

They moved over to a window next to the front door, but it appeared to be locked or nailed down. Wilkins squinted through the glass into the dark school. He saw a dim outline of a statue of a man with arms outstretched.

"We'll just have to break it," Calcagno said.

"Hey," said a voice from on high. "What are you doing down there?"

The Outcast looked down at the men from a second-story window. He was eating a drumstick with one hand. Barbecue sauce was all over his cheeks.

"You're under arrest," Calcagno said. "Come out of there with your hands up."

"Oh gee, like I'm so scared," the Outcast said. "Wait, I'll be right back."

The head vanished from the window, then reappeared. He had put down the drumstick, but he hadn't wiped his face. The Outcast pointed a rifle at them. "Nice costume," he said.

"Don't talk to me about it," said Calcagno.

"You're just about the sorriest-looking cop I've ever seen," said the Outcast. "You make getting arrested into an embarrassment."

"I'm going to give you ten seconds to put that gun down and come out of there," Calcagno said.

"Or what?"

"Yeah, or what?" Wilkins whispered.

"You don't want to find out," Calcagno said. "Something bad."

"Yeah, right," the Outcast said. He fired. A cloud of dust to their right shot up out of the ground. "You boys better be moving on."

"Wait," Wilkins cried. "Is there a young woman with you named Judith? Judith Lenahan?"

"Jeez, I don't know. Wait a minute."

The Outcast disappeared from the window for a moment. They could barely hear his voice speaking to someone in the room with him.

The Outcast reappeared in the window. "Yeah, she's here," he said. "If you're Wilkins, she doesn't want to talk to you."

"Why not?" Wilkins said.

"Hey, what am I, psychic?" said the Outcast. "Now you boys skeedaddle. Before things get ugly."

Another shot was fired; this time a piece of the sidewalk cracked.

"We better get out of here," Wilkins said.

"Right."

The men ran back to Wilkins' car. The shots kept firing from the window. Suddenly the glass in the rear window shattered.

"Drive, man, drive!" shouted Calcagno.

Tires squealing, they drove out of the driveway of James Buchanan Memorial High School. When they were about half a block away from the school, Calcagno said, "All right, pull over here."

Wilkins stopped the car.

"What are you going to do?" Wilkins said. "We can't attack them like this."

"You wait here," Calcagno said. "I got a plan."

He started to walk away from the car, then came back, reached through the broken glass, and retrieved the wand and the pointed hat from the back seat.

"Just in case," Calcagno said. "I need a disguise."

Wilkins looked in the rearview mirror and watched the black-robed figure recede. Soon Calcagno had vanished completely, and Wilkins was left alone, waiting in a car, somewhere in the coal country of Pennsylvania.

He did not quite know what was ahead of him, nor could he have said with any certainty where he had been. He had a great feeling of hollowness, as if he were no longer quite human.

"Let me out of here," Corky Chorkles said.

He turned on the radio in his car. Strains of classical music came to his ear. The music was both sad and light. The sadness of it touched him, making him think back on the long road to this moment. But there was something that shone in the sounds as well, something that picked him up, as if he were suddenly weightless and buoyant.

Wilkins drummed on the windowsill. He thought about the moment he had seen the tears pouring from Judith's eyes, as the two of them lay in bed together in Centralia. The ball of string. The orange firelight dancing on her body.

Calcagno returned. "What's that?" he asked. "What's that you're listening to?"

"I don't know," Wilkins said. "It's pretty, isn't it?"

"Yeah," said Calcagno. "I recognize that. That's something you hear all the time."

"What is it then?"

"Beats me. Kind of spooky, though, isn't it?"

Wilkins shrugged. "I like it."

They stood there listening to the music.

"Sounds like those clarinets are doing a kind of dance," Calcagno said.

"Clarinets?" Wilkins said. "You mean bassoons. Those are bassoons."

"Well, what do I know about music. I played trumpet in third grade, my parents made me stop. Said I was going to make the milk turn sour."

Wilkins drummed his fingers on the steering wheel. "I never played a thing," he said. "Maybe I should have."

"Listen," Calcagno said. "I don't think they saw me. I went back to the van, used the radio. It'll be a while, but I think we're going to get some state troopers in here. In the meantime, I got these." He held up some metal canisters.

"What is that?"

"Tear gas," Calcagno said. "Hydrogen. We can get in there and gas 'em. Knock 'em out so they don't drive away. They got the keys to the van with 'em in there still. We don't want to lose 'em."

"But how are you going to get in? They've locked the doors and windows, haven't they?"

"I know how," Calcagno said. "I done this before. Back in the sixties the kids used to seize control of this dump all the time."

"Why?"

"They said if the Vietnam War didn't end, they'd blow up the high school. We just said, well, go ahead, blow it up. That usually got 'em. Thinking about it now, maybe we should have let them. Seems a shame to have held on to this place just to keep some damn war going. Anyway that's all hindsight."

The men looked at each other.

"You can get in through the roof. There's a ladder, up the side of that smokestack. You jump on the roof and go in through the fire door."

"It sounds dangerous," Wilkins said.

"We can do it," Calcagno said. He took his magic wand and touched Wilkins' head with the twinkling star. "Deputy."

Wilkins sighed. "All right," he said, and got out of the car. He would do it for Judith. He owed her at least that.

Calcagno was looking at his magic wand. It seemed to glow with a soft blue light. "Gee whiz," he said. "I shoulda gotten one of these years ago."

•   •   •

Ten minutes later they were creeping around the back of the school, approaching the west wing. Wilkins and Calcagno each had two canisters of tear gas attached to their belts.

"Sshhh," Calcagno said.

"I didn't say anything," said Wilkins.

"I know."

They moved forward, past the quiet waters of the Catawissa, past the pit of greenish water with the cupcakes floating in it, past the long windowless wing of the school built from cinder blocks painted vomit yellow.

"What is that?" Wilkins whispered.

"Arts Center," Calcagno whispered back.

They moved along the wall, crouching, until they came to the windows of the school cafeteria. They got down on all fours and crept along the ground.

Wilkins and Calcagno reached a disgusting crook formed by the intersection of the cafeteria wing, the Arts Center, and the old mansion. The ground back here was black and brown. There was a lot of old garbage standing in piles, lunch bags and milk cartons and wrappers from straws.

The incinerator stood before them. The door was still open.

Next to the door was a set of iron rungs that led upward along the edge of the furnace, then followed the ascent of the smokestack. There were some paint cans on the ground near the open incinerator door.

"Ready?" Calcagno said.

"Ready," Wilkins whispered.

"You first," Calcagno said.

"Why me first?"

"I weigh more."

"So what?"

"In case there's any problem with the rungs snapping, we want you first."

"Why would that happen? Is that going to happen?"

"It might," Calcagno said. "They're kind of rusty."

"Jesus," Wilkins muttered. He stood next to the incinerator, grasped the first iron rung, and pulled himself up.

"Upsy daisy," Calcagno said.

Wilkins began to climb upwards into the sky.

When he had reached a height of twenty feet, he looked down. Calcagno was still watching him.

"Aren't you coming?" he whispered.

"Soon," Calcagno said.

He reached up and grasped the next rung. It was scary, being this high up in the air, and it was getting scarier with each step. Orange rust flaked off in his hands.

Still he climbed. He was up past the first floor now. Below him, Calcagno was grasping the first rung. He seemed to be having some trouble with it.

And looking down at the ground, Wilkins had a sudden attack of vertigo. The world spun around him. He closed his eyes, pulling himself closely to the smokestack.

Why did I ever agree to do this, Wilkins thought. Was it only out of guilt, for betraying his wife? But she betrayed me. What was her penance for that? Was Tawny hanging on to a smokestack of her own, even now, gasping for breath above the skyline of Saginaw, Michigan? Would that make things equal?

He opened his eyes again, resolved not to look down. Just one step after another. The ladder went up another fifty feet, then there was a kind of a scaffold you could climb down to the roof. He wouldn't have to go all the way to the top. For a moment he imagined the very top, the rim of the smokestack, and himself peering over the edge into its vast, gaping darkness. Clouds drifting by. The stench of all those burning milk cartons, spewing out into the universe.

Further. One step after another. The scaffold was only about ten feet away now. The roof of the school was below him now. One good jump and he could almost have reached it.

From below came a sudden scream. He looked down. Calcagno was falling. He was rushing through the air, facing the sky, looking at Wilkins. He held a broken rung in one hand.

Calcagno hit the ground. He hadn't fallen very far. Far enough to make his back hurt, but not far enough to do any real damage. He lay on his back in his black robes, gritting his teeth, watching Wilkins ascend.

Wilkins had another attack of vertigo. He closed his eyes and breathed hard. Just a few more steps. Just up to the scaffold and it would be over. Then he could go in and rescue poor Judith.

"I'm coming, sweetheart," he said. "I'm coming."

He reached up and grasped the next rung and pulled down hard. There was a snapping sound, of fatigued metal cracking in half.

Wilkins rushed through the air, not fully understanding what had happened. But his sense of gravity was inverted. He felt one of his feet brush against the smokestack. Below him he saw Calcagno, still lying on the ground, looking upward. He felt himself falling, still holding the broken rung in one hand.

For a moment the image of Edith Schmertz came into his mind. They said she had done it on purpose. *I just wanted people to like me.*

Johann moved a razor over his skull. Wilkins was crying. *Ja, ja,* votevah you say. *Your name is not Private Alfalfa. Your name is Private Aerhart.* It was hard to get people to like you, harder than Wilkins had imagined.

Something square loomed up below him. He was going to hit

it. Wilkins closed his eyes, preparing to become the ghost of Edith Schmertz, preparing to smack like a cannonball through layers of shingle and fiberglass. But something was wrong. He was in the air again. He came down a second time, but in seconds he was airborne again.

He was bouncing on a trampoline.

Up he went into the air once more, and down he fell, into the canvas. Time after time, up then down. There was no telling how long this bouncing would go on. Wilkins hoped it would wear itself out. There was a law of physics. Any solid body set in a bouncing motion gradually comes to a nonbouncing state.

Until then he'd just have to wait it out. It wasn't a perfect landing, but it was a landing nonetheless. You had to take what you got. He was on earth again. *The mouth is not a perfect place.*

At last the bouncing concluded. Dent Wilkins sat up. He checked himself to make sure none of his bones was broken. It was lucky his tear gas canisters hadn't exploded. He looked up for a moment at the massive tower of the incinerator. The sun was dropping lower now, and the smokestack's great shadow fell across the trampoline.

"All right," Judith Lenahan said. "Get up."

Wilkins looked over towards the entrance to the school. Judith stood there, wearing a prom dress. Her shoulders were exposed, and the skirt had hoops in it. She held a shotgun under one arm.

"At last," she said. "Bastard."

N E P T U N E

○

The Mystic

*The planet is enveloped in an impenetrable layer
of helium.*

Mrs. Mary Hackles, seated behind an elegant table in the observatory, held her fondue fork up in the air like a trident. She looked at the glistening tines, listening to the sounds in the warped old school. The whine of a band saw echoed from the basement. Her son Morty and his friends were sawing off their handcuffs. From down the hallway came the sounds of Judith locking the intruder in the principal's office. To think that these men thought they could just break into the school without being noticed. Did they think she was without senses? Judith's footsteps drew nearer now, clicking on the tile floor. Mary Hackles listened for the sounds of Foucault's Pendulum, swinging softly. If you were silent enough, you could almost hear it sway.

Judith came back into the circular chamber, leaned the rifle against the wall, and sat down at the small table. She picked up her napkin and stuffed it into the neck of her dress.

"Have some more fondue," Mrs. Hackles said. "Before it gets clammy."

"It already is clammy," Judith said.

"Did you get some brains?"

"I think they're disgusting."

"Don't whine. Here. Do as I do."

Mrs. Hackles stabbed a forkful of brains, then dunked them in the creamy cheese sauce simmering above the Sterno can. She lifted the brains, dripping with melted cheddar, towards her mouth.

"See?" Mrs. Hackles said, chewing. "Brains fondue. Now you try."

Judith curled her lip.

"You said you'd be my pupil," Mrs. Hackles said. "Do you or don't you want to learn about the world?"

"All right already," Judith said. She cut some brains with the side of her fork and dipped them in the sauce.

"Interesting," Judith said, chewing. "It's almost not as revolting as I thought."

"Wait," Mrs. Hackles said. "It will be. Just a little practice."

"I've never had brains before," she said.

"It surprises me how few people eat brains anymore," Mrs. Hackles said. "It's remarkable. I see them for sale in the grocery everytime I go. I can't be the only person buying them, can I?"

"I don't know," Judith said, eating some more brains. "I wouldn't buy them. They're kind of putrid."

"That's exactly right!" Mrs. Hackles said. "Oh, how I dislike eating! It's such a loathsome process!"

"Unavoidable, though," Judith said, chewing.

"Well, that's what they say. But's it's such an inefficient way to run a living being. Having to stop whatever you're doing every three hours to cram more garbage down your throat. Why can't people be more like snakes? You eat once every six months, unhinge your jaw, and that's that. Then you have your time to yourself."

"Maybe you'd like eating more," Judith said, "if you ate things besides brains and fondue."

Mrs. Hackles narrowed her eyes and pointed a long finger at Judith.

"I've just about had it with your suggestions!" she said.

"Well, don't get sore," Judith said. "You know, you blow up at the slightest little thing!"

"If you knew what I knew!" Mrs. Hackles said. "You try walking around in my shoes for a while, then we'll see if you're hungry or what!"

From down the hall came the muffled sounds of Dent Wilkins crying for help.

"Was that him?" Mrs. Hackles asked. "The banker?"

"Yeah," Judith said. "Just as you predicted. I still don't know how he found me here, unless maybe he got my message."

"They always come after you," Mrs. Hackles said, shaking her head contemptuously. "Men are like boomerangs with hair."

Wilkins' cries came through the air once more.

"Didn't you gag him?" Mrs. Hackles said.

"I put a sock in his mouth," Judith said.

"A sock? Where'd you get a sock? You didn't go through my drawers, did you? Who gave you permission to go through my things?"

"Oh, just relax," Judith said. "It's one of his socks."

"You put one of his own socks in his mouth? No wonder he's yelling!"

"Maybe I should let him out," Judith said. "He sounds unhappy."

"No, no, no!" Mrs. Hackles said. "Listen to you! I can't believe what I'm hearing. This is the man who hit you on the head! Who abandoned you! And you want to show him mercy? Let's make this lesson number one, girl: no sympathy to anyone, okay?"

Judith ate her brains in silence.

"I said okay?"

"Okay," Judith said, without conviction.

"What's wrong?"

"I just don't know. Maybe sometimes you should give people a little latitude."

"Why? Tell me that. Why should you ever trust people to do anything that's not idiotic? Have you ever known such a person? Tell me about this wonderful human kindness you've seen out there in the world. The way everything makes perfect sense. I want to know all about it."

Judith did not reply.

"I thought so," Mrs. Hackles said. "You see? All you have to do is think about it for half a second and you know I'm right.

The only thing to do with people is stay away from 'em. If you give them the slightest leeway they've got you."

Judith looked at Mrs. Hackles, simmering with resentment.

"Don't give me a look like that," Mrs. Hackles said. "I'm not the one who shaved her head. Who sits around naked in her spare time. I'm not the one who left her family."

"They left me," Judith said. "My family left me."

"Listen, honey. I'm only talking common sense. You and me, we're peas in a pod. That's what I like about you. All those stories you told me, about the way you live in this world. You're not stupid, and neither am I. The idea is to live life to the fullest, without illusions, without anything that's pretend. If you want to live life full measure, you have to cut out other people. They lead you astray."

Judith looked around the observatory. There was an enormous crack in the dome.

"How'd that get there?" Judith said. "The crack, I mean."

"Did that myself," Mrs. Hackles said, swirling some brains around in the cheese. "With the shotgun. Something got me ticked off, I forget what." She looked at Judith's dress. "You look nice in that. Like something on a wedding cake."

"I feel kind of weird. You said the girl who owned this dress died?"

"Well, she's dead, yes, now she is. She didn't die *in* it, though, if that's what you mean. Melinda Carbuncle. Went into a coma in the middle of the junior prom." Mrs. Hackles slapped her thigh and laughed. "You shoulda seen her date! What an idiot! Ha ha ha! He kept trying to get her to drink some coffee!"

"You think that's funny?" Judith said. "I think that's sad. Some girl, just falling asleep in the middle of a dance, and not waking up."

"Funny, sad," Mrs. Hackles said, eating brains. She shrugged. From downstairs came the sound of the band saw.

"How long have you lived here?" Judith asked.

"Here? In this abomination?" She smiled. "Since my house was torn down. Nineteen eighty. Same month we got that Reagan I moved into this dump."

"But you taught here before that? What did you teach?"

"English," Mrs. Hackles said. "Eleventh grade. But I was only here one year before the place closed. Before that I taught in Oil City."

"English was always my worst subject," Judith said.

"Nonsense. Your teachers were cretins, that's all, cretins. There's so much to like about poetry. Byron, dead at thirty-six! Shelley, dead at thirty! Keats, dead at twenty-six!"

"That's my age," Judith said. "Keats was dead when he was my age."

"That's right. Shortest English poet, too. Tallest was John Stuart Mill. Fattest was Robert Burns. Coleridge had the longest beard. You see how much you could have learned? It grieves me to think of your education wasted. What you need is a good teacher to make poetry come alive like this."

In the distance there was the sound of a dog barking, and the Outcast laughing.

"God," Mrs. Hackles said. "There goes that hyena again."

"Why do you hate him?" Judith asked. "He's your son, isn't he?"

"Morty? Ugh, he's an imbecile. Can't you hear him bellowing down there? That boy's been nothing but a quagmire since the day he was born."

"Why?"

"Oh, he's so damn jolly all the time. It drives me batty. He's got such an attitude about everything. He simply *adores* his stupid life, can't get enough of it. He wakes up in the morning and bounces out of bed. Sings opera in the shower. Eats cake for breakfast. God, to think I should have such a son!"

"What was his father like?"

"Ah, there was a man," Mrs. Hackles said. "If only you could have met him! What a family the three of us could have been, Judy, if only we'd gotten you instead of that bellowing baboon! James Hackles was the one man in my life. There'll never be another."

"What attracted you to him?"

"Oh, well, everything. The first time I met him was right after the Korean War. He was in his captain's uniform. I'm a sucker for costumes, I suppose. But what a gentleman, honestly! And he could sharpen knives sharper than anyone I've ever known. Maybe that seems silly to you, that he could sharpen knives so good. But just try to carve a roast sometime without a sharp knife! Just try!"

"He's dead now?"

"Yes, yes, of course. He must be. Left me in nineteen fifty-seven, he'd be eighty-something by now."

"Why did he leave you?"

"Out of respect."

"Respect?"

"Yes, of course. In time we came to understand just how terrible things really are. Staying together, being a little wife and husband together when things are as horrible as they are, it was just ludicrous. So we parted. It's better this way. By which I mean to say they're worse. More true. More what they are."

"You sure have lived an interesting life," Judith said. "I don't know. Sometimes I feel as if I haven't done anything with my life except be angry."

"That's something!" Mrs. Hackles said.

"You think so?"

"Oh, Judith, you'll like living here. You floating down that river today was the best thing that's ever happened. At last I have someone to give all this to, someone who'll appreciate it."

"You don't even know me," Judith said.

"I know all about you. From what you've said, you're a girl after my own heart. I've never met anyone who hates people more than I do! This is so exciting! Oh, how happy you've made me today! I feel like punching out some windows with my bare fist!"

The sun was drawing lower in the sky, sending long shafts of gold through high white clouds. The blossoms of spring were blooming on the trees. Birds sang.

"God, I hate this time of day," Mrs. Hackles said.

• • •

Downstairs in the wood shop, Morton Hackles was sawing Phoebe free from her father. Buddy sat near the band saw, staring towards the potters' wheels. He whimpered softly.

"Gimme that drumstick," the Outcast said to Dwayne.

"This one?" Dwayne said.

"The one you're holding," the Outcast said. He looked at Vicki and winked; Vicki and Dwayne's cuffs had already been severed. "Your boyfriend's a real deep thinker."

"Oh, there's more going on there than meets the eye," Vicki said.

"Well, I'd hope so, little lady, that's all I can say."

"Dwayne," Vicki said.

"Careful," Wedley said. "Would you watch what you're doing? You're going to cut my hand off."

"Nobody's cutting nobody's hands off. You just gotta hold still."

"What?" Dwayne said.

"Gee, they sure make these things strong."

"Daddy, are there police outside?"

"He asked you for the drumstick, Dwayne," Vicki said.

"Yes, honey," Wedley said.

"Oh yeah, here." Dwayne held up the chicken.

"Boy, those things are sure messy," the Outcast said, reaching for the barbecued leg. He still had barbecue sauce all over his cheeks.

"Are we under arrest?" Phoebe said.

The band saw cut through the chains, and the Outcast turned off the saw. Phoebe and Wedley rubbed their wrists, where the bracelets of the handcuffs still remained.

"Yes, sweetheart," Wedley said. "Technically, we're still under arrest."

"Aw, wouldn't ya know," the Outcast said, chewing. "I got me a gristly piece." He threw the drumstick over one shoulder.

"When are we going to go home?" Phoebe asked.

Buddy fell over suddenly and made a groaning sound.

The Outcast reached into his pocket and got out a Snickers bar.

"That's a very good question," Vicki said, looking at her nails. "Dwayne, I would like to go home soon."

"We have to, uh—"

Dwayne stared off into space.

"Ah, shit," the Outcast said, looking at the chocolate bar. It had gotten limp in the heat of his pocket. He bit into it.

"What?" Vicki said. "We have to what?"

Dwayne was looking at Buddy. The dog's eyes were rotating in opposite directions.

"Thmelted," said the Outcast.

"We have to wait," Dwayne said.

The Snickers bar fell onto the floor. The Outcast was covered in chocolate mess and barbecued chicken.

"Duth ennbuddy heff uh nepkid?" he said.

"What did he say, Daddy?" Phoebe said. The Outcast was holding up his soiled hands.

"I'm not sure," Wedley said. The Outcast was looking at Buddy.

"He wants a napkin," Vicki said.

"Oh well," the Outcast said. "Ull juthth uth the dawg."

The Outcast leaned over and wiped his chocolaty hands on the dog's coat.

"What did you do that for?" Phoebe said, putting her hands on her hips.

"Sorry, honey," the Outcast said, smacking his chops. "Your dog here's the only towel around!"

"You're a bad man," Phoebe said, pointing at him. "You're a *very* bad man."

"Now, now, Phoebe," Wedley said. "You be polite."

"Naw, she's right," Hackles said. "I got a lot to learn. But hey, at least I'm enjoying myself. How 'bout you? You guys enjoying yourselves? You want any more barbecued ribs? I bet my Ma's got some more upstairs! Some brains, too!"

"I'm fine, thank you," Vicki said.

"Brains?" said Phoebe.

"Dwayne?" the Outcast said. "What about you?"

Dwayne was still looking at Buddy, who now had barbecued

chicken and chocolate on his coat. Phoebe patted the dog's head.

"Wuh," Dwayne said.

"He's all right for now," Vicki said.

"All right, suit yourself. Now then, you all, as long as I got you here, take a look around! You see this shop of mine? Isn't this a miracle? God, I love it here!"

They looked around at the shop. It was filled with fine equipment for woodworking and pottery. Four table saws stood next to one another in a corner. There was an oak workbench with a steel vise and a shining shop vacuum. Other desks for students lay around the shop, each equipped with a small vise. There was a lathe and a circular saw and a device for melting Plexiglas.

"Quite a setup," Wedley said.

"Stolen," the Outcast said, folding his arms proudly on his chest. "Every square inch of it liberated from hardware stores from here to Wilkes-Barre!"

"You must be very proud," Vicki said sourly. She touched the bun on top of her head.

"Wait, let me show you my pride and joy," the Outcast said. "Wait here."

He went to a corner behind the table saws, pulled forward an odd stainless steel machine, and plugged it in.

"Okay, say you got some paint you want to mix up. You could pry the lid off the can with a screwdriver, then stir it around with a wooden stick for fifteen minutes, sure. But looka here."

The Outcast picked up a can of paint, and locked it into the metal arms of the machine. He flicked a switch and the machine began to shake the can violently.

"How about that!" the Outcast said. "My very own electric paint mixer! Ha ha!" He spread his arms out wide in rapture. "Get me! I'm the very first name in hardware!"

Phoebe looked at her father and rolled her eyes.

"What a dope," she said.

Vicki sniffed. "God, what is that smell?"

Everyone sniffed. "Yuck," the Outcast said. "Boy, that's awful. Like something rotting."

They all looked at Buddy.

"Sometimes he gets like this," Phoebe said quietly. "If he's not eating right. If he's upset."

"Boy, I'd hate to smell him when he is eating right," the Outcast said, then burst into laughter again. On the pavement outside they heard the sound of tinkling glass.

"What's that?" Vicki said, afraid.

"Aw, don't you worry," the Outcast said. "That's just my maw. Punching out windows. Looks like I'll be using the glass cutter a little later on. She smashes 'em, I repair 'em." He smiled. "Checks and balances, hah?"

"When are we going home?" Phoebe said. "Buddy wants a Milk-Bone."

"Yeah, can we talk about this?" Wedley said. He ran his fingers through his long black hair. "We've gotten the cuffs off, like you wanted. Now we'd like to go."

"Go?" the Outcast said. "Go?" He looked from face to face. Dwayne was standing near one of the workbenches, looking at a small blue vise.

"Yes, go," Vicki said.

"Hey, wait a minute," the Outcast said. "Weren't you all under arrest when I met you? Sure you were. Disturbing the peace or something? Don't look at me like I'm keeping you here against your will. You all helped steal that squad car same as me. We're accomplices. And there's cop cars outside, you know that. You think you can just go waltzing out the front door? No, sir. We gotta get ourselves a plan. Figure a way of getting back on the road. I'm not going back to Cheyney State Prison just like that, I don't know about you."

"We weren't *in* Cheyney State Prison," Wedley said. "We were just sitting in our living rooms when Dwayne threw a rabbit through our window."

"My bunny!" Vicki said suddenly, sniffing. "My little funny bunny!"

"Ah jeez, I'm gonna be sick," the Outcast said.

"This one used to be mine," Dwayne said, pointing at the vise.

"What?" Wedley said.

"Tomorrow was going to be my bunny's birthday," Vicki said, "as if anyone cared!"

"This one was mine," Dwayne said. "In high school. This was my workbench." His voice seemed oddly sentimental.

The Outcast narrowed his eyes. "You went here?" he said, in amazement. "You went to high school in this place?"

"We both did," Vicki said.

"Me and Vicki and Edith," said Dwayne.

Buddy looked up suddenly. He groaned to his feet, then took a step forward. He walked towards the shop vacuum, raised a front paw, his tail stiffening. Buddy growled suspiciously at the vacuum hose.

"I never knew anybody that went here," the Outcast said. "We only moved here the year before they closed it."

"My old vise!" Dwayne said. It sounded like he was going to cry. "Ol' Faithful! This vise never let me down. Anything I put in it, stayed there."

"Dad," Phoebe whined. "I wanna go home!"

"All right," said the Outcast. "Here's my plan. I put my gun to Vicki's head, see, pretend I'll shoot her if they don't let us make a getaway. We all get as far as the car, then presto, we vamoose!"

"Why me?" said Vicki. "Why am I the one who has to get shot?"

"You're the cute one," Hackles said.

"This is so sexist!" Vicki said. "Just because I use a moisturizer, I have to get shot in the head?"

"You think they'll care if I shoot Wedley?" Hackles said. "Or Dwayne?"

"Aw, Dwayne's cute," Vicki said. "He's so soulful!"

"Wuh," Dwayne said.

"Mr. Hackles, are you sure you have enough bullets?" Phoebe said. "I thought you used them all up shooting out the window."

"Dammit to hell," the Outcast said. "She's right!"

"Thank goodness," Vicki said.

"Wait a second, sister," the Outcast said. "My maw's got bullets. Let me just go get some shells offa my maw. Then I can shoot you."

"What are we supposed to do in the meantime?" Vicki said. "Just stand around this wood shop? It's so dull!"

"We can go exploring," Phoebe said. "Buddy wants to go exploring."

"ATTENTION MORTON HACKLES," said a voice from outside. "YOU HAVE FIFTEEN MINUTES TO COME OUT WITH YOUR HANDS UP."

Buddy barked at the shop vacuum. He sunk his teeth into the hose.

"We're in trouble," Dwayne said.

• • •

Dent Wilkins, tied to the principal's desk with a ball of string, a sock in his mouth, tried to think happy, pleasant thoughts. Into each life a little rain must fall, he thought, tasting the taste of his own foot. Everytime it rains, it rains pennies from heaven.

In rooms nearby he heard the sound of smashing glass, followed by wild laughter. One of the voices was Judith's. It occurred to him that he had never heard her laugh before. What was it about her that kept her so morose and detached from things? He felt tears burning in his eyes. To think of all he had risked to come and rescue her, only to have her treat him like this. She wasn't right in the head, that much was becoming increasingly clear. He was amazed at his own gullibility. Why had he taken a U-turn in the midst of Route 61? To give her the opportunity to put his own sock in his mouth?

He looked around the principal's office. There were certificates on the wall, attesting to the school's compliance with hundreds of outdated regulations. There was a tall stool in the corner, and a broken phone on the floor. It looked as if the phone had been blasted with a shotgun.

Wilkins struggled in his chair. If he collected all his strength, it was possible to wiggle just enough to make the chair move around slightly on the floor. But what good was that? The door was locked, and the ground was too far away for him to jump out a window. He looked at the ball of string on the floor. It was really a rather large ball of twine, like the kind one saw on television now and then. People who save string, roll it into a ball that gets so big they have to keep it outside in the garage. That's a form of illness, Wilkins thought. Whenever you saw that, you knew you were witnessing the slow decay of an imagination. People saving their toenail clippings in an envelope. Pasting stamps in albums. Buying bras for their cars.

Wilkins tasted his own sock, thinking about his job. He had to be back at work on Monday, meet with the executive officers and come up with a budget plan for the coming year. It seemed funny to think about, here in the principal's office. He was overwhelmed with a sense of shame. Everything I've done has turned out wrong, he thought. You slave for years and years trying to work your way up to the top in your field. Finally, you're there, where you've wanted to arrive for decades, and then what? You wind up in the principal's office with a sock in your mouth. It was no sense trying to have any ambition.

He shoved his chair forward. It moved almost six inches this time. Maybe if he were able to get over to the window he could attract attention. What was Calcagno doing back there on the ground? Had he ever gotten up? His last view of Calcagno had been of him lying on his back, watching Wilkins fall towards the earth. That was just before he hit the trampoline.

Wilkins shoved himself forward again, and then again. He was getting closer and closer to the window. Just a few more shoves would do it. The sound of smashing glass had stopped. The school was strangely quiet now, waiting. Wilkins moved forward again, and looked out the window.

A half-dozen police cars had pulled into the driveway. Men in Smokey the Bear hats were speaking into radios. A man in a trench coat was checking the batteries on a bullhorn. One of the squad cars had a searchlight that stabbed across the lawn.

The Catawissa flowed slowly past the school. The sun was setting over the Appalachians to the west, and the clouds were turning blue and gray. A burro was chewing grass in the kickball field, moving closer and closer towards a pit of green water.

• • •

"Oh, Dwayne," Vicki was saying, as they walked through the deserted corridors of the school together. "It's all so changed."

"No," Dwayne said, looking down the long hallway, the beat-up lockers on the walls. "This is the same."

"But without all the kids," Vicki said. "It doesn't seem right, being here alone."

Dwayne took Vicki's hand.

They walked down the hallway, past the empty cages for the kinkajous and the science lab.

"Look," Vicki said. "Here's ol' Flatbottom's class. Remember Flatbottom?"

"Ol' Flatbottom," Dwayne said.

They entered the room. A giant slide rule hung on the wall.

"This was my seat," Vicki said, sitting in the second row.

"I forget which one mine was," Dwayne said.

"Here," Vicki said. "Back row, second column. This one."

Dwayne sat down.

"I remember sitting at my desk just trying to think of a good reason to turn around, to see if you were looking at me."

"I was," Dwayne said, and smiled. "Looking at you."

"Oh, Dwayne," Vicki said, putting her hand at the bottom of her neck.

Dwayne shifted in his seat uncomfortably.

"I don't fit in this chair," he said.

"Well, you're bigger, Dwayne," Vicki said. She smiled. "Look at that old slide rule. Can you believe all this stuff is still here?"

"They should of taught us how to use calculators."

"What?"

"Instead of slide rules. No one uses slide rules anymore."

"Yeah, but some people couldn't afford calculators. They were only trying to be fair."

"That was wrong. People laughed at me."

"Who laughed at you, Dwayne?"

"At work. I wanted to know the mileage I was getting. On the truck. If I had a calculator they wouldn't have laughed."

"You were trying to figure out your gas mileage on a slide rule? Well, no wonder they laughed."

Dwayne looked hurt.

"You can't do it on a slide rule, Dwayne! A slide rule's for exponents. Sines and cosines. You don't need that stuff to figure out the mileage on your truck, honey!"

Dwayne shook his head.

"Sometimes I wish you'd stick up for me, just once."

Vicki looked confused, stood up, and went over to him. She sat on his desktop. "What do you mean, Dwayne? What are you saying?"

"Nothing."

"Yes you are, you're trying to tell me something. Just tell me what you're trying to say."

"Nothing. I just want you to stand up for me sometimes."

"But not when you're wrong, darling." She laughed. "You don't want me to stand up for you when you're wrong, do you?" She cocked her head to one side.

Dwayne's lips moved, as if he were reading an invisible book.

"Yeah," he said. "I do. Once in a while why can't you stand up for me when I'm wrong?"

"Oh, Dwayne," Vicki said. She pinched his cheek. "You're not thinking clearly. You want me to love you, I know. But loving someone means pointing out their little mistakes! Oh yes indeedy!"

Dwayne's lips moved again.

"Come on, honey," Vicki said. "Let's explore some more, while we have the time left. There's so much I want to see!"

She walked to the front of the room, moved the cursor of the slide rule. She got dust on her fingertips, which she sifted distastefully between her fingers and thumb.

She turned back to Dwayne.

"Coming?" she said.

But Dwayne was looking at one of the vacant desks. Next aisle over, one desk forward. He could almost see her still sitting there, writing his name over and over in the margins of her notebook.

"Dwayne? Come on. Let's go." Vicki walked out into the hall.

Dwayne remained in the classroom, looking at the surface of his desk. It was still there: the heart he had gouged into the wood, day after day, along with his initials, and the initials of Edith Schmertz.

He stood up, moved towards the giant slide rule at the front of the room. The classroom was silent.

Dwayne touched the cursor of the enormous slide rule, and moved it back into its former position. He took one look over his shoulder, at the seat in the back of the room near his. He could almost see Edith now, looking the way she had looked back then.

"Dwayne!" Vicki called. "Look what I found! It's Dr. Parsons' music room! I'd totally forgotten."

"I didn't," Dwayne said to himself, and moved out into the hall.

Dr. Parsons' music room was down two doors. The broken piano stood next to the blackboard, surrounded by boxes of percussion instruments.

"Ta, ta, *ti-ti,* ta!" Vicki said, imitating Dr. Parsons' high-pitched German accent. "Remember that? And those hand signals we had to make? God, that was crazy. Whatever got into them, it makes no sense."

"It makes sense," Dwayne said. He put out a fist. "Doh," he said. He cupped his hand, palm facing floorward. "Re." He flattened his palm. "Mi." He pointed towards the floor. "Fa." He turned his flat palm to the wall. "Sol." He cupped his fingers again. "La." He pointed to the ceiling. "Ti." He made a fist again. "Doh."

"But Dwayne," Vicki said, "what good was that? Why did we have to know that?"

"It's good to know things," Dwayne said.

"I know that, darling, but children should know useful things. Like using calculators and how to keep themselves clean. Why learn that weird sign language? You can't communicate with it!"

Dwayne looked through the box of percussion instruments. There were maracas and finger cymbals and triangles.

"Dildocks," Dwayne said.

"What?"

"Dildocks," Dwayne said. "That's what Dr. Parsons called us. If we were unmusical. He said we were dildocks."

"I don't remember that," Vicki said. She picked up the sheet music in the stand. "Oh, but this! *The Mikado,* remember, Dwayne? *So let the throng our joy advance,*" she sang. *"With laughing song and merry dance, with laughing song, and dance!"*

Dwayne smiled. "I remember that." He sat down at the piano and played some chords. *"With joyous shout and ringing cheer inaugurate our new career."* Dwayne was a good pianist, but a terrible singer. His voice sounded like water going down the drain in a bathtub.

"Oh, Dwayne, I love it when you play. Play something else."

"Okay."

His fingers ambled over the keys, starting the piece even before his brain knew what it was doing. But soon Dwayne realized what he was playing. *Clair de Lune.* The pretty music, played on the out-of-tune piano, echoed through the old school.

Dwayne's mind drifted. He thought about adolescence. Going out with Vicki. Driving his car. Eating lunch in the cafeteria. Trying to do his homework. There was this feeling of dread upon him then, that no matter what he did it would never be enough to satisfy the world. There was always more homework to do, always more games for the Fighting Weasels to play and lose. Braces on his teeth. Rubber bands in his mouth. Hormones in his glands undergoing nuclear fission. If only I hadn't had so many glands, Dwayne thought, everything would have been all right. Salivation glands, pituitary glands, lymph glands, gonads. All those juices frying up his insides like gasoline.

He saw himself standing out in front of his parents' house, before he had his license, waiting for the school bus in the rain. Water pouring off his rain slicker. Safety slogans printed on the lining of the slicker. *Green means go, red means stop. Walk on the right. Don't take candy from strangers. Don't fidget when you eat. Keep your elbows off the table. Don't cross your eyes or they'll stick that way.*

He saw himself driving his truck, going out to Edith's house. The enormous tree down across the road, the severed electric lines buzzing ferociously. The way she had stood in the window of her house, watching him work. And that day he had buried his cat. If only he could have relived that day. Given her something of himself, instead of that tag that said JOCKO. If only some stranger had owned a cocker spaniel named DWAYNE, then everything would have been all right. He colored, and was filled with a sense of regret and shame.

"Dwayne?" Vicki said.

Dwayne looked over at her.

"That was beautiful," she said.

He had not realized he had finished the composition.

Vicki had this beatific smile on her face. There were tears in her eyes.

"No one plays like you do," she said. "Thank you, honey. That was special."

Dwayne shrugged. "I wasn't really thinking," he said.

There was a silence in the room for a moment as Dwayne and Vicki looked at each other. The sounds of the piano music seemed to linger in the air.

"Dwayne, honey," Vicki said. "Do you ever think about getting married?"

Dwayne looked around the music room at the broken percussion instruments, the rows of empty desks, the upended kettledrum. He started moving his lips again, reading from something Vicki could not quite see.

"Sweetheart?"

Dwayne looked over at her.

"I asked if you ever thought about getting married."

"Maybe," Dwayne said. "When the time comes."

"When will that be, though?" Vicki said, standing up. "I'm twenty-five years old now. I'm running out of time!"

Dwayne's eyes crossed slightly.

"No you're not," he said. "Twenty-five is young. You got lots of childbearing years."

"Oh, that's just like a man to say!" Vicki said. She sat down on the piano bench next to him.

"Can't you hear my biological clock, ticking away? It's going to be too late for me, too late!"

Dwayne wrinkled his nose, and looked as if he were trying to think of something to say. He said nothing.

"Oh, I'm sorry, sweetheart," Vicki said. "I'm just getting emotional. It's this old school, and getting arrested. I'm all topsy-turvy. We don't have to talk about this now. Here. Let's play something together."

"I want to get out of here," Dwayne said.

"Oh, no, wait, Dwayne, let's just play one more piece together. A duet."

"I want to get out of here," Dwayne said, and stood up.

"Please wait," Vicki said. "Can't we play a duet together?" He was already at the door.

"I mean it," he said, and walked out into the hallway.

Vicki, alone at the piano, felt tears coming to her eyes. She hated herself for them, but they came anyway. Her fingers fell onto the piano keys, but the sound did not seem like music. Tears rolled down her cheek, and fell on the ivory keys.

•   •   •

Wedley stood with his daughter at the window of the science classroom, looking at the swelling numbers of police outside.

"Are we going to jail, Daddy?" Phoebe asked.

"I'm not sure," Wedley said. "If only they'd give us a chance to explain. We didn't plan on any of this."

Buddy sat next to Phoebe on the floor. His front legs wouldn't support his body, though, and he kept slipping forward into a lying-down position.

"Are you mad at me?" Phoebe asked her father.

Wedley looked at her.

"Why would I be mad at you?"

" 'Cause I got us arrested."

"You?" Wedley sat down at a desk in the classroom, picked his daughter up, and sat her on his knee. "Why do you think that?"

" 'Cause it's true. I started throwing eggs at the wall. And when that policeman came, he hit Buddy with his stick. He was wrong to do that, wasn't he, Pa?"

"Yes, sweetheart, he was." Wedley hugged Phoebe. "I don't know what caused this, angel," he said. "But it's not your fault. It's no one's fault. These things just happen."

Music from an out-of-tune piano drifted through the air. It was soft and sweet.

Buddy looked up suddenly. His ears pricked up.

"Awoo," Buddy said quietly.

The dog stood up and shook, as if it had been covered with water. Buddy perked his ears again. His tail grew stiff.

"Awoo," he said again, and walked out of the room, as if he were on the track of something, or sleepwalking.

"Buddy," Phoebe said, snapping her fingers. "Here, boy."

The dog did not come back.

"Maybe I should go get him," Phoebe said.

"Oh, leave him be," Wedley said. "He'll come back. Funny how he's following that music, though."

"He's a musical dog," Phoebe said proudly.

"I know it, angel."

Phoebe looked at her father, wrinkled her brow. She stuck her index finger in her mouth and wiped her father's cheek with her saliva.

"What are you doing?" Wedley said.

"You still have some chimney on your cheek. Soot, I mean. I hate that."

"Thank you," Wedley said. "Is it off now?"

"Yeah, I got most of it. Why don't you wash your face, Dad?"

"I don't know," he said. "I just get dirty again."

"You shouldn't think like that," Phoebe said. "You should be clean every day, or you get germs. Pinkeye. I don't want you to wind up like Mr. Hackles, Pa. He's a disgusting blob. Like a big potato tick."

Wedley shook his head. "Phoebe," he said, "you're a doodle."

Phoebe stamped her feet. "I hate it when you say that."

"MORTON HACKLES," said a voice on a megaphone. "YOU HAVE TEN MINUTES."

"Uh-oh," Wedley said.

"Are they going to storm the place, Pa? Tell me, are they going to storm the place?"

"I don't know," Wedley said. "But we'd better stick together."

"Buddy," Phoebe said suddenly. "Where's Buddy?"

"Stay with me," Wedley said, but Phoebe was already out the door.

"Here, boy," Phoebe said, and whistled. Her voice echoed in the empty hall. "C'mere."

"Come back, Phoebe," Wedley said, following her, but Phoebe was already growing distant. He watched as his daughter ran away from him, growing smaller and smaller in the dark halls of school.

* * *

Judith Lenahan stood by the stairwell, watching the pendulum. The music had stopped now, making the old school seem more lonely. She hoped Mrs. Hackles' son had a plan for extricating himself. She had seen the troopers gathering outside. There was going to be trouble.

That sad-looking Dalmatian came down the hall towards her. He looked bewildered, as if he had misplaced the scent he was tracing. The dog came up to Judith, and she put out her hand to pet him.

"Good dog," Judith said.

Buddy wagged his tail, then moved on.

Judith looked at her fingers. There was melted chocolate and barbecue sauce on them.

"Yech," she said.

Down the long hall came the form of a tall man. His pale eyes bulged out of his head, as if he were holding his breath. Dwayne looked at Judith, standing there in her prom dress.

"Have you seen—uh . . ." He licked his lips.

Judith looked at the man, waiting for him to finish his sentence.

"Have you seen—uh . . ."

"Have I seen who? Mrs. Hackles' son? No. I thought he was in the wood shop."

Judith detected a distant scent from the man, a faint but unmistakable smell of chocolate milk.

"Buddy," Dwayne said. "I have to find him."

"Who's Buddy?" Judith said.

"The dog. You've seen him. I know."

"What do you want that dog for?"

Dwayne leaned forward, urgently. "We have to talk."

Judith backed off. "He went down the hall. That way. Less than thirty seconds ago."

"Thank you," Dwayne said. He started walking briskly down the hall, practically running.

Judith looked after him, shaking her head. Mrs. Hackles was right. People were crazy. She had known this all along, had made this her motivating force since she'd quit the theatre. There was no point in trying to make sense of things.

She ran her fingertips over her smooth skull.

At that moment a little girl, wearing a party dress, walked towards Judith. She was out of breath, and seemed slightly afraid.

"Are you a witch?" she asked Judith.

"A witch? Me? No."

"Have you seen my dog?"

"The Dalmatian? Yeah, he just went down the hall. That big man was after him."

"Dwayne?"

"Yes."

"Oh no," Phoebe said, "I have to hurry. Buddy's in trouble." She ran off down the hallway, in pursuit of her dog.

"Boy, that dog is sure popular," Judith muttered.

At that moment Wedley Harrison came round the corner, and walked towards Judith. He seemed nervous, and kept pushing his long hair out of his eyes.

"Let me guess," Judith said. "You're looking for Buddy."

Wedley smiled. "Did my daughter just go by here?"

"First the dog. Then Dwayne. Then that little girl. Now you. You're her father?"

"Yeah," Wedley said. "I try, anyhow."

"They went that way," Judith said, pointing down the hall.

She looked in the direction her finger was pointing. The school was getting dark now; long shadows gathered in the deserted halls.

"What's that?" Wedley said, looking at Judith.

"What's what?"

"That sound. Don't you hear it? Sounds like someone weeping."

Judith listened, and heard it too. It sounded like someone was crying out her heart.

"Ghosts, maybe," Judith said.

Wedley walked down the hall, towards the shadows, and Judith followed him. Her prom dress rustled as she walked.

"There," Wedley said, moving towards a dark room.

In the room were rows of desks on the floor and a broken piano. A woman sat in one of the desks, holding her face in her hands, sobbing.

"Hey, Vicki," Wedley said, moving towards her. "Hey."

Judith stood at a distance from Wedley and the sobbing woman, next to the piano. She didn't want to get involved in this, but she couldn't quite abandon the situation, either. She stood by the piano, self-consciously looking on.

"What's the matter?" Wedley asked. "Vicki?"

"Oh," she said, choking on a sob. She looked up at Wedley for a moment, displaying her changed face. Her cheeks were red, and tears were all over her. She snuffed some mucus in her nose.

"Here," Wedley said, reaching into his pocket. "Use this bandana."

"Thank you," Vicki said. She took the bandana from him, clutched it in her fist, and started sobbing again.

"There, there," Wedley said, and put his arms around her. "It's all right."

"I'm so ashamed," Vicki said.

"Stop," Wedley said.

She cried on his shoulder for a few moments, while Wedley stroked her hair. The scene went on for some time, Vicki crying and sniffing, Wedley holding her, Judith standing by the piano watching.

"I'm all right," Vicki said at last, raising her head.

"Look at you," Wedley said. "I've never seen such a mess."

"Is my mascara running? It's supposed to be waterproof."

"No," Wedley said, taking the bandana from her, dabbing at her cheeks. "You look fine. You're a regular Cosmopolitan Girl."

Vicki shook her head and smiled. "Don't try to make me laugh," she said.

"I think I will," Wedley said. "I think I will try to make you laugh."

"Yeah, well, good luck," Vicki said, as Wedley folded up his bandana. "It's going to take a lot."

"Now what's all this about?" Wedley said. "You want to talk?"

"Oh, Wedley, you don't want to know about it. I know what you think about me."

"What? What do I think about you?"

"You think I'm stupid." Vicki smiled and wiped her eyes. She shook her head. "I know what you think."

"I don't think you're stupid," Wedley said.

"Of course you do. And you're right. I am stupid. I'm a complete nincompoop!"

"Vicki," Wedley said, "I don't actually know you at all."

"Wedley, will you tell me your honest opinion about something? What do you think of Dwayne? I mean really?

Wedley sighed. "What do I think of Dwayne? I don't know, Vicki. I know he means a lot to you."

"But what do you *think* about him? What's your *opinion?*"

"Well, jeez. He's a very unusual man, that's for sure."

"Yeah. You got that right."

"Sometimes I think he's very troubled."

"Yeah, me too! But how? What's eating him?"

"I don't know."

"Neither do I! What do I have to do to break through to him? Do I have to learn a foreign language?"

"Maybe all you need is patience."

"Patience!" Vicki said. "I've been waiting and waiting for him. I know he loves me. If you loved a woman, wouldn't you ask her to marry you? Would you just keep her waiting and waiting?"

"I can't answer that," Wedley said.

"Well, I can. I think if you love someone you should tell them, tell them all the damn time. But Dwayne hardly says anything. It's too hard for him to sort things out. I know that's how he is, but it just hurts me all the time."

"Have you ever told Dwayne that?"

"No," Vicki said. "You know Dwayne, he doesn't listen."

"I think you can get him to listen."

"Really?"

"You go tell him what you just told me. See what he says."

"What if he tells me to get lost?"

"Then you deal with it. You're a strong woman. You don't have to depend on him for your life. He's the one who needs you. He just doesn't know it yet."

Vicki stood up. "You're right. I'm going to go tell him. Only, where is he?"

Judith spoke up. "He's chasing Buddy. They went down the hall that way about five minutes ago."

"Hello," Vicki said. "I didn't even know you were there."

"I'm here," Judith said.

"You two must think I'm a real nitwit," Vicki said, touching the back of her hair with her palms.

"We don't think you're a nitwit," Wedley said. "Do we, Judith?"

"I don't think you're a nitwit," Judith said. "Considering."

"Why are you being so nice to me?" Vicki said. "You don't even like me!"

"Maybe I never knew you before," Wedley said.

"I never knew you either," Vicki said. She looked into his eyes for a moment, then hugged him. Wedley put his arms around her. Vicki looked up and kissed his lips.

"Oh, Wedley," she said. "You're special."

She seemed to jerk suddenly, to come back to life. "But I have to find Dwayne!" she said. "I have to find him right away! While I still have everything clear in my mind! I'll talk to you later, Wedley," she said, running towards the door. She stopped for a second, took off her high heels, and held them in one hand.

"It was nice to meet you, miss," she said to Judith. "I adore your hair!"

She ran out the door. Wedley and Judith heard the sound of her soft feet padding rapidly down the hallway.

Wedley put his hands in his pockets and sighed.

"She was right, wasn't she?" Judith said.

"What?" He turned to look at her. "About what?"

"What she said was true. You don't really like Vicki very much."

"Ah, well, what does it matter," Wedley said.

"That was very good what you just did for her. I'm impressed."

"Well," Wedley said, "you got to look out for people."

"You're a wise man," Judith said. "I never saw anyone do that for anyone before."

"What? Be nice to them?"

"It was the way you were nice. Not cloying and fake. You really wanted to make her feel better. Even though you don't like her."

"Jesus, it's not some miracle, being kind to people."

"Well, I never saw it before."

"I don't believe you. You just haven't been looking, is my guess."

"Aw, what do you know about it?" Judith said. "What are you, Ann Landers?"

"Well, you know best," Wedley said. He looked at the floor. "I guess I should go. I got to find out what happened to my daughter."

"She said I looked like a witch."

Wedley laughed. "Well, you do look kind of unusual. Where'd you get that getup?"

"Mrs. Hackles gave it to me. I lost my clothes earlier today. I had a kind of an accident. She's got all kinds of clothes up in the observatory."

"And your head? What happened to your hair?"

"I shaved it off."

"Why?"

"Because," Judith said. "It's bullshit."

"What do you mean?"

"Just what I said. It's all fashion. I wanted to get out of the cycle."

"What cycle?"

"Making statements about myself. Giving creeps the chance to make snap judgments about me. This way they can just guess. Anyway, don't you think it looks kind of cool?"

"It takes some getting used to."

"Well, that's true, I guess. I'm still getting used to it myself. I only got it done last week."

"It is eye-catching," Wedley said. "I guess there is something kind of haunting about it."

"Thank you."

"Well, anyway, I don't think you look like a witch. You look like nobody I've ever seen before. That's something."

"Goddamn," Judith said. "You really are a nice guy, aren't you? It's kind of creepy."

Wedley shook his head sadly. "My daughter's lost," he said, and walked down the hall.

Judith sat there on the piano bench, in wonder.

What kind of life, she thought, might I have had if I'd had someone like this Wedley for a father? Or a boyfriend? Everything might have been different. I could have been someone else entirely, the kind of person who sang in the Glee Club and played trombone. Terrific, Judith thought. Just what the world needs.

There was an odd taste in her mouth that lasted a moment and disappeared. That green elixir. That small green glass.

"ATTENTION MORTON HACKLES," the policeman on the megaphone said again. "YOU HAVE FIVE MINUTES. COME OUT WITH YOUR PRISONERS."

"Prisoners?" Judith said. She did not feel like a prisoner. She put her hands out to touch the keys of the piano, but drew them back. Judith did not know how to play.

She leaned over to the box of percussion instruments on the floor. Was it possible, this late in life, to learn to play an instrument? The trick was to start with an easy one.

She thought about what Mrs. Hackles had said, in speaking of
her former husband James. The importance of a sharp knife.
Judith thought of the cafeteria downstairs, and remembered all
those terrible knives and cleavers hanging in a row. An idea came
to her slowly, an idea that would solve her problem. All she
needed was a sharp knife.

She picked up the finger cymbals, put one on each hand.
Bringing her hands together, the cymbals made a small, soft
chime.

"Ting," she said.

•   •   •

"You hate me," Morton Hackles yelled at his mother.

"So?" Mrs. Hackles poured some coffee from a thermos into
a wine glass. Lifting a bottle of Listerine she poured herself a
capful into the coffee, then picked up a can of Reddi Wip and
shook it. She squirted the whipped cream onto the top of the
coffee.

"Here," she said. "Drink your Irish Listerine."

"I don't want an Irish Listerine," Hackles said. "I want you to
help me get out of here."

"You want my help but you won't even drink the supper I
make for you." She sipped her Irish Listerine. "Yech," she said.
"Repulsive."

"You're all screwed up, you know that, Maw?" Hackles said.

"Oh, I suppose I should just follow your example. Hold up
hardware stores on a little donkey!"

"At least I enjoy myself!" Hackles wiped the sweat off his
forehead with his hand. "You don't take any pleasure from
nothing."

Mrs. Hackles sipped her coffee. Her rifle lay next to her,
leaning against the wall.

"ATTENTION MORTON HACKLES," the man with the
megaphone said. "YOU HAVE THREE MINUTES."

"You'd better think of something," Mrs. Hackles said.

"How can I do anything if you won't lend me some more
bullets."

"When are you going to grow up? Be a man?"

"I am a man," Hackles said.

"You're a buffoon." Mrs. Hackles put her Irish Listerine down on the windowsill. "Now you either give yourself up or figure a way out of here without shooting people. That's so tiresome, when you start shooting at people! You make me feel like I'm in some Wild West stampede or something!"

"How can I get out of here without a gun, Maw? Tell me that!"

"Well, you figure it out, sonny-boy! This is your problem, not mine. Anyway, you should have remembered to save your bullets before you started shooting at those two baboons."

"You never let me do what I want," Hackles said. "Why do you hate me so much?"

"I call it 'tough love,' " Mrs. Hackles said.

"Not letting me have any more bullets isn't tough love, it's just meanness. You know I'm going to go to jail again."

"It's *really* tough love."

"What's the difference between tough love and hating me, then? You tell me that."

Mrs. Hackles shrugged her shoulders. "Beats me." She picked up her rifle.

"Go on," she said. "Have some brains."

"I don't like brains," Hackles said.

"If you eat some brains I'll give you my rifle," Mrs. Hackles said. "This has a couple shells in it still."

"Really?" Hackles said. He looked excited. "If I eat some brains you'll let me have your gun? No shit? How come?"

"I worry about your diet," Mrs. Hackles said. "You don't eat right."

"Well, let me set your mind at ease, Maw! Where are the brains! Serve 'em up! I'll have a whole platter!"

"You're a good boy, Morty," Mrs. Hackles said, scooping out a healthy portion of brains onto a paper plate. "There. You eat that all up."

Morton Hackles sat at his table, eating his brains. "Mm-hm," he said, chewing. "Not bad!"

"I knew you'd like them," Mrs. Hackles said. She aimed the rifle at him. "That's my boy."

"Okay," he said, dropping his fork into his empty plate. "Now give me your gun."

"Forget it," Mrs. Hackles said.

"You said you'd give it to me if I finished my supper!"

"I lied! Ha ha ha!"

Morton stood up, reached out, and grabbed the end of the rifle. Mrs. Hackles cried out as the gun was wrested from her grasp. For a moment Hackles stood there, holding the rifle high, as if considering striking his own mother with it.

"I'm in charge now," he said. "You understand that, Maw? You take orders from me."

"You're a bad boy," Mrs. Hackles said.

"It runs in the blood."

"Ah, you're no son of mine." She sighed, and turned away from him. "Everything has disappointed me."

• • •

Wedley was walking briskly through the halls of the Arts Center, searching for his daughter. There was a small gallery with green finger paintings on the wall. "Hello?" he said. "Is anybody there?"

"I'm here," said a woman's voice. Vicki came running towards him, carrying her high heels in one hand. "Did you find Dwayne?"

"No. Did you?"

"No."

"Damn."

"I'm worried," Vicki said. "Those police are going to come in here any second. We have to find Dwayne."

"And Phoebe," Wedley said.

Vicki dropped her shoes onto the floor, and stepped into them.

"Where do you think they are?" she said. "Do you suppose they're all together?"

"Maybe. I hope so."

They turned away from the gallery and walked back towards the main building of the school.

"I wanted to thank you for being so nice to me," Vicki said. "You made me feel much better."

"That's all right," Wedley said. "I was glad to help."

"If only I could find Dwayne right now and tell him what I'm thinking."

"You'll find him."

"Have you ever been in love like I am, Wedley?" Vicki said.

"I don't know, Vicki. Sure. I mean, I love Emily. My wife Emily."

"She left you, though."

"Yeah."

"I'm sorry."

"It's all right. It's getting to be a long time now."

"Still, that must be hard," Vicki said. "Being left by someone you love."

"What's hard is not knowing why. She never even explained. One day she was just gone."

"You poor man," Vicki said. She stopped and turned to him. She reached out with one hand and held his cheek.

"I hope you fall in love again someday," she said.

"Vicki," Wedley said.

"Well, well, well," said a loud, booming voice. "What do we got here?"

The Outcast walked towards them, holding a shotgun. Vicki took her hand away from Wedley's face, and blushed.

"What's going on here? You two having a little smooch or something? A little tête-à-tête?"

"We happened to be talking," Vicki said, putting her hands on her hips.

"Looked like more than that, haw haw haw."

He pointed the gun at her. "You want I should tell your boyfriend about this?"

"You tell him what you want," Vicki said. "I've got nothing to hide."

"What's this all about, Hackles?" Wedley said.

"We're moving out of here." He put the rifle to Vicki's head. "You first, sweetheart."

"Help!" Vicki cried. "He's going to shoot me!"

"I'm not going to shoot you," Hackles said, exasperated. "Not now! Wait till we get outside."

"Oh, Dwayne," Vicki said, full of panic. "Where's Dwayne? Help! Help!"

"Now stop that," Hackles said. "I'm not going to kill you."

"Then why do you have your gun at her head?"

"To make them think I will. It's an illusion."

"Could have fooled me," Wedley muttered.

"Look you, we have to work together on this. Otherwise it's curtains. You got that?"

"I'm frightened," Vicki said. "Dwayne, I'm frightened."

"I'm right here," Wedley said.

"You're not Dwayne!" Vicki said. She bit her lip.

"Where is that boyfriend of yours?" Hackles asked. "We got to round up the troops. It's time to make our escape."

"I don't know where he is," Vicki said. "He left me. I looked up one moment and he was gone."

Suddenly they heard a loud sound. A dog was barking and snarling, as if it was trying to defend its master. It sounded as if the dog was being attacked.

"Holy shit," Wedley said. "That's Buddy."

• • •

Judith Lenahan climbed the spiral stairs, clasping a sharp knife from the cafeteria. The light from the sailing ship in the window was fading now. She wondered where everyone was. There was a long line of people tracking each other somewhere in the building. Wedley looking for Phoebe, Vicki looking for Dwayne, Dwayne and Phoebe looking for Buddy. Following each other's traces.

She reached the third floor. All was still quiet up here. Slowly, delicately, she moved towards the principal's office.

He was still there, tied up in the ball of string. The sock dribbled out of his mouth.

Judith held up the sharp knife. Wilkins whimpered something. She pulled the sock out of his mouth.

"Judith," he said. "I'm sorry."

"Yes," Judith said. She pointed the knife towards him and kneeled. "You are."

"I'm sorry," he said. "You never gave me a chance to explain."

"You don't have to explain," Judith said. "It doesn't matter now."

"Please," Wilkins said.

"It's too late," Judith said. "Just listen. This is the last thing I'm going to tell you."

She put the knife on the floor. She raised her hands over her head, and held her body in the form of a frozen pirouette. Once again she moved herself into the form of a question mark.

"Judith," Wilkins said.

"Sshh," Judith said. "Just let me finish what I started."

She walked across the room, balancing on an invisible line, then put out her arms to feel a wall she could not see. She moved her arms all over that wall, looking for the opening, but it appeared to be gone.

She turned back to Wilkins, balancing along the line once more, and raised her arms out in a flourish. Her hands went to her breast, covering her heart, then she held them out to Wilkins. She looked at him, longingly, achingly, for a moment, then pulled back. Suddenly she threw her hands up, as if throwing her heart into the air. She looked up at the ceiling, watching her heart ascend.

Judith stood there in her prom dress, and Wilkins sat on his chair. The two of them looked up at the ceiling, waiting for the heart to come back down. It didn't.

Judith sighed, and walked back over towards Wilkins. She picked the knife up off the floor.

"Now," she said. "It's time."

She held the knife next to his ribs, and cut the twine.

She sawed through the cords that bound him to the chair. The string fell onto the floor next to him.

"Go," she said.

"I'm free?" Wilkins said, suspicious.

"Yeah. You're free. I want you to go out the way you came, though. Don't let anybody see you. Climb back out on the roof, and follow the scaffold up to the smokestack. Take the ladder back to the ground."

"There are rungs missing. It's dangerous."

"You can get down, though, right? If you're careful?"

Wilkins nodded. "Yeah. I think so."

"Okay, then. Go."

"But what about you?" Wilkins said. "What will happen to you?"

"Don't worry about me," Judith said. "I'll get by. I always get by."

"There's so much I wanted to say to you," Wilkins said. "About everything. About the way I acted."

"Save it," Judith said. "We don't have the time."

"I was afraid," Wilkins said. "I was afraid of screwing up my life."

"You don't have to apologize for being afraid," Judith said. "I was afraid, too."

"You were?"

"Yeah. I was wrong about you. I thought you were just some banker I was going to take for a ride. I wasn't prepared for you to be more than that."

"I can be more than that," Wilkins whispered, urgently. "I've changed, I swear it."

"It's too late," Judith said. "You should just go."

"Sweetheart," Wilkins said, and put his arms around her.

"Don't say sweetheart," Judith said. "God, everybody says that. It's such a stupid word. Why does everything about love have to be sugary? What does sugar have to do with anything?"

"Sssh," Wilkins said. "Just relax."

"All right," Judith said. "Maybe I'm too critical of things. Maybe—"

"Quiet."

"All right."

They kissed. Wilkins put his hand on Judith's cheek.

"Oh, Judith," Wilkins said. "My love."

"Quiet," Judith said. "Don't spoil it."

In absolute silence they held each other tightly, moment after moment, in the old school.

Judith kissed him again, then looked around.

"Now," she said. "You have to go."

"No," he said. "I want to be with you. I can't leave you here."

"Go," Judith said.

They stood up. Judith looked down the hall. "The coast is clear," she said. "You get out of here."

They walked arm in arm past the old gym, out to the door marked ROOF. The smokestack was lit by a spotlight. Wilkins walked past the rusted weight machines and the trampoline, up to the foot of the scaffold.

"Goodbye," Judith said.

"Tell me one thing," he said. "Why the change? Why did you let me free just now?"

"I saw something," she said. "I saw somebody do something nice for somebody else. It made me think."

"Thank you for giving me a second chance," Wilkins said. "You won't be sorry. I saw something, too."

"Goodbye," Judith said.

"Bye, Judith."

They kissed. The shadow of the smokestack fell across them. Wilkins turned his back, climbed up the steps to the iron ladder.

"Bye-bye," Judith said, and ran back to the school. She did not want him to see her on the verge of tears.

She closed the door marked ROOF behind her, and held her hands over her eyes. Judith Lenahan bit her lip, blinking back tears.

"Pathetic," said a voice from the opposite end of the hall.

She looked up, and there stood Mrs. Hackles, all in black, watching her.

"You let him go, didn't you?" she said.

Judith nodded her head. She was biting her tongue.

"I knew you would," Mrs. Hackles said. "I knew it all along."

She turned her back on Judith, walked back towards the observatory.

"Mrs. Hackles—" Judith said. "I'm sorry—"

"Don't talk to me," Mrs. Hackles said. "I don't even know you. Judas! Benedict Arnold!"

"I'm sorry," Judith said again, more softly.

Mrs. Hackles went into her observatory alone. "I have no children!" she said.

• • •

On and on Dwayne walked, following the music in his soul. It was not the kind of music you heard, it was the kind of music you lived. Dwayne was getting closer and closer. He sniffed. You could almost smell the music getting closer. There was a place where everything was in tune.

If you tuned a piano correctly, Dwayne thought, striking one string would make all the others resonate, in accordance with the harmonics of the instrument. All the tones and overtones. That was what he wanted his brain to be like, for all of his constantly competing emotions to ring in unison.

Twice in his life his soul had rung like a bell—the day he went over to Edith's after Hurricane Hildegarde, and the day he met Vicki in the Wurlitzer showroom. Now he could feel it coming on again. Everything was going to be in alignment.

He entered the auditorium. There before him were all of the science exhibits on plywood tables, collecting dust. There was the miniature volcano that erupted with Mrs. Butterworth's syrup and the Play-Doh structure that said MOTER and the teeth in a little jar. There was a fully functioning crossbow. There were lungs of cows floating in formaldehyde. There was a cross-species examination of the differences in paws. There was a small model of Benjamin Franklin holding a kite and a key dangling on the end of a string. *Touch Here,* said a small sign. Dwayne reached forward and touched the key. Electricity raced through his body.

"Ow!" Dwayne said, holding his hand. The exhibit was still live, wired up to a car battery. "Dammit." He looked around to see if perhaps there was a first aid exhibit. But you couldn't take anything for shock.

He heard a soft growling sound.

In front of him was Buddy. The dog seemed to be in another world. He was standing in point position, one foreleg raised, the hairless tail erect. He was pointing at a skeleton hanging from a hook.

Dwayne stepped forward.

Buddy growled again.

What was it the dog was seeing in the skeleton? She was swinging from a hook, all the bones marked with little signs. Clavicle, scapula, humerus, ulna, radius, carpus, metacarpals, phalanges. There was the zygomatic arch. Mandible and vomer.

"Buddy?" Dwayne said.

The dog blinked, looked over at Dwayne, then back at the skeleton. He swayed. There was a remarkable abundance of brown jam on Buddy's face. It seemed like there was more of his insides on the outside than not. The dog was turning inside out before Dwayne's eyes.

Buddy looked back at the skeleton, then at Dwayne again. He barked.

Dwayne had a feeling of anticipation, as if he were about to sneeze with his entire being. He waited for his feeling of mystical alignment to become complete, to feel that sense that everything he knew and felt was in harmony.

Buddy began to vibrate.

If only he could see the world as Buddy saw it, Dwayne thought. To live a life of sensations rather than thoughts. Then he would never have known a sense of shame, a sense of not living up to the expectations of his lovers. There had to be a way of being himself without living a contradiction. It was just a moment away.

The dog looked at Dwayne, shaking like a paint mixer. Buddy took a step towards him.

Maybe if he could somehow get inside the dog.

That would do it. If he could switch places with Buddy he could know the secrets that Buddy knew that continually eluded Dwayne. Somewhere in the science fair perhaps there was one of those machines you saw in movies, that would move Dwayne's brain into Buddy's body. Then Dwayne's insides would be external. He could live a life in tune.

"Buddy," Dwayne whispered, holding out his hand. "Tell me, tell me, tell me . . ."

The dog growled, showing Dwayne his canine teeth. Dwayne thought, well, technically all of his teeth are canine teeth. But the long ones in particular. The ones for being a vampire.

Dwayne looked up at the skeleton and suddenly saw Edith standing there. She was watching Dwayne, looking at him with love and disappointment. Her features were covered with little signs. Her lips were marked *Orbicularis oris.* Her eyelids, *Orbicularis oculi.* The chin, *Mentalis.*

"I'm sorry," Dwayne said. "I'm sorry, honey."

He looked at Buddy, as if the dog could explain the riot and chaos that had led him to betray her.

"Tell her," Dwayne whispered. "Show her what it's like to be a man."

But Buddy just growled some more. The dog was looking very angry.

The only way I can explain it to you, love, Dwayne thought, is if I'm Buddy myself. I've got to figure out a way of getting inside that dog.

"Help me, Buddy," Dwayne said. "Help me."

He reached out his hand. Buddy froze. For a moment the two of them stood there, like frozen reflections.

Then Dwayne dove forward, tackling the dog. Buddy groaned and fell over. Dwayne grabbed Buddy by the throat, shaking him. The dog barked angrily and pushed Dwayne over. The two of them were rolling on the floor underneath the science exhibits. "Help me, Buddy!" Dwayne was yelling. "Help me!"

A glob of green Play-Doh hit Dwayne in the head. Then another, blue this time. Small pieces of a miniature car engine were bombarding Dwayne. They hurt. He looked up.

Phoebe Harrison was holding part of the MOTER in one hand. "Stop it!" she yelled. "Stop it! You're hurting him!"

She threw an orange Play-Doh carburetor at Dwayne. It hit him on the forehead.

Dwayne blinked. Buddy was lying motionless on the ground. Dwayne had chocolate and barbecue sauce all over him. Brown goo from the dog's eyes was smeared on Dwayne's cheeks.

"You've killed him," Phoebe said. She went up to Dwayne and grabbed him by the throat. "You've killed Buddy!"

She punched Dwayne in the stomach. Dwayne rolled over in pain.

"Jerk," Phoebe said.

She went over to her dog and held him in her arms. "Roll over," she said. "Good dog. Play dead."

•   •   •

That was how Judith, Wedley, Vicki, and the Outcast found them, a few moments later, when they entered the gymnasium.

"Jeezo-peezo," said the Outcast. "Look at this. Looks like a battlefield in here."

"Honey?" Wedley said. "Are you all right?"

"Buddy," Vicki said. "He killed Buddy."

"He's still breathing," Judith said. "I can see his ribs moving."

"He's dead," Phoebe said miserably.

Dwayne sat up, holding his stomach. Vicki went over to him and held him. "What happened, Dwayne?"

"Buddy and me—" Dwayne said.

"Yes? Buddy and you what?"

"Buddy and me—" Dwayne said.

"What? Tell me, Dwayne. Concentrate."

"We had a—a falling up."

"Out, you mean," Vicki said. "You had a falling out."

"I know what I mean," Dwayne growled.

"All right, everybody's all right down here," the Outcast said. "Let's get up. We're leaving."

"Yay!" Phoebe said. "We're going home."

"Not quite," Wedley said. "We're leaving but we're not going home."

"What's—what's happening?" Dwayne said.

"The Outcast here is going to pretend to shoot me unless they let us go," Vicki said.

"I got the bullets!" the Outcast said. "Ya-hoo!"

. "What happens if they don't let us go?" Dwayne said, still rubbing his stomach.

"You just leave it up to me," the Outcast said. "We're going to have some fun."

"Is the witch coming with us?" Phoebe said, pointing to Judith. "She wasn't with us before."

"Yes, I'm coming with you," Judith said. "Mrs. Hackles says I can't stay here anymore."

"You don't know how lucky you are," the Outcast said. "Believe me, if you'd a stayed here she would a made you into a cuckoo clock."

"I'm scared," Phoebe said. "Is Buddy going to be okay?"

"He'll be fine," Judith said, going over to Phoebe. "I think he's just stunned." Judith ran her fingers through Phoebe's hair. "Everything's going to be fine," she said.

"Hey," the Outcast said, picking up the crossbow from the table. "Looka here! Do you think this works?"

"Careful," Vicki said. "You could hurt somebody with that."

He fiddled with it for a moment, then put it back on the table. "Piece a shit," he said.

Dwayne was rubbing his head, still looking at Buddy. He seemed to be deep in thought.

"Hey, is everybody having a good time?" the Outcast shouted. "If we're gonna be partners in crime together, let's at least enjoy ourselves!"

Everyone looked around uncomfortably.

"Boy, I haven't been in this old gymnasium for years," the Outcast said. "Look at all this stuff. The old Science Fair! Whoopdy doopdy!"

He looked at the skeleton hanging from the hook. "Hey! The

anklebone's connected to the thigh bone! The thighbone's connected to the hipbone! I never realized that before!"

"Edith," Dwayne said, shaking his head.

"Stop it, Dwayne," Vicki said.

"Something's happened to Edith," he said.

"You're being morbid," Vicki said.

"She's gone," Dwayne said, and shuddered.

"Moron," Phoebe said. She was still mad about Dwayne's attack on Buddy.

"Hey, what do you know?" the Outcast said. "The hipbone's connected to the backbone!"

"I am the mother of an idiot," Mrs. Hackles said, entering the gymnasium.

"Hiya, Ma!" Hackles said.

"Haven't you left yet?" Mrs. Hackles said. "I thought you were on your way out."

"We're going," the Outcast said. "I just wanted to take a last look around. You sure got a lot of disgusting stuff in this old place!"

"Mrs. Hackles—" Judith said.

"You be quiet," Mrs. Hackles said. "I don't want to hear a word out of you! Benedict Arnold! Brutus! Tokyo Rose!"

"Hey, Ma," the Outcast said, pointing to some rubbery-looking objects on a table. "What the hell are these?"

"Those are weather balloons," Mrs. Hackles said. "They were going to fill 'em up with helium and let 'em go. See where they were going to come down. Ask people to write letters. Where they found them."

Her son shook his head.

"Buncha dumb kids," he said.

"What's this?" Wedley asked.

"Well, that's the dental decay booth. Those teeth in the ginger ale bottle are decaying, right? Whereas these teeth here are in water. They're fine."

"What's this, Ma?" Hackles said, pointing at the remaining slabs of Play-Doh and the sign that said MOTER.

"That was Ray Baxter's," Mrs. Hackles said, sighing. "He made a car engine out of Play-Doh and put a lot of little signs on toothpicks showing what each part of the motor was."

"Phoebe threw part of it at me," Dwayne said.

"You deserved it," Phoebe said.

Wedley looked carefully at the crossbow Hackles had left on the table. If it worked, perhaps it could be used. What would happen if he grabbed the crossbow and aimed it at the Outcast? He could order him to leave, to let the rest of the party stay behind. Then this nightmare could be over.

But the Outcast might just as well shoot him. Hackles was unpredictable. One minute he was jolly, the next minute he was out of control. It was a big risk to take.

The Outcast moved onward, towards a wall of cylindrical tanks. "Whatcha got here?" he said. "Ozone?"

"That's helium," Mrs. Hackles said. "For the weather balloons."

"Helium!" he shouted. "And they're full? This is terrific." He put his lips over the nozzle of one of the tanks and inhaled.

"My name is Donald Fuckin' Duck," he said, in a voice high-pitched and squeaky. "My name is Donald Fuckin' Duck. My name is Donald, ah well, that's it. It only lasts for a few seconds. See what happens is, the helium freezes your vocal cords. Just for a few moments. While they're frozen your voice sounds like it's going at forty-five. Like on an old record. Is that a laugh or what?

"Here," he said. "Everybody try."

The prisoners looked at each other nervously. "Come on!" he said. "Let's have some fun. What about you, Harrison? Why don't you loosen up?"

"I don't feel like it," Wedley said.

"Come on," the Outcast said. "You all gotta try some helium. I can't believe this. Look at all these tanks. You got gallons and gallons of this stuff."

"Morton," Mrs. Hackles said, "I want you to leave. Now."

"Okay, okay," he said. "Hey, wait a minute. Holy cow! Am I brilliant or what? This is incredible. I am having a brainstorm.

A way to get us out of here. Right in our hands. Each one of us grabs hold of one of these balloons, see, we go up to the roof and float away. They'll never catch us! They won't even see us go!"

"What?" Vicki said. "What are you talking about?"

"Them weather balloons. We fill 'em all up with helium, jump off the roof, we're airborne! Escape! It's brilliant!"

"What if they shoot at us?"

"They'll never know we're gone! It don't make no noise. By the time they figure it out we'll be sky-high! Look, you, your name is Judith, right? You start filling these things up. Vicki, you get a bunch of rope together from all this trash, help set up something to tie us to the balloons. This is incredible. Hackles, you amaze me."

"You'll need more than one balloon to make each person float," Judith said.

"It won't work," Wedley said. "We'll all be killed."

"That would at least be something," Mrs. Hackles said.

"It might work," Vicki said. "It's very interesting! It's kind of an experiment!"

"It's an experiment in stupidity," Wedley said. "I won't do it."

"Okay, fine," the Outcast said. "You stay here and get your ass shot off."

"We should name each one," Phoebe said. "Like the Nina, the Pinta, the Santa Marie!"

"ATTENTION MORTON HACKLES," said the voice on the megaphone. "YOU HAVE ONE MINUTE."

"Move it," Hackles said. "You start filling up them balloons. We gotta get this factory going."

Judith went to the pile of weather balloons and started filling one up with helium. Vicki was already poking around the exhibits, looking for rope. Wedley stood by the MOTER, his hands folded across his chest.

There was a hissing sound as helium rushed out of the tank and into the balloon. Judith watched the rubber balloon inflating.

"Jesus Christ," Hackles said. "You done already? Those things fill up fast."

"All you do is turn the nozzle," Judith said. "It's easy."

"Dwayne, come on," Vicki said. "Help out."

But Dwayne was still sitting near Buddy, lost. He rubbed his cheeks, and looked at the brown goo on his fingers.

"That's one," Judith said. Vicki tied some rope around the base of the enormous balloon.

"You better tie that down to something or it'll wind up on the ceiling," Hackles said.

"Tie it to the leg of the table," said Judith.

"What are we doing?" Wedley said. "You actually think this will work? It's the dumbest thing I've heard all day."

"Oh, Pa," Phoebe said. "Try to have a sense of humor."

"It's dangerous," he said.

"Hey, life's an adventure!" Hackles said. "Just another couple balloons and we'll all be—" His expression changed suddenly. "Ah, shit," he said.

"What's the matter?" Wedley said. "You suddenly remembered about reality or something?"

"Naw, man, it's Gomez! My little friend! I can't go noplace without Gomez! You, Judith, make sure you inflate some balloons for my donkey!"

"How are you going to get him?" Mrs. Hackles said. "He's outside, lapping water out of the open sewer. To get him, you'll have to go outside."

"Anyway, we don't have enough balloons," Judith said, tying off another one. "I think we'll need two for each person."

"Aw," the Outcast said. He sniffed. "Poor little Gomez. Left behind! My best friend."

"Oh, stop," Mrs. Hackles said. "You make me want to throw up."

"My only friend! Gone, forever. Those floppy ears! That happy tail! Buh, buh, buh."

"Oh, Morty," Mrs. Hackles said. "Stop it. I'll look after your goddamned burro. He'll be all right."

"Oh, Ma, will you? You're the best!" The Outcast hugged his mother.

"Morty, stop it. This display of affection is inappropriate!"

He slapped his mother on the rear end. "I *love* this gal!" he shouted.

"All right, freeze!" Wedley yelled suddenly. He held the crossbow in front of him. "Get your hands up in the air. I'll skewer you if you don't."

"What is this?" the Outcast said. "What the hell you got there, boy?"

"It's a crossbow," Wedley said. "And it's aimed at your fat face."

"It's from Ecuador," Phoebe said.

"Yeah, well listen, Pedro, I got a rifle here that's aimed right back at you."

"I'll take you with me, Hackles," Wedley said. "Drop your gun."

"Dang it, Wedley," Hackles said, pulling off the safety on the rifle. "You just made a big mistake. A big mistake."

At that moment a door at the far end of the auditorium opened.

A man with a strange haircut came rushing towards them, yelling like a warrior. He took something from his belt and threw it. There was a sudden explosion of orange smoke. Judith felt light-headed, as if she were drifting through the air. Through the smoke she saw Wilkins' face, floating above the mist like a summer moon.

"Daddy, help!" Phoebe cried.

"Dwayne!" Vicki screamed. "Save me, oh save me!"

The smoke billowed through the room, engulfing everything. Judith felt her eyelids growing heavy. The exhibits of the old science fair came in and out of focus: the grinning skeleton, the lungs in formaldehyde, the charred remains of Skylab.

"I'm here," Wilkins said, and she looked up at him. She couldn't understand how he came to be there, holding her as the world disappeared.

"I came back," he said.

The smoke grew thicker, enveloping all. People were gasping and coughing, crying out for help. The last thing Judith remembered was the sight of many men in uniform pouring through the walls, like the sunlight streaming through the blue stained glass in the stairwell.

• • •

It must have been ten or fifteen minutes later when Judith came to. She opened her eyes and once again saw the silhouette of James Buchanan Memorial High School in the twilight. She recalled setting eyes on it for the first time earlier in the day, how lonely and forlorn it had looked. It didn't look much better now, bathed in spotlights.

Someone had carried her outside. Most of the prisoners from the school were lying near her, in various stages of unconsciousness. Vicki was lying on her back with her eyes closed. Mrs. Hackles was being fed oxygen by a paramedic in a white coat. Wedley was kneeling on all fours next to her, choking and coughing.

Dent Wilkins sat next to her, rubbing her scalp with his fingertips. Blue police beacons flashed off of his face.

Policemen were talking into radios, waving flashlights. There were dozens and dozens of officers, their numbers ridiculously out of proportion to the situation. Some were still rushing in and out of the old school. Orange smoke was drifting from the windows. Judith thought about the smoke she had seen puffing out of the fields in Centralia. The whole town was still on fire, underground, she thought. Moving closer and closer.

She looked at Wilkins. "I told you to get lost," she said.

"I am," he replied.

Judith sat up, rubbing her head. The tear gas made her temples throb.

"I went almost all the way back down that smokestack," Wilkins said, "before I realized I still had those canisters. I didn't want to leave the job unfinished."

"Well, you finished it," Judith said, her lids still heavy.

"Isn't he something?" said a man in a long black robe. "Official deputy."

"Who's that?" Judith said.

"This is Officer Calcagno," Wilkins said. "A man after my own heart."

"Why's he dressed like that?"

"Hey," Calcagno said, "you should talk." Judith looked down at her prom dress. She'd forgotten.

"How's it going?" Wilkins said.

"We still got a couple missing persons," Calcagno said.

An angry-looking, lobster-red man approached, mopping his forehead with a handkerchief. "Well, where the hell is he?" the man said.

"We don't know yet," said Calcagno. "We're looking."

"Don't tell me you *lost* him! I don't want to hear you even *think* that! If you've lost him, I'll have your badge. I'll cut your stinking *head* off." The man in the trench coat looked at Calcagno, clenching his teeth. "And get out of that costume," he said. "You're the sorriest-looking cop I've ever seen."

"You haven't met my boss yet, have you," Calcagno said. "This is Lieutenant Stroke. Lieutenant, this is Mr. Wilkins. I deputized him. He's the one who set off the tear gas inside."

"Who gave you authority to do that?" shouted Stroke. "What do you know about this man? A deputy? He could be anybody!"

"We have to go," Calcagno said. "Police business."

"Pleased to meet you, Lieutenant Stroke," said Judith.

Stroke growled at her, and the policemen stalked away.

"Who are they missing?" Wilkins said. Judith looked around. Wedley was standing up, looking anxiously towards the school.

"Phoebe," Judith said. "Phoebe and Buddy."

"And Dwayne," said Vicki, crawling towards them. "Where's Dwayne?"

"And the Outcast," Wilkins said. "That's what the cops are most upset about. They didn't even get Hackles yet."

They looked at the old school. The beams of flashlights flickered in the windows. Judith had a sudden vision of the face of the man she'd seen in the painting, illuminated by flashlight. Fenton Weems. Fourth Principal 1889–1892.

"Phoebe," Wedley said. "Phoebe darling."

An ambulance pulled up quickly, tires squealing to a halt, behind the row of flashing police cars. Mrs. Hackles was sitting on the tailgate of a station wagon, apparently receiving oxygen from a paramedic against her will.

"There!" Wilkins said suddenly, pointing to the roof. "Someone's up there."

Judith watched, amazed, as the figure stepped to the edge of the roof, the balloons tied around his waist. He looked out over the chaos below him, hoping that he would have enough buoyancy to elude the pull of gravity.

Judith imagined his escape route, running from the science fair up to heaven. He had run up the spiral stairs, hauling the balloons behind him, the immense, silent pendulum swaying back and forth to his left. She saw him dragging the balloons through the smoke, getting to the third floor, yanking them through the old hallways out to the roof. Tying them to his waist. Looking out on all creation now, wondering if this departure would malfunction.

Dwayne stood there, next to the trampoline, feeling the tug of the balloons. It took all his strength to hold on. If he let go of the railing now he would ascend to paradise. For once he would be free from the relentless drift of smoke.

He looked up into the night sky. Somewhere up there was a place where all things were in harmony, where there was solace for those feeling grief, where joy did not contradict itself. He looked up into the night. The heavens shimmered and twinkled beyond his grasp.

"Edith," he said.

Dwayne let go of the railing and slowly rose into space.

Judith, lying on the ground, watched him drifting past the stars. There was something beautiful about seeing him up there. He took on an unexpected grace, like a fat man floating in the ocean.

"Dwayne," Vicki said, watching him soar overhead. "Dwayne."

She turned to Wedley. "I'm losing him," she said. "He's never coming back. He's going to keep going and going until he disappears! Oh, somebody do something! Help me! Wedley, please help me."

"I can't do anything," Wedley said. He raised his fists, then opened his hands, helpless.

"Goodbye, darling!" Vicki said, waving to him. "Goodbye, my love!"

He was already growing smaller. Dwayne drifted over their heads, receding, until he was almost beyond the perimeter of the school grounds. Inside the school the beams of light stabbed in and out of windows. Flashing police beacons illuminated Dwayne's silhouette with pulsing blue light.

Suddenly, from the rooftop, came a piercing shriek. It was Phoebe.

"Phoebe!" Wedley yelled. "Come down here this instant. What are you doing up there?"

Buddy was standing next to her, his paws up on the railing. He had the crossbow in his mouth.

"Stupid jerk," Phoebe said. "Moron!"

"Darling," Wedley cried. "Sweetheart!"

The policemen aimed their searchlights at her.

"What's she going to do?" Vicki said.

She took the crossbow from Buddy's mouth and aimed it at Dwayne.

"Stop," Wedley cried. "Phoebe!"

"She's going to kill him!" Vicki screamed.

Phoebe closed one eye.

"Come down here!" Wedley cried. "Please, honey. Stop what you're doing."

"I can't watch," Vicki said, covering her eyes.

The crossbow made a clicking sound as the arrow was released.

"Jerk," Phoebe said.

It was an exceptionally good shot. Even at this distance hitting one of Dwayne's three weather balloons would have brought him down. But the arrow punctured first one, then another. There were two almost simultaneous explosions, then Dwayne's soft exclamation of surprise and regret.

Screaming softly, Dwayne fell to earth, still grasping one of the enormous balloons.

"Is that him?" Lieutenant Stroke shouted. "That's gotta be him. Get him, men!"

The policemen ran towards the place where Dwayne's impact seemed most probable. He rushed down at them, still drifting to the south, still screaming. He was moving farther and farther away. The policemen stopped on the bank of the Catawissa River and watched the enormous descending form.

Dwayne splashed down into the river, coughing and sputtering. The policemen on the bank began to applaud and cheer.

"We got him!" Lieutenant Stroke shouted, moving towards the river. "We got him!"

Dwayne, however, was not quite done. He was trying to grab onto his one remaining balloon. If he could sit on it, Dwayne could float downstream.

"Stop him," Lieutenant Stroke shouted. "Don't let him get away."

There was a sudden shot, and the last balloon burst. Dwayne was thrashing in the water. There was another shot.

"They're going to kill him!" Vicki shouted. "Wedley, stop them."

But Dwayne had already been shot. He raised his arms to his side, motionless, and began to move with the current. A cop jumped into the river and hauled him to shore.

"You killed him!" Vicki shrieked. "You killed Dwayne!"

"He's all right," Calcagno said, coming over to them. "Just a tranquilizer. He'll wake up in a few minutes."

"A tranquilizer?" Vicki said, weeping. "You tranquilized him?"

"Daddy!" Phoebe said. She had climbed down from the roof, and was now standing next to her father. Buddy was with her, wagging his tail.

"Phoebe, what was the idea of shooting Dwayne with the crossbow?" Wedley said. "That was very naughty, young lady."

"But, Pa! He was mean to Buddy!" she said. "He tried to strangle him!"

"I know, darling," Wedley said. "But Dwayne could have gotten hurt. Even killed."

Buddy fell over.

"That's right," Phoebe said.

"I want you to promise me you'll never do anything like this again," Wedley said.

"I promise," Phoebe said, and smiled. "It was a good shot though, wasn't it, Pa! I got him!"

"Phoebe," Wedley said. "You're a doodle."

They hugged each other.

"Aw, Pa," Phoebe said. "This is the best birthday I ever had."

"Hey," Lieutenant Stroke said. "This isn't Hackles! This is one of the hostages!"

"That's right," Calcagno said.

"You knew that?" Stroke yelled. "You *knew* that?"

"I was going to say something," Calcagno said.

"Where's Hackles, then?" Stroke yelled. He was turning purple. "Where the hell is goddamn *Hackles?* Jesus!" He stormed away. "Keep searching the building!" he yelled. "I'm going to talk to you later, Calcagno!"

Calcagno sat down on the tailgate of a station wagon, next to Mrs. Hackles. Two paramedics were still giving her oxygen.

"God, I hate him," Calcagno said.

Mrs. Hackles tried to say something.

"You want that mask off, ma'am?" Calcagno asked.

Mrs. Hackles nodded. "Take it off, boys," Calcagno said.

"But Lieutenant Stroke said we had to—"

"Take it off," Calcagno said. "I'll assume responsibility."

The men took off the oxygen mask, and put the tank back in the truck.

"You all right, ma'am?" Calcagno said.

"Of course I'm all right. Stupid kids want to pump me full of so much oxygen I'll blow up." She looked over at him, surveyed his long robes. "What are you supposed to be?"

"I'm a cop," he said.

"You wear a magician's robes to work?"

"I had an accident today," he said. "Lost my pants. You don't want to know about it."

"You're right," she said. "I don't. I had an accident today, too."

"I don't care," Calcagno said. "Drop dead. I could give a shit."

Mrs. Hackles looked over at him. "Why, you're a very interesting man!" she said, beaming.

"That's the problem," Calcagno muttered. "I keep getting more and more interesting. What would be so wrong with being boring? God, I'm so sick of everything!"

"What's your name?" Mrs. Hackles asked.

"Calcagno."

"I'm Mrs. Hackles," she said. She nodded to him. "You may call me Mary. Officer Calcagno. Would you like to come inside the school, after the smoke clears? Are you hungry?"

Calcagno looked over at this strange woman in her black dress and long braided hair. He was kind of hungry.

"What you got?" he said.

"Oh, I don't know," Mrs. Hackles said. "I could whip up a bit of something." She moved closer to him. "I know recipes nobody else knows!"

"Well, okay," Calcagno said. "Maybe I will go in with you. After the smoke clears." He looked at her. "But only for a minute. I got to get home."

He sniffed the air. There was a strange and unexpected smell, like plastic and rubber melting on a distant radiator in the land of dreams.

"Dwayne," Vicki was saying, bent over his prostrate form. "Say something. Anything."

Dwayne's lips were moving. He was in another land, drifting and floating. "Wuh," he said.

"Honey," Vicki said. "Please. Talk to me."

"Wuh. Wuh. Wuh."

"It's me. Vicki."

She patted his hand, trying to squeeze the life back into him.

"Coconut," he said.

"What? Dwayne? What did you say?"

"Coconut," he said, his eyes still closed.

"Oh honey, yes, it's me! Coconut! It's Vicki!"

"Coconut," Dwayne said, as if from a deep cave. "Edith. My love. Edith my Coconut. Edith my only."

"Oh no," Vicki said, beginning to weep. "Don't say that."

"Edith my true."

"Oh, I'm so stupid," Vicki said.

"Edith my Coconut."

She took off the bracelet he had given her, and put it into his hand. "Oh no," Vicki said, holding the hand. "Oh Dwayne."

"I love you," Dwayne said.

Vicki sniffed back her tears.

"I love you, too."

She looked up. Wedley was still holding Phoebe, cradling her in his arms. Wedley and Vicki looked at each other for a long, odd moment.

"I love you, too," Vicki said again, not looking at Dwayne.

Across the wide lawn of the old school, on the other side of the pit of green water, Judith Lenahan and Dent Wilkins walked together, towards the moving river. They did not touch. Now, at the end of things, they found their earlier shyness restored, all the awkwardness and reticence of the previous night renewed. Wilkins looked over at Judith, wanting to speak, but words would not come. They reached the edge of the water, and Wilkins put his hands in his pockets.

"So, Judith. What now?" he said.

Judith put her hands on her hips and bent backwards, looking at the sky. The spring stars were coming out now, the Lion and the Virgin and the Twins. A crescent moon was sinking along the ecliptic.

"It's so pretty," Judith said.

"Yes," Wilkins said, looking at her.

They stood in silence for a long time, moment after moment passing them by. At last Wilkins moved towards her, kissed her cheek.

"I guess we say goodbye again," Wilkins said.

"Yeah," Judith said. "I guess that's about the size of it."

"You don't think," Wilkins said, "I mean, you don't suppose there's a world where we could go out together? Date?"

Judith shrugged. "It's nice to think about, isn't it? Somehow that you and I could stay friends. But what would all your banker friends say, if they saw you with me? Could you really go out with me and keep doing what you do?"

Wilkins looked at the ground. "I don't know."

"I mean, you're not going to give up your whole life for me. Are you?"

Wilkins shook his head. "I can't," he said. "I'm sorry."

Judith put her hand on his cheek and kissed him. "Don't be," Judith said. "You're sweet. We had an adventure. And that kiss up on the roof. Don't forget that. Thanks."

"Thank you," Wilkins said.

They stood there in silence for a long time, watching the river move before them.

At last Wilkins said, "Do you want me to drive you home? To take you back to Bryn Mawr? At least let me do that."

"No, Dent," she said. "We should part, here, now. I'll get home somehow. You know me, I always get by."

"All right," Wilkins said. He kissed her again. "Goodbye, Judith."

"Bye," Judith said.

She turned her back and walked towards the school, where the flashlights of the police were still strobing and searching. Wilkins watched her walk away, shaking his head, until at last he returned his gaze to the river. Down these waters she had come, hours ago, asleep and unconscious. Where was the vessel that had brought her here? What tale downstream still awaited its end?

He turned to look at her again. Already she was vanishing; he could see the swaying skirts of her prom dress, the silhouette of her smooth skull, receding towards the school. His heart filled with a vast zodiac of complex passion. What is it I'm trying to save by losing her, he thought. What life am I trying to preserve? He recalled the dance she had done for him, and the way she had thrown her heart into the air. They had both looked up, waiting for it to come down. What was he supposed to do now, he wondered. Live the rest of his life with someone's heart floating over his head? Was that even possible?

It suddenly all seemed very simple to Wilkins. He laughed aloud. It was obvious.

"I'm free," he said to himself.

He looked up at Judith. "Judith," he said, raising his hands into the air. *"I'm free!"*

Wilkins was startled, for the voice issuing from his lips was not his own.

Corky Chorkles started laughing. *I'm free,* he cried, running in circles. There was something vaguely frightening about the voice. Wilkins ran on the green grass, waving his arms like some strange bird of paradise.

Judith turned and looked back towards the river.

In a moment she would focus her attention on him, and make her decision. In a moment she would decide whether or not to run back to him, arms outspread, whether to join his dance or to turn her back again, to carry on alone, naked and free.

But for that second, Wilkins vanished from Judith's mind. Her attention, instead, was captured by a figure on the opposite side of the riverbank, sitting on the back of a burro, eating a leg of barbecued chicken with one hand.

"Giddyap," Hackles said to Gomez, and kicked his spurs into the donkey's ribs.

The stars and moon shone down on the twinkling waters. *I'm free,* said Corky Chorkles. *I'm free.*

The Outcast, on the opposite bank, pulled on the reins, and rode off on his burro into the soft Centralia night.

PLUTO

◑

The Bringer of Night

It is not known whether it is dim because it is small or because its surface reflects poorly.

By nine o'clock evening had finally settled onto Columbia County. The few remaining citizens of Centralia were in chairs, illuminated by the blue light of televisions, or lying in their beds reading books. The smell of skunk hung in the air. In the morning employees of the Department of the Interior would start their cranes again, begin anew the desperate process of slowing the spread of the invisible fire. Bulldozers would again begin demolishing the last few houses in the impact zone, leaving a few more brown holes in the earth.

For now, though, all was quiet. A few cars passed through town, moving south towards Ashland. Rain had fallen earlier, but the skies were now clear. Easter was all but past.

At the edge of town, standing not quite thirty feet away from a cloud of smoke rising from the ground, a single figure remained, his bag by the side of the road, his thumb outstretched. He liked the drama of it, his silhouette looming up at people through the fumes. The man from beyond the grave.

Billings was surprised how few things he owned. Most of the stuff in the basement belonged to Dent and Tawny Wilkins. It was a shame to leave all those good tools behind, the screw gun and the bubble level and the electric sander. But it had to be done. No one would ever come to reclaim the house now; that hole in the ceiling would slowly let more and more of the outer world in, until the floorboards began to warp and squirrels and badgers would nest in the foundation. In the end sunflowers would grow through the floor, raising their faces to heaven.

So Billings had taken flight. It was an interesting moment, he thought, an interlude. In a moment someone would pick him up, a stranger, and it would be off to the next adventure. A woman. She would drive up out of the smoke, open the door, and the two of them would intertwine. Not all at once, of course. He'd have to be polite. Women are suspicious of men, and no wonder. Women are afraid if they pick up men that they'll be kooks and weirdos. George Billings wanted to let this stranger know that she did not have to be afraid. He would try to concentrate, so hard that she could read his mind. Know in her heart that he could be trusted. Then he'd tell her about the angel of death, the value of basements, the power of gum. She'd know that he was unusual.

You got messages all the time. It was frightening. The universe sent you Morse code. Semaphore. Sometimes you got false messages, too. But there was this big bell out there. Sometimes you heard it ring. You'd look into the sunset and you'd hear that big bell. Or in the voices of children. Even your grandparents sometimes. He'd heard it from them. Just the way his deranged grandmother used to laugh. Gumpy laughed kind of like a chimpanzee, like something screaming into its banana. But you could tell from Gumpy's laugh that she loved life. Even if she was a pain in the butt. She loved life, and she loved her children. So. Even there, in Gumpy's simian scream. The big bell.

A car approached.

He heard the tires moving across the wet pavement. Rubber on water. The headlights, dim now, approached the far edge of the cloud of smoke. Billings kept his hand out. He hoped that she was going his way. There was music. Loud music, as if an entire orchestra was approaching. The smoke filled with light.

Demmie almost passed him by, then at the last minute she jammed on the brakes. What the hell. She opened the door.

He had a nice face. Weird little Casey Jones hat.

"How far you going?" she said.

"As far as you'll take me," Billings said.

"Well, I'm not sure," Demmie said. "I think I'm going to Philly. Maybe New York. I haven't figured it out."

"I'll go wherever you want to go," Billings said.

"Hop in."

Billings got his bag. "You want me to put this in the trunk?" he said.

"Yeah. If you can fit it. Wait. Let me open it for you."

Demmie got out of the car, unlocked the trunk. It was hard to wedge it in, but somehow she managed. The trunk was over-flowing with household appliances. Blenders. Coffee grinders. A microwave. Answering machine. Cuisinart. A television.

They got back in the car, took off. Billings noticed that the back seat of the car was filled with appliances too, as well as a large amplifier and an electric guitar. There were clothes strewn all over the floor.

"Jeez, you sure got a lot of stuff," Billings said.

"It's not mine," she said.

He had noticed her unusual looks from the moment he got in the car. She was wearing a torn black shirt that had eight zippers on it. Her pants looked like they were some kind of leather. Oily. She was wearing black lipstick and had a lot of smudgy-looking shadows around her eyes.

"Whatcha doing?" Demmie said. "Leaving town?"

"Yeah," Billings said. "I can't take it anymore."

"Lemme guess," Demmie said. "They don't understand ya."

"Well, that's part of it. But I've always wanted to leave. Finally I just had the reason to."

"Yeah? Me too. I hate this place. Such a dump. I'm going to the city. You know, I'm in the music business."

"Really?" Billings said. "I like music."

"Oh yeah, good." She switched on the radio. A loud song was already in progress. "Music is my life," Demmie said.

They drove along for a while, as the loud music serenaded them. Demmie drove with the windows down and the heater going full blast. A heavy metal band sang: *Oh-ho the Wells Fargo Wagon is a-comin' down the street, oh don't let him pass my door.*

Demmie turned to him. "Is that all you got?" she said.

"Is what?"

"That pack? Is that all the stuff you own? I mean in the world?"

"Yeah," Billings said. "All that matters. Some clothes. Some pictures."

"Jeez," Demmie said. "You really are cutting out, aren't you."

"Yup," he said.

"Whad you do for bucks? In Centralia?"

"Caretaker," he said. "A carpenter sometimes too. I looked out for this guy's house. He was never there, though."

"Jeez, you musta partied up," Demmie said.

"I partied up," Billings said. "I partied down."

"I like to party," Demmie said. "You like to party?"

"Yeah," Billings said.

"Hey, this is great. 'Cause like I said I'm leaving too. Jeez, what a weirdo town."

"It was all right," Billings said. "Useda be, anyway."

"Nah," Demmie said. "It sucks. Always sucked."

"Whatever," Billings said. "It's over now."

"So listen, my name's Demmie."

"I'm George Billings. But you can call me Billings. Everybody calls me Billings."

"You can call me Demmie if you want. I'm trying to think of something new, though, like a stage name."

"I think Demmie's a beautiful name," Billings said.

"Do you really?"

"Yeah. It's nice. I never knew a Demmie before. Is it short for something?"

"Yeah, I think it must be. I don't know what, though. My ma thought it up."

"She must be very pretty," Billings said.

Demmie looked over at him suspiciously.

"I'm sorry," he said. "I didn't mean to say the wrong thing."

"No skin off my butt," Demmie said. "My mom checked out a few years ago."

"I'm sorry," Billings said.

"It's all right," Demmie said. "You get over stuff. So. What do you think my name should be? I was thinking of Zeena for a while. You like it?"

"Zeena?"

"Too metallic? How about Scabbaxx?"

"Scabbaxx?"

"Yeah. With two *x*'s."

"I just like Demmie," Billings said.

"I was thinking, Scabbaxx, and no last name. Like Cher or Sting or somebody. Just plain Scabbaxx. *I am Scabbaxx.* I like the sound of that."

"Well, whatever. Like I said, I still like plain Demmie."

"Yeah?"

"Yeah. I do. It sounds like you're half of something. You know, like hemi demi semi. Sounds like you're supposed to be part of something bigger."

"You mean like semi colon. Maybe I could change my name to Demmie Colon."

"Or Demmie Tass."

"What's that? Like the Russian guy?"

"No. Demmie Tass. When you only have enough coffee for a little cup."

"I don't know anything about that."

"Well, you could. It's interesting. Demmie. Half of something else."

"Oh yeah? I never thought of it like that. Like what am I supposed to be part of?"

"I don't know. Some mystery."

"Yeah!" Demmie said. She pulled onto the turnpike.

"Some mystery! You got it, Billings! Hey, you're all right! You get it. You'd be amazed how many people in Centralia just didn't get it at all. They didn't have a damn clue."

"Well," Billings said, "you know how people are."

"All right, so listen. You know anybody in Philadelphia who could help like set us up?"

"What do you mean?"

"Set us up, man! Like let us crash out until we unload all this junk I got."

"What do you mean, junk?" Billings said. For the first time he was afraid. "You mean like drugs?"

"No, no." Demmie said. She rolled her eyes. "Get with it. I mean all this junk in the car. The toasters and shit. I got 'em coming out the gazoo."

"Oh," Billings said. He was relieved. "I get it."

"I gotta dump this car someplace too. It's hot as shit."

"You mean like you stole it?"

"Well, it's my dad's. He'll blow his stack when he finds out I swiped it. Course that might not be for weeks. He's in jail."

"Jail," Billings said. "Hey, you had it rough, didn't you, Demmie."

"Yeah," Demmie said. "I come from a deprived area."

"Me too," Billings said.

"Where's that?"

"Centralia," he said. "Same place as you."

"Oh yeah."

Demmie turned up the volume of the radio. She was drumming her fingertips on the steering wheel. She turned to her left and spat her gum out the window. He could tell from the smell it was Fruit Stripe. His favorite.

"Anyway, we need to figure out a way to pawn all this stuff. You know. On the sly. You ever pawn anything?"

"Once," Billings said. When he was small he had pawned an autoharp that belonged to his music teacher.

"You have to sign something, don't you. See, I don't want to sign nothing. I just want to get the cash and run. Go to the city and join a band. Hey, can you sing, Billings?"

"Yeah. I can sing. A little. In the shower and stuff."

"Great. You can be our lead vocal." She honked the horn. "Asshole!" she yelled. It was hard to hear her over the music. "I hate people who drive the speed limit."

"What about all this stuff," Billings said. "Is it your dad's, too?"

"Nah. I swiped it from the people next door. They're real jerks. This caveman dude and his girlfriend from Bloomingdale's. Dwayne and Vicki. Like they really need this junk. When was the last time you think they used that hot-air popcorn popper? Anyway, I figure after I cut the album I'll buy 'em all the stuff back. Maybe go down to the same pawn shop, get 'em their own things. That would be the best."

"Hey, you smell something?" Billings said. He could swear there was the scent of Menthol shaving cream in the car.

"Hah? No. Not unless it's you. You know how some people have a stink?"

"Do I stink?"

"Nah, Billings. You have a certain something, though. Maybe it's not you. Like smoke."

A song came on the radio. Demmie turned it up. "This is excellent," she said.

"What?"

"This is excellent."

"What is it?"

"Huh? I don't know."

A reedy voice sang: *"Words are flowing off like endless rain into a paper cup, they slither wildly as they slip away across the universe."*

"John Lennon," Billings said. "That's on *Let It Be*. The Beatles. 'Across the Universe.' "

"John Lennon," Demmie said. "He's the dead one."

"Yeah," Billings said. "Must be. They're all dead now."

"So you know anybody?" Demmie said. "Who can help us out?"

"I have to think," Billings said.

"Even a place to crash tonight would be good. I'd hate to have to blow all my money on some Howard Johnson's."

"Well, there's always Wilkins," Billings said. "That guy whose house I watched. He lives in Bryn Mawr. You think we can find Bryn Mawr?"

"I got a map. You think you could find where he lives?"

"How hard can it be?"

"We won't be getting there till like two or three in the morning. He won't mind us coming in then, will he?"

"Oh, no," Billings said. "He loves me. He'll be glad to see me."

"What if he's not home?"

"Then we can stay at his house until he gets back. He won't mind. He trusts me."

• "Jeez, well, it's all set then."

"*Sounds of laughter, shades of life are ringing through my opened ears,*" Lennon sang, "*inviting and inciting me.*"

"What'd he say?" Demmie said.

"Inviting him and inciting him."

"Oh. This is good. I should learn this."

"*Limitless undying love which shines around me like a million suns and calls me on and on across the universe.*"

"It doesn't sound hard."

"Nah," Demmie said. "I don't believe in that. Things being hard."

He looked out the window, at the dark cornfields whizzing past. There were billboards for Hershey's Chocolate World and Indian Echo Caverns. A line of sparrows slept upon a telephone wire.

"*Jai Guru Deva. Om,*" Lennon sang in refrain. "*Nothing's going to change my world.*"

"What's he saying?" Demmie said. "Jack aroo dave blob?"

"I don't know. It sounds like nonsense," Billings said.

"Nah, nobody sings nonsense."

"I can't make it out."

"Like a new day of love?" Demmie said. "Maybe he's saying 'Like a new day of love.' That's kind of pretty."

Billings was still looking out the window. It would be a few hours before they got to Wilkins' house, but he'd be glad to see them. He'd understand. People were forgiving. It was in the nature of men and women to be kind.

"What'd you say?" he said over the loud music.

In the rearview mirror a white cloud stood above the mountains. Billings wasn't sure if it was a cloud or just the ghost of smoke, rising up over Centralia. It didn't matter now. They were moving at incredible speed, out into the beyond. He looked over at Demmie, a vision in black. A great gonging bell rang in his heart and lungs.

"I said it's pretty," she yelled. " 'A new day of love.' "

The car, moving quickly, passed beyond Chocolate World and Indian Echo Caverns and Pennsylvania Dutch Anti-Gravity Park. Windows open, music thundering, they climbed a small hill, balanced precariously at the summit, and crossed over to the other side.

Demmie and Billings, singing at the top of their lungs, vanished into the wide, loving beyond of vast and limitless space.